'The novel provides a meticulously researched, oppressive and always instructive piece of German post-war history. Further sequels are absolutely welcome!' KSTA

'A captivating and authentic portrait of post-war Germany immediately before currency reform' Oberhessic Press

'A captivating, dazzling narrated crime novel that comes to the point without bloodthirsty gimmickry' City Advice Westfalen

'[*The Murderer in Ruins*] Undoubtedly the most powerful work of crime fiction I have read this year' *Independent*

'Vivid and harrowing' *Sunday Times*

'Once again, Rademacher combines an exciting crime story with a detailed description of Hamburg in the post-war period' *Aachener Nachrichten*

'Rademacher succeeds in describing history with tension' *Neue Presse*

'Rademacher understands how to draw a living picture of the post-war period. *The Wolf Children* allows its readers to embrace history without an instructive tone, wonderfully packaged in a thriller' *Hessische Allgemeine*

'With his follow-up to *The Murderer in Ruins*, Rademacher has once again captured an intriguing view into a not-so-distant world in which everyone is fighting for survival' *Brigitte*

'Impressively, Rademacher describes life in 1947 with all its hardships and hopes. A piece of history comes alive and is immensely touching' *Hamburger Morgenpost*

# THE FORGER

CAY RADEMACHER was born in 1965 and studied Anglo-American history, ancient history and philosophy in Cologne and Washington. He has been an editor at *Geo* since 1999, and was instrumental in setting up renowned history magazine *Geo-Epoche*. *The Forger* is the third novel in the Inspector Stave series, following *The Murderer in Ruins* and *The Wolf Children* (both Arcadia Books). He now lives in France with his wife and children, where his new crime series is set.

PETER MILLAR is an award-winning British journalist, author and translator, and has been a correspondent for Reuters, *The Sunday Times* and *Sunday Telegraph*. He has written a number of books, including *All Gone to Look for America* and *1989: The Berlin Wall, My Part in Its Downfall*. He has also translated, from German, Corinne Hofmann's best-selling *White Masai* series of memoirs, Martin Suter's *A Deal with the Devil* and Cay Rademacher's Inspector Stave *trilogy*.

# THE FORGER

CAY RADEMACHER

Translated from the German by Peter Millar

Arcadia Books Ltd
139 Highlever Road
London w10 6PH

*www.arcadiabooks.co.uk*

First published in the United Kingdom 2018
Originally published as *Der Fälscher* by DuMont Buchverlag 2013
Copyright © Cay Rademacher 2013
English translation copyright © Peter Millar 2018

A catalogue record for this book is available from the British Library.

The translation of this work was supported by a grant from the
Goethe-Institut, which is funded by the German Ministry of Foreign Affairs.

ISBN 978-1-911350-32-3

Typeset in Garamond by MacGuru Ltd
Printed and bound by TJ International, Padstow PL28 8RW

ARCADIA BOOKS DISTRIBUTORS ARE AS FOLLOWS:

*in the UK and elsewhere in Europe:*
BookSource
50 Cambuslang Road
Cambuslang
Glasgow G32 8NB

*in Australia/New Zealand:*
NewSouth Books
University of New South Wales
Sydney NSW 2052

# The wound

*Wednesday, 31 March 1948*

A bullet travels faster than sound. It hit Chief Inspector Frank Stave in the chest, before he even heard the noise of the gunshot. Struck him just below the heart, throwing him backwards into a pile of bricks from a collapsed wall. No pain, he thought to himself, I don't feel any pain. That frightened him more than the blood streaming down his stomach from the wound, warm and sticky. Breathe slowly. The taste of iron in his mouth. A rushing in his ears. Stave pressed his right hand against the entry wound. He was lying on his back, staring upwards through the remnants of a roof into a low grey sky. Dust clouds danced in the air. There was a stench of mould and old mortar. He wished the pain would suddenly overwhelm him. But instead of pain it was darkness that overtook him, as his mind sank ever deeper into a sea of dark water. Please, pain, come. Now. If I don't feel any pain, it means I'm going to die, thought Stave, before he stopped thinking altogether.

When he came to again, the pain was finally there: a fiery band of it burning through his chest, accompanied by a knife blade stabbing through his body with very breath. The chief inspector smiled with relief. White walls, blinding bright light eating its way into the back of his brain, the smell of disinfectant. A hospital. This time he didn't fight back: he just let himself drift off. Sleep.

He was awakened by the sound of ragged breathing, as if someone buried up to the neck in fine sand was gasping for air. Stave opened his eyes. He listened to the gasping sound somewhere to his left.

His breast was on fire. Carefully he touched the bandages, thick as blankets. He sat up. A thousand needles pierced his body. He felt faint and just managed to suppress a cry of pain; only a heavy sigh escaped his lips. The jagged breathing nearby stopped for a moment then started up again, still struggling. A ray of bright light to his right, coming through a half-open door. The hallway, Stave guessed. A hospital room. To his left he could make out the outline of a folding screen, obscuring from view his suffering neighbour.

Stave didn't know which hospital he was in. He didn't know how much time had passed since he had been shot. The Homicide Department had been looking for a man who had stabbed his wife to death outside their apartment in St Pauli. A ship's mate who had been on the warship *Tirpitz*, sunk in a Norwegian fjord in 1944. The junior officer had survived and had been captured in Scandinavia in 1945, but was soon released and came back to his family to one of the few houses in St Pauli that hadn't been destroyed. All in all, someone who had come through the war relatively easily.

No obvious reason for the killing, though there were more than enough witnesses who had seen him attack his wife with the knife outside the door. He had fled and an arrest warrant had been issued. An evening call. Somebody had seen the suspect getting out of a tram on line 31 at the Baumwall stop, only a few hundred metres from the scene of the crime.

Stave had dashed there with all the uniformed police available. And indeed the former ship's mate had still been standing there at the tram stop, with no idea where he was going or what he was doing. He looked younger than the chief inspector had imagined. It was only when he spotted the patrol cars that he took off, eventually hiding in the bomb-blasted ruins of a chandler's shop. The chief inspector had some of the rubble moved to one side and crept carefully into the fire-blackened rooms. Not carefully enough. He had been expecting a killer armed with a knife, not a gun.

He wondered to himself if the murderer had shot more of his colleagues. If he had got away? Or if he had been overwhelmed and captured by the police? Maybe they had had to shoot him? He hoped they had managed to arrest him without further bloodshed – even if the result would be the same in the end: an English judge would send the killer to the gallows. It was even possible that it would be his friend, Public Prosecutor Ehrlich, who would make the speech calling for the death penalty. Stave would be called as a witness in court, his testimony the foundation stone on which the judge and the public prosecutor would build their case for the death penalty. He closed his eyes and hoped to fall asleep again.

But he was wide awake and there was nothing for him to do but lie there staring for hours into the darkness, occasionally touching his bandaged wound and listening to the hoarse breathing coming from behind the screen, breathing that seemed to get weaker as the night went on.

In the grey light of dawn the door opened. A young nurse came in, her pretty face narrow under her high starched hood. The Wehrmacht soldiers had called the nurses '*Stukas*' because their hoods had bent wings like those of the dive bombers. Stave's son Karl had told him that. She wore a badge on her chest with her name: Franziska. He wished for a moment he could greet her with a joke, but nothing came to mind. 'Where am I?' he asked instead. He was horrified by how flat his voice sounded.

She gave him a brief smile. 'Just a second, please,' then she disappeared behind the screen. It was only then that it occurred to the chief inspector that it had been a long time since he had heard any breathing. The nurse hurried out of the room, then came back with another nurse; a doctor rushed past Stave's bed without even glancing at him. Whispered words behind the screen, surreal, like in one of those modern plays that were banned in the 'brown' days.

Eventually a bed was rolled out of the room. The CID man spared himself the pain of trying to sit up. Somebody folded up the screen, and all of a sudden his pillow was flooded with light from the high window. The space next to him was empty.

'You've had a long leave of duty, Chief Inspector.' It was an elderly doctor, with cropped steel-grey hair, a scar on his left cheek. A former army doctor, Stark reckoned.

'Where am I?'

'In Eppendorf University Hospital. Only the very best for servants of the state. You wouldn't have survived your wound anywhere else. A bullet lodged in your lung. A few years ago there would have been nothing much we could have done. But we've had an enormous amount of experience with bullet wounds over recent years.'

'I'm one of those who profited from the war.'

The medic laughed. 'Aren't we all?'

'How long was I unconscious?'

'You spent two weeks hovering between this world and the next. It was a close thing, but I've seen worse. In case you were hoping for early retirement I'm going to have to disappoint you. You'll recover.'

'Did they get the guy?'

The doctor shrugged his shoulders. 'Not my department.'

'Did he wound any of my colleagues, or even...' Stave didn't finish the sentence.

'All I can say is that no other policeman was brought in here. Relax now. Sleep.'

'I've been asleep for half a month.'

'That's an order.'

Stave looked after the white coat as it waved its way towards the hallway. At first he thought the doctor's last sentence had been a joke, but then the chief inspector realised he had meant it seriously.

That afternoon they brought in a young man, little more than a child, barely conscious, his forehead covered by a thick bandage. As the nurses were pushing his bed in and setting up the screen, someone else came in: Stave's son. Very tall, very lean, his light blond hair a tad too long for Stave's liking, deep blue eyes. Damp patches on his faded coat and shoes that squelched on the linoleum floor.

'Happy birthday,' Stave mumbled. 'I'm afraid I slept through it.'

Karl gave him a surprised look for a moment, then smiled briefly and was serious again. He had turned twenty on the second of April. 'We can eat my birthday cake when you're out again. If I'd known you were going to regain consciousness today I would have brought you flowers.'

'From your allotment?'

'Only tobacco growing there. I'd have taken some tulips from my neighbour's.'

'Stolen goods? A fitting present for a copper.'

'I'm glad to see you're doing better.'

'I'll be back on duty tomorrow.'

'Leave it until the day after.'

Silence. Stave looked at his son who was making awkward gestures to suggest he might help the nurses set up the screen, but he was actually getting in the way rather than helping them. What was Karl doing these days? As far as Stave knew, ever since his son had been released from a POW camp in Russia he'd been earning a living from the tobacco he grew on his allotment. I've only just come to, and already I'm worrying about him, he thought to himself. It'll never end. He would have liked to go and see his son on the allotment more often, but somehow Karl had made him feel that he didn't like having his father there.

He nodded towards Karl's coat. 'Is it raining?' The question was hardly necessary but he didn't want to prolong the silence.

'Nobody in Hamburg is in danger of dying of thirst at this time of year, that's for sure.'

'Is that good or bad for tobacco-growing?'

The boy shrugged his shoulders indifferently. 'Apropos tobacco,' he whispered, leaning closer to his father. 'I guess the *Stukas* would object if I lit up a cigarette?'

'Sometimes it helps if you just stick a ciggy between your lips, but don't light up. It calms the nerves. You shouldn't smoke so much, it's not good for your lungs.'

Karl laughed so loud that Sister Franziska shot him a warning look over the top of the screen.

'Your lung has more holes than mine,' Karl said.

'Do you know if they arrested the guy who did it?'

'Yes, they got him. The shot got your colleagues' adrenalin flowing. They overpowered him in among the ruins and…' Karl hesitated briefly, 'gave him a bit of a going-over.'

'A going-over?'

'The guy must have looked pretty bad by the time they finally had him behind bars. There was an article about it in *Zeit*. Just the one though, and it was short,' he added quickly when he saw his father close his eyes.

That's something I'm going to have to explain to Cuddel Breuer, Stave thought. Maybe Prosecutor Ehrlich too. When something goes wrong, it goes really wrong. Even so, at least we got the killer.

They spent the next half hour in awkward chitchat. Stave had lots of things he would have liked to ask his son. When will you finally start doing something sensible? Have you made some new friends? Maybe a girlfriend? But Karl was always so evasive when things got personal. And the chief inspector didn't have the energy to be persistent and perspicacious at the same time. The boy just made small talk, about the bad weather and an HSV football game. He flexed his hands and Stave noted the yellow nicotine stains on his fingers.

'Go and have a smoke,' he said. 'I need a bit of a snooze.'

Karl nodded, obviously relieved. 'I'll come again in a day or two.' He held up a hand, awkwardly, not quite a wave and something almost like a *Heil Hitler* gesture, then closed the door behind him.

The boy on the other side of the screen was humming a melody. Jazz, Stave thought to himself, as he closed his eyes in exhaustion.

But the pain, the pain he had longed so much to feel after being shot, now would not let him sleep. His thoughts wandered to Anna. How long had it been since he had last seen her? Six months? Was she even aware that he was in hospital? Don't feel sorry for yourself, he cautioned.

His lover. Or rather his former lover. He remembered how last summer, at a jewellery pawnshop in the colonnades, Anna von Veckinhausen had exchanged a few thick bundles of Reichsmarks for a wedding ring. Had it been hers? He knew almost nothing about her life before she fled to Hamburg. Maybe there was somebody who knew more. The chief inspector recalled her irritated conversation with the public prosecutor in a café. The secret mission she was performing for Ehrlich: tracking down the pieces of his art colllection that had been stolen by the Nazis. And the sad words she had spoken to him, Stave.

They had only been a couple for a few months, been to the theatre a few times, to restaurants, spent a few nights together, rare weekends of stolen togetherness. He had always had too much to do. And then Karl had come back from the war, and Stave hadn't been able to deal with a son who had become a stranger and keep Anna at the same time. They had split up, without bitterness, more with resignation at having lost a battle.

He longed for Anna's smile, the scent of her hair, her skin. He thought of the meaningless chitchat with Karl. Of the days he had already frittered away in this hospital, and those he would still have to waste here until he had cobbled enough of himself back together again to leave. Of the 'going-over' his colleagues had given the shooter. Of CID Chief Cuddel Breuer, who was definitely going to want to know how this arrest had gone so terribly wrong.

Everything's gone wrong, the chief inspector said to himself, absolutely everything. In hospital with a perforated lung, and I have to lie here until I get the all-clear.

Stave counted every day he spent in that room. The grey light trickling through the window. The smell of disinfectant that permeated his pores. The tunes hummed from the other side of the screen. He didn't exchange a single word with the boy, and the boy got no visitors, even though the hummed tunes, or so he imagined, got more light-hearted, louder. He even managed to force himself out of bed. What a triumph to be able to go to the toilet on his own, wobbling along the corridor, with his head spinning and his lung burning to be sure, but it was better than relieving himself on the shiny bedpan and then having to wait for the nurse to take it away.

Karl came by again four days later. They still didn't have much to say to one another. On the fifth day Lieutenant MacDonald popped in.

'I'm bringing you two medical items,' the young British officer, with whom Stave had already solved two cases, told him, nodding at the brown paper bag in his hand. He dramatically pulled out a huge bar of chocolate. 'Hershey's, genuine American calories. A comrade from the US Army gave it to me, but your ribs have more need of them than mine.' Then he glanced at the screen, lowered his voice conspiratorially and pulled out of the bag a bottle full of amber liquid. 'Whiskey, also from the American officer. "Old Tennessee", lovingly nicknamed "Old Tennis Shoes" by its devotees. It's not exactly a Scottish single malt but it will get your pulse back up to speed.'

Stave gave a dry smile. 'A couple of sips and on his next visit the doctor will have to revise his diagnosis.'

'It's a miracle cure.'

'How are Erna and the baby?' Stave's former secretary and the young lieutenant had become involved in a relationship, with a few serious consequences: a chubby, healthy daughter called Iris, born the previous summer; a horrible divorce case in which she had lost custody of her eight-year-old son to her former husband, a bitter, cripple Wehrmacht veteran; her resignation from the CID 'in best mutual interests', because she could no longer take the looks her colleagues gave her; and her wedding, carried out by a British military chaplain, which had transformed her into 'Mrs MacDonald'.

'The little one's teething,' the officer answered with a laugh. 'I'm nostalgic for the war. The nights were quieter.'

'Teeth won't take as long to come through as peace did.'

'Put a word in God's ear. That would be one thing less for Erna and me to worry about.'

Stave thought of Karl and the old saying that worries about children grow with them, but he didn't mention it.

'We need to get you out of here soon,' MacDonald said, serious again. 'We want to say goodbye properly.'

The chief inspector hoped his shock at the announcement didn't show. 'You're being transferred?'

'It looks as if I'll be out of here this summer. Rumours going around the Officers' Club suggest I can count on a posting within Europe.'

'Will Erna and Iris go with you?'

'Of course.'

'And Erna's son.'

'I hope it won't break her heart to have to leave him here in Hamburg.'

'Won't you make another attempt to get custody?'

'The judge was very clear on that. My superiors too. A good soldier knows when a battle is lost.'

Erna MacDonald, formerly Erna Berg, was paying a high price for her new life, Stave thought to himself. But then she wasn't the only person in Hamburg who had paid a high price to be able to start over again after 1945.

Another day he had a more surprising visit: Police Corporal Heinrich Ruge, a young uniformed policeman who had accompanied him on several cases. Stave hardly recognised him because it was the first time he had seen his colleague in plain clothes – a dark suit with jacket sleeves far too short so that his skinny forearms stuck out like those of a wooden puppet.

'I brought you something,' he said, embarrassedly setting a thin wrapped-up parcel on the bedside table. Chocolate. A small fortune for a young uniformed policeman. I must really look emaciated, Stave thought, very touched. Ruge was the only one of his colleagues who had come to see him.

They chatted a bit. The longer the conversation went on, the more self-confident Ruge became. 'It's a pity Frau Berg is no longer there.'

'Mrs MacDonald now.'

Ruge blushed. 'That takes a bit of getting used to. It sounds a bit different to "Müller" or "Schmidt".'

'You mean not "Germanic" enough?' the chief inspector asked in the mildest of voices.

The policeman's face went even redder. 'New times, new names. I don't have a problem with that, quite the contrary. The lieutenant is…' he searched for the right word, 'so worldly wise. But some of our older colleagues have difficulties with the Veronikas.'

'The Veronikas?'

'That's what they call girls who go out with the Tommies.'

'Is this just a CID thing? Or is it common all over Hamburg?'

'All over. You know how it is, Chief Inspector. Suddenly a nickname like that pops up, from nobody knows where. But all of a sudden everybody's using it.'

'I know how it is well enough. After 1933 overnight there were a few funny new names for certain people.'

'Anyway, I want to join CID,' Ruge suddenly let out. 'I've already applied to do the entrance exam.'

The chief inspector looked at him long and hard. Should he encourage the kid? 'Who was it gave the "going-over" to the Baumwall murderer after he was arrested?' he asked eventually.

'Chief Inspector Dönnecke.'

That old battleship. Cäsar Dönnecke, the man who'd been in CID since the days of the Kaiser. The man who, during the 'brown years', had carried out investigations with 'colleagues' from the Gestapo. And who had nonetheless somehow managed to get through the English 'cleansing' after the end of the war, even though the victors had fired men with less dirt on their hands than Dönnecke.

'You can learn from people like him how not to behave.'

'I'll watch out for him. Maybe I might begin in your department.'

Ruge gave a shy laugh, then blushed again. 'I mean, if I'm accepted, that is.'

And if I'm back in harness by then, Stave thought, but said nothing.

Later, after his visitor had left, the chief inspector stared up at the ceiling thinking to himself. About Erna Berg, Erna MacDonald. He wondered if she knew what her former colleagues were calling her? Of course she did. She knew everything that went on in CID; in fact she was usually the first to know. She probably knew before her pregnancy was that advanced that she wouldn't be able to hold down the job. A 'Veronika'. An Engländer flirt who abandoned the husband who'd lost a leg on the Eastern Front. Erna might not be so unhappy after all about her new husband's move.

Cäsar Dönnecke, Gestapo Dönnecke. The colleague who could give prisoners a 'going-over' without fearing the consequences.

'I don't belong there any more,' Stave mumbled, half to himself. Suddenly the humming from the other side of the screen stopped. The chief inspector suppressed the curse that nearly escaped his lips. He had made a decision: I need to change departments, he told himself. Homicide is no longer for me.

# Department S

*Friday, 11 June 1948*

Stave was standing next to the bronze elephant that the CID had nicknamed 'Anton'. A work of art from the days when the CID head-quarters had still been the head office of an insurance company, back in the long gone world of the twenties, before the war, when even the cold-blooded bean counters of a company could afford luxurious jokes such as a three-metre-high tonne-weight statue of an animal by their entrance. It was just 7 a.m. Even though it was one of the longest days of the year, the city was sunk in a grey light, fine veils of water hanging in the air, too heavy to be fog, too insubstantial to be rain; cold weather for an early summer day.

The chief inspector took off his thin, square-shouldered overcoat while he was still in the stairwell. He took his time. There was nobody to see him at such an early hour. He limped up the steps, with their crazily patterned tiles; his old ankle wound from the bombing nights was playing up. He felt his more recent wound too, although not so obviously: a scar across his chest, still rather red, longer than his index finger, but already well healed, the doctors had assured him. Every now and then there would be a pain, or rather a twinge when he moved too quickly. And the occasional difficulty breathing if he exerted himself. That would pass. In civilian clothes nobody noticed anything wrong with him, except that he was a bit more gaunt than he had been.

The corridor on the sixth floor was as abandoned as the Führ-erbunker had been in April 1945. The anteroom to his office had been the realm of Erna Berg. Erna MacDonald. He didn't have a new secretary. Why would he? Initially, after the birth of Erna's daughter, there had been no qualified candidate. And then nobody had seen the point of installing someone as the secretary to a chief inspector lying in the University Hospital. The heavy black typewriter that had sat on her desk was gone. One or another of his colleagues had seen to that, Stave thought. Not that it mattered.

His office. A thin layer of dust on the desk, no new files, no new reports, no photos from the lab, no autopsy reports from Dr Czrisini. He pulled open the drawer of a metal filing cabinet with hanging folders containing the files of his solved cases. The unsolved ones must have been taken and given to another officer. A drawer full of cardboard files, the achievements of a career. Doesn't exactly look impressive, the CID man thought. But what matters is the things you can't see: the jailed murderer. The justice handed down by the court. The compensation for the relatives of the victim – not much in the way of compensation, but all the same. And above everything, the satisfaction, the pleasure even, of having solved yet another puzzle.

'But they don't have to be murder cases,' Stave mumbled, pushing the drawer back in so that it made a metallic clang as it hit the cabinet.

He cleared out his desk systematically, throwing away bits of paper and notebooks filled on every page with his scribbles. In the end he was left with a few pencils and notebooks, his certificate of promotion to the CID, in itself a relic of the long gone Weimar Republic, his card index files with hundreds of addresses of culprits, victims, contacts, informants, suspects, that he had put together over the years, a map of pre-war Hamburg and a new Falkplan map showing the bombed-out districts in red and blue lines to indicate the British no-go area along the Alster river. A magnifying glass, a penknife. He had never bothered with souvenirs and other bits and pieces that some of colleagues collected. And he had never wanted to have photos of Karl or his late wife Margarethe in the office; and certainly no photo of Anna. It only occurred to him now that he didn't even have a photo of her at home.

He bundled it all into a leather briefcase, the lock of which no longer worked. He had picked it up on the black market – a good job none of his colleagues knew. Then he heard voices down the corridor, footsteps, doors opening and closing. Stave was about to officially report for duty and his boss wasn't going to like what he was going to tell him.

Cuddel Breuer forced his massive muscular body out of his seat as Stave entered, genuine pleasure on his face. Not making things any easier for me, the chief inspector thought.

'I'd like to change departments,' he said straight away.

'Did that guy down at Baumwall shoot you in the head?' his boss asked, falling back into his seat. He was still smiling but somehow a light in his eyes had gone out. 'Come back here initially. Let yourself get back into the way of things. You don't need to take on a new case straight away. Don't need to plunge straight back in.'

'Homicide just isn't right for me any more.'

'A gunshot wound like that can knock you off the rails. I mean not just physically. Think it through. Give yourself a bit of time.'

'I had enough time in the hospital to think it through. It's not that I've suddenly become scared of something similar happening to me again.'

'So why do you want to change? Only the very best get to work in Homicide. It was me who oversaw your transfer. The work was surely much more interesting than what you had been doing before.'

It was an oblique reference to the fact that the Nazis had put Stave on ice – and that maybe the same thing could happen again. What was he to say in response? That he didn't want to keep bumping into people like Dönnecke? That from now on he would be asking each and every one of his colleagues if they had labelled his former secretary a 'Veronika'? That working in Homicide had got him so involved in his work that he no longer had time for his son or the only woman he loved?

'It's a complicated story,' he replied.

'It's part of my job to get to the end of complicated stories,' Breuer grumbled. 'Are you afraid I'm going to blame you for getting shot? Or that I'm going to ask you about the "going-over" the guy in the ruins got?'

'No. The former is a risk of the job. The latter a matter for you and Chief Inspector Dönnecke.'

Breuer mumbled something Stave couldn't make out, but he took out a folder and began leafing through the files in it. 'Where do you want to move to?'

'Department S.'

His superior slammed the folder shut. 'What's up with you, Stave? Why would somebody of your calibre want to work in the department that deals with the black market?'

'It's important work.'

'Important work! Were you totally unconscious during those last weeks in the hospital? Haven't you heard anything?'

'You mean about X-day.'

'X-day indeed. There have been rumours going round for weeks. We're getting new money. Out with the old worthless Reichsmark. That's just so much waste paper. Sometime soon the Allies are going to give us a new currency. Nobody knows when, nobody knows how it's all going to work out, but everybody is hoping for the best. Shop windows are emptier than they've ever been. People are gathering together their stocks of Reichsmarks and handing them over in bundles for anything they can still buy. You wouldn't believe how full the cinemas and theatres are. There's never been such an interest in culture before, if only because culture effectively costs nothing any more. Who knows whether in a week's time the only use you'll have for a thousand-Reichsmark note will be as toilet paper?'

'Sounds like a golden era for the black market.'

'Nonsense. This is the first time since the disappearance of the Nazis that I've seen the black marketeers look nervous. Nobody knows what the new currency will mean. Maybe the economy will collapse altogether and we'll all become farmers digging up the fields in Holstein. But maybe it will work, and then people will have real money again and be able to buy real things in real shops, just like back in the good old days. One way or the other: who's going to need a black market? And you want to go over to Department S where the black market is what they deal with!' Breuer thumped the folder in front to him. 'I have a dozen requests in here from other colleagues wanting to be transferred out of Department S, no matter where! If I wanted to punish you, Stave, I would be transferring you to Department S.'

'You're rewarding me.' For the first time the chief inspector smiled. 'In the hospital there wasn't a lot to do, apart from counting the cracks in the wall and thinking. I didn't just think about the black market, I thought about the ruins, the destroyed streets, the electricity that keeps cutting out, the bombed docks, the ruined stations, the rickety, screeching pre-war cars with wood-burning engines, shoes made out of cut-up car tyres, clothes out of cut-up parachutes. There isn't going to be a German marching into Russia or anywhere else in the world for the foreseeable future. The world has had enough of us. We're on our own and there's nothing for it but to take the heap of rubble we're left with and start to rebuild everything. A golden era for people with initiative, whether they're black marketeers or honest businessmen. There's going to be a lot of money flowing, a serious lot of money. In whatever currency. And wherever there's money flowing, there are criminals not far behind. It may be that Department S itself ceases to exist, but it will be reincarnated as a department dealing with economic crime. It's inevitable. That's the future and that's where I want to be.'

'Smugglers and fences instead of corpses and killer.'

'Doesn't sound such a bad alternative to me.'

'You're hearing a tune that nobody else in these corridors has heard yet.' Breuer gave up trying to hide his disappointment. 'Very well. I have a dozen officers here who would kiss the worn-out soles of my old shoes if I transferred them to Homicide. I'll pick one of them. You can take up your new position straight away. You know where it is. Go and report to Bahr and find yourself a new office. There's more than a few empty.'

As Stave walked through the Homicide Department one last time to fetch his briefcase, an officer aged around sixty with a large, heavy skull ringed with hair like a laurel wreath on the head of an emperor and deep-set piercing eyes came up to him. Cäsar Dönnecke.

'Welcome back, colleague.' He held out his hand.

'*Auf Wiedersehen,*' the chief inspector answered. 'I'm going to Department S.' He tried to push past, but Dönnecke laid his great paw on his shoulder.'

'I always knew you were too soft for this kind of work, Stave,' he whispered, his breath reeking of cold tobacco. 'But I didn't think you were that soft. One bullet wound and then crawl away to somewhere nothing's going to happen. The black market is finished. Haven't you heard? It's only a question of time before the Americans give us new money. Then Department S's clientele will disappear like a fart in the north wind.' He made an astounding lifelike imitation of the sound and waved his hairy right hand. 'Then? What'll you do then?'

'Then I'll stand on a tub on Stephansplatz and direct the traffic.'

'That might be better.' Dönnecke laughed and let him past.

Stave took two steps, then turned round. 'What did you actually do to the guy down at Baumwall?'

The thickset old man blinked in irritation for a moment, then rearranged his flabby features into a joyless grin. 'That's all been sorted out. You could read all about it in the files, if you were still with Homicide.'

Stave had just reached the door to his office when Dönnecke called after him, deliberately loud enough for all their colleagues to hear: 'How's your secretary, by the way, that Erna – what was her surname?'

'Veronika,' Stave replied every bit as loud, and turned the door handle.

A few minutes later he was standing in an identical corridor a few metres lower down. The CID allocated floors to departments according to their status. Homicide was right at the top. Department S was only one storey below, because from 1945 onwards the black market had become a leading priority. The chief inspector looked around: there was nobody in the corridor, the office doors were all ajar, he could hear no clicking of typewriters. It looked as if this floor was about to be taken over by another department

He went up to the only door behind which he could hear a voice. Someone on the telephone. He knocked and went in.

A colleague who must have been somewhat corpulent before the war set down the heavy black receiver with a resigned gesture. Wilhelm Bahr was head of Department S – the depredations of recent years had melted his fat away and his old skin now hung from his cheeks and neck like torn sails on a still sea. The last time Stave had worked with him was in organising a raid in the case of the murderer in the ruins. Back then he had been happy and energetic, now he looked at his visitor wearily. A man afraid he had lost.

'I'm your new colleague,' Stave said, holding out his hand.

'You must be crazy. I've just been talking to Cuddel Breuer.' Bahr tapped the telephone, but still shook his hand.

'Even you think this department is done for?'

'No, we'll expand and thrive, but nobody in his building believes that.'

'Well at least there are now two of us,' the chief inspector replied.

Bahr shook his head incredulously and handed him a pile of paperwork. 'Read that.'

Stave lifted the first page, lined, apparently ripped out of a school exercise book, written on in black ink and in an uneven hand: 'I hereby declare that the transport worker Kröger, 102 on Kiel Strasse, has stored a big load of oats in his yard. Some of it has already been eaten by vermin. But with need so great why is this? The car Herr Kröger owns is private but he uses it as a taxi and gets fuel for it.

Now he moves wood brought to his yard for building timber a few hundred metres further on as firewood.'

'What is it this poet is trying to get across to us?' Stave muttered.

'That he failed his German lessons.' Bahr tapped the pile of papers dismissively. 'Whistleblowers! We get stuff like that in here every day. We used to ignore most of it and concentrate on the big fish. Now we investigate this shit. My colleague, we work a standard 56-hour week here, with no overtime payment like in Homicide, but I can promise you one thing, it can be a tough 56 hours.'

'Can I find an office for myself or will you allocate me one?'

'Take next door. It has a nice view out on to Karl-Muck-Platz, gets the sun, the window closes properly. That's important if we're still here next winter. But you don't get a secretary of your own.'

'I'll get used to that.'

'One more thing: do you want to spend the day settling in to the office, or do you want to take on a case straight away?'

'A corrupt oats transporter on Kiel Strasse?'

'No. Artworks hidden in the ruins. Might be the work of a fence, might even date back to before the war. No other department is interested so it's ended up with Department S.'

'Sounds more interesting than spending the day "settling in". I can take my time over that. Not that it'll be a lot of work.' The chief inspector nodded at his briefcase.

'Good. Off you go then: the Reimershof accounting house on Reimersbrücke. The uniformed police are already there. I'll order a car for you. It would appear there's another case to be dealt with there, one a colleague from Homicide is already working on. But it has nothing to do with our case.'

'Which colleague?'

'Chief Inspector Dönnecke.'

'Fucking shit.'

'I did warn you: we're not on the winning side.'

The dark grey blanket of cloud lay so low in the sky it looked as if it could fall on to the ruins at any moment. A fine drizzle swirled in the wind, a precursor of heavier gusts. Stave pulled his coat collar up high, even though he only had a few metres to dash from the head office to the patrol car parked on the square. The radio patrol car – nicknamed 'radiwagon' – was an angular Mercedes Benz, previously used by the Wehrmacht as an ambulance, now used by his colleague from police station 66 on Lübeck Strasse to patrol the streets of Hamburg. The chief inspector wondered how it was that Bahr could get hold of this vehicle in particular. Maybe he had worked at that police station. He nodded to the elderly uniformed policeman behind the wheel.

'To the Reimershof…'

'I already know. Watch out for the passenger door, it can spring open sometimes while we're driving.'

Am I just imagining this, the CID man wondered. I've only just left Homicide, but already the guys in uniform treat me with less respect.

It wasn't far. Stave would happily have walked, despite the foul weather, but he didn't want to turn down a favour Bahr was doing for him on his first day on the job. The old Mercedes rumbled along Kaiser Wilhelm Strasse past the ruins on the bridge by the city hall: the exterior wall of a building had been blown out. On the way past the chief inspector glanced into the remnants of an exposed office on the first floor where the showers of rain were drawing strange patterns on the sodden wallpaper. It seemed almost like a grimace. In between two collapsed walls an organ grinder was turning his handle. The CID man wondered who would bother to waste a coin in weather like this in such a desolate part of town. On Rödingsmarkt they drove under the grey stilts that held up the overhead railway, the only stop between Baumwall and the ruins where he had been shot. Don't think about it, Stave told himself.

He could soon see the Nikolaikirche, or what was left of the church. Its narrow, neo-Gothic tower had soared above Hamburg for as long as he could remember. At one time it had even been the tallest church tower in the world. Now it stood there like a rotten tooth, still almost a hundred metres high, but torn on both sides as if someone had taken out two of its four walls with a hammer and chisel. The interior staircase was exposed and the remains of a huge set of bells glistened in the rain. Three, maybe four, black-scarred remnants of the nave walls still stood, with battered pillars, steel window frames and rosettes, missing the glass that had been melted by the firestorm.

The old uniformed officer drove around the church ruins. The Reimersbrücke bridge went over the Nikolaifleet river directly behind it. It was ebb tide. Cracked bulkheads and oak beams sunk down into the soft ground generations ago to support the houses stuck up out of slimy brown water barely half a metre deep.

'I'm not sure the bridge will support the vehicle's weight. I'm going to park just before it,' the driver said, standing hard on the brake.

Stave muttered a few words of thanks.

'Should I wait for you, Chief Inspector?' The CID man was about to shake his head, seeing as however long it took here, he could easily walk the few hundred metres back. But then it occurred to him that among the ruins of the office blocks on either side of the little river there wasn't going to be a telephone and it would be useful to have a radio, in case he had to call in specialists.

'Make yourself comfortable,' he replied.

The policeman nodded, obviously relieved. It was fine by him if he could just doze in the Mercedes.

Two of the uniformed police on the spot had closed off the Reimersbrücke bridge and the street beyond – not that it was necessary given that there was hardly a passer-by to be seen. Stave flashed his yellow CID pass.

'Ludwig Ramdohr,' one of the policemen said, introducing himself and saluting. 'It was the *Trümmerfrauen*, the women clearing the rubble, who discovered the whole heap. They were working on the remnants when a gust of wind blew down a whole wall. They were very lucky not to have been crushed to death. When the dust died down, they found a skeleton. And a work of art.'

'One of our colleagues is dealing with the skeleton. I'm interested in the work of art. What sort of work?'

An indifferent shrug of the shoulders. 'Modern stuff.'

Stave thought of Anna, who earned her money by unearthing antiques and works of art from the ruins to hive them off to the English and black marketeers. 'Can you be more precise? A painting? A statue?' His voice was sharper than it needed to be.

'A statue, I suppose you could call it. As far as I'm concerned it doesn't look any prettier than the skeleton next to it. Not something I would want in my living room.' Sergeant Major Ramdohr rubbed the badge on his uniformed chest: a little metal clasp with the word 'Hamburg' at the top, then the city crest below and his four-figure identification number. He was doing it subconsciously until he noticed Stave watching his right hand.

'I can't get used to this English invention,' Ramdohr apologised.

'It shines well enough though.'

'Unlike the work of art. That needed a good polishing. I'll take you to it.'

The Reimershof was the first office block on the left after the bridge, or rather what was left of it. Originally an eight-storey building, plastered white once upon a time. The two equally damaged buildings on either side were made of brick. The chief inspector surmised that the white plaster had been intended to show that this was a more modern building. Built in the twenties maybe, he reckoned, not that it mattered now. There were brown and yellow damp patches in the white plaster and each window was surrounded by red rust. And above it all was open sky. The roof had gone. Direct hit, Stave thought to himself. A firebomb in the attic, and nobody had ventured out in the hail of bombs to extinguish the flames. Fire had consumed the attic, then spread to the floor below until the whole building – and anything it had contained – collapsed in an avalanche of stone and wood. There were hundreds of houses like this in Hamburg with their exterior walls almost intact, without glass in the windows, without roofs, their interiors a heap of rubble.

In the entrance, where the charred remains of a heavy oak door still hung at an angle, Ansgar Kienle, the police photographer, nodded to him. 'I'm dealing with the corpse first, Chief Inspector,' he said apologetically. 'Then I'll deal with your case.' Stave glanced at him, a jolly, freckled face looking at him from under a tent-like rain cape. He was holding the cape's waxed cloth out over his expensive pre-war Leica, the sole camera in the possession of Hamburg CID.

'That stuff isn't going to rust away on me,' Stave replied, thinking, he already knows I'm no longer with Homicide. Word gets around fast. 'Very well,' he added. 'But I'm going to take a look at the scene anyway. I'll be careful not to trample over any traces.'

'That's what they all say,' Kienle sighed, tinkering with his Leica.

'Where are the *Trümmerfrauen?*'

'Behind the Reimershof,' Ramdohr replied. 'After the wall came down and they found the corpse, they didn't want to hang around in here any longer. You can interview them after...' He hesitated.

'After the Homicide colleagues have finished.'

The interior of the Reimershof was surreally quiet. Heaps of rubble between the walls, some of them no higher than his hip, but others three, four metres high. A mountain of broken bricks, blackened beams, tangled cables and shattered tiles. Grass was growing over some of the flatter areas and in the midst of the ruins there was already a tall birch tree growing as high as where the second storey floor must once have been. There was no level ground; with every step he took something crunched beneath his feet and sometimes he sent stones rolling down slopes. Thanks to the outer walls protecting him from the wind, the drizzle came straight down, making the rubble glisten, and Stave felt as if it was raining harder here than outside.

On the side that looked away from the Reimersbrücke there was a huge gap. A section of the wall about five metres across had fallen in.

'Luckily the *Trümmerfrauen* were standing on the outside,' Ramdohr told him. He had automatically lowered his voice.

The chief inspector nodded and moved closer. A vaulted roof that must previously have been concealed by the rubble had been smashed through by the weight of the falling bricks. The cellar, the CID man assumed. In a spot that must once have been a storage room but now looked like a ditch that stones had fallen into from every side, stood several police in uniform and a plainclothes colleague Stave didn't recognise. He nodded at them but didn't go over to join them. He could make out the body – a skeletal corpse, with remnants of clothing on bones and leathery skin, the death grin of a skull. Not just been here since yesterday, he reckoned. Then he shook his head. Not your business.

The sergeant major led him to an indentation on the edge of the collapsed cellar, little more than a dent in the rubble.

'This is your case, Chief Inspector.'

At first Stave couldn't make out anything at all. But then as he went down into the dip he stopped in shock for a moment, because he had almost trodden on a face. A head, half buried under the pulverised remnants of bricks turned by the rain into a gravelly paste. The chief inspector carefully brushed the dirt aside. The head of a woman, life-size, made of reddish brown metal. Bronze, the CID man assumed, not that he was an expert. In most places the metal was covered with verdigris or a scabby white layer, almost like something woven. Even so he could make out some of the features: big eyes, the nose slightly bent to the left, a smiling mouth. One part of the neck had been broken off, but otherwise the bust was relatively unharmed. Modern art indeed, even if he had never seen this sculpture before. It would have been great if Anna were here. And not just because of the artwork. Stave shook his head, annoyed with himself. This is your first case in this field, don't get distracted.

'The *Trümmerfrauen* certainly wouldn't have reported this thing,' Ramdohr mumbled from the edge of the dip. 'They'd have wrapped it up under their aprons and taken it to a scrap-metal dealer. It was only the skeleton over there that made them act as they did. They were scared and rang us up.'

'Nor is it the only treasure in this heap of rubble,' the uniformed policeman said dismissively, nodding towards an area several metres away from the bronze.

Stave went over and whistled in appreciation. 'You obviously have an expert's eye,' he said, only half sarcastically.

Three fragments of a figure, a woman perhaps, although the nose had been broken off, the cheeks were scarred and the fragments of the torso looked more like a rough block so that he couldn't properly decide its gender. At first Stave thought he might be looking at some statue of an Egyptian god, its shape was so archaic. Light grey stone, he thought to himself, but it was only when he lifted the first fragment that he realised how familiar the material was: 'This is concrete,' he muttered. What sort of artist would work in concrete? It definitely had to be modern.

Systematically he began to work his way through the rubble. On two occasions he thought he had found something but it turned out to be only the silvery glistening end pieces of a British firebomb. These narrow weapons, as long as an arm, looked harmless, almost like over-large fireworks. They had been dropped in their thousands out of the planes, coming through the roofs and setting off phosphorous fires in the warehouses, yellow and red flames like flickering flowers blooming in the city night. The heavy metal end pieces of the bombs were to be found stuck in the asphalt of the streets the morning after an attack and would be hauled out by the children who had survived.

After half an hour, during which the sodden uniformed man gave him ever more morose looks, Stave found something at the edge of the depression in the ground: the bottom half of a man's head cast in black glazed ceramic. The nose, eyes and hair were missing, the broken edges sharp. It reminded him of a shattered skull he had had to deal with in one of his first cases as a detective. But no matter how hard he looked he couldn't find the upper part, or even fragments of it. Instead he just came across a few coins, one or two mark pieces, Reichsmarks from the thirties, their top side melted. The night of the firestorm, he thought.

'The artworks weren't in the cellar,' he eventually told Ramdohr, as he struggled to climb out of the ditch. 'If everything had collapsed on top of them they'd be a lot worse damaged.' He nodded at the coins. 'These must have been kept upstairs, either in the attic or one of the upper storeys, where a firebomb had burst. But the other objects weren't in the same place. The bronze hasn't melted, and the concrete isn't blackened. They must have been one or two storeys lower. The fire upstairs, and maybe also explosive bombs, damaged the office building to the extent that eventually all the floors collapsed right down into the cellar and brought these with them.'

'Like a pile of plates falling out of your hands,' Ramdohr replied. 'Bang, bang, bang, the plates hit the ground one after another, and then you've got a right mess.'

'You're speaking from experience?'

'My wife complains constantly I have two left hands.'

It was a good job that the ordinary beat policemen didn't carry guns, Stave thought to himself. 'The Reimershof was hit in the summer of 1943,' he said. 'This art therefore must date from then or the previous few years.' Not a hiding place for a fence or a black marketeer, who regularly made hiding places in the ruins. But not in ruins like this, and not goods like this, the detective thought. That meant that if it had nothing to do with the black market it wasn't a case for Department S. But if the black market collapsed, what else did they have to do?

'Doesn't look very valuable if you ask me,' the sergeant major said dismissively.

'In that case I won't ask you.' Stave was thinking of Anna and the bundles of Reichsmarks she had got for some of the things she found in the ruins; and Public Prosecutor Ehrlich who would have paid any price to get back the art collection stolen from him by the Nazis. 'It just might be that we could make someone unexpectedly happy,' he mumbled. 'We just need to find out who rented rooms in the Reimershof in 1943.'

To his amazement Stave noticed that Ramdohr had suddenly adopted an almost military stance. 'Chief Inspector Dönnecke is coming,' he hissed.

Stave's massive colleague was climbing over the rubble, accompanied by three younger officers. 'You've only just left our department and already you're getting in my way, Stave,' he grumbled.

'Your corpse, my artworks.'

'You artworks don't look in much better condition than my old corpse.'

'The two things may be related.'

'And the world is flat and the Führer is just hiding in the Alps. Don't tell me fairy tales, dear colleague. You're not getting back into Homicide, even by the back door.'

'The dead body and these objects are in the same building.'

'Now that you mention it, I see what you mean. Maybe they were both taken out by the same bomb. So what? I will ascertain that the cause of death was the result of the war, and then I'll find out who the victim was. You deal with your own discovery. It may well be that my corpse was the owner of your artworks. In which case we can pool our files and hand them in to the store for files to be forgotten. But until then, do not set foot in my office. Is that clear?'

Ramdohr grinned, then noticed that Stave was looking at him and straightened his face. 'Always a pleasure to work with you,' Stave replied, and made a gesture to the uniformed policemen: 'Get hold of crates or cartons. When Kienle has finished taking his photographs we'll pack these things up and take them in the patrol car to headquarters.'

Stave followed the sergeant major who had disappeared through a gap in the wall, then glanced briefly at Dönnecke who hadn't even bothered to get down into the trench where the body lay. A couple of younger officers were crawling around in a manner that suggested to Stave they didn't really know what they were doing. A third stood next to their boss with a notebook out, ready to take dictation. But it seemed Dönnecke hadn't much to say; the pencil with its chewed end hardly moved. He's not even pretending to take the case seriously, Stave thought, and then shrugged. Why should he? Tens of thousands died in the bombing raids on Hamburg. Police had been finding bodies for years and it would probably continue for years. Not my problem any more, he told himself.

Dr Czrisini, the pathologist, turned up, dragging his doctor's bag as if it was filled with lead plates. Normally rather portly, he had lost weight and the skin of his face had a yellowish note to it, his eyes sunk deep in black-rimmed holes in his face. Only the Woodbine glowing between his lips was the same as ever.

'You need a holiday,' Stave said. 'A couple of weeks on the North Sea would do you good.'

'I can have a rainy summer just as easily here in Hamburg,' Czrisini answered, spluttering. Then he lowered his voice, 'I believe you're no longer one of the team?'

'I'm in art and embezzled butter now.'

'There's no future in the black market, Stave. Department S is a dead end.'

The chief inspector laughed. 'I thought your department was a dead end.'

'Not for those who can still walk on two legs. Take this as a piece of medical advice: move back to Homicide.'

'So that you don't have to deal only with the Dönneckes?'

'I don't care about Dönnecke,' Czrisini managed to say before succumbing to a coughing fit.

Stave had a long wait before Kienle arrived. 'Did you know that my Leica used to belong to a war reporter,' the photographer said, as he clambered down into the dip where the CID man was standing. 'The French campaign, Norway, the Eastern Front, a U-boat expedition, it came through all of them. But this goddamn Hamburg rain is going to be the ruin of it.'

'How did you get your hands on a war reporter's camera.'

'I was the war reporter,' Kienle laughed. 'One of my pictures even made it on to the front of *Signal* magazine. After 1945 the Tommies wouldn't let me continue to work as a photographer, but when Cuddel Breuer offered me a job with CID, they had no objection. There's no understanding the English.'

'Did you take a lot of photos, over there?'

'Of the corpse? No, I didn't even use up half a 24-frame film roll. I'll use the remainder on your discoveries, then it's off to the lab. I just hope I don't get them mixed up afterwards. This head doesn't look much better than that of the guy in the other ditch.'

'Bomb victim?'

'That's what Chief Inspector Dönnecke suspects.'

'What about you?'

'I don't have suspicions, I take photographs.'

Stave got out of Kienle's way and watched the young man crawl around the objects, getting down on his knees, changing the aperture on his Leica, occasionally clicking the shutter, all the time making sure his own shadow didn't fall on the artworks. He would need all he could get of the pale light. Kienle wasn't one to waste expensive flashbulbs.

As he listened to the clicks of the shutter and the quiet scrape of the film moving on in the Leica, Stave wondered to himself why Kienle had been passed over: he didn't just take photographs, he was the CID's only crime scene expert. After three years with CID in which he spent practically every day examining crime scenes, he was an experienced man, whatever job he might have done before – much more experienced than many officers who only saw the scene of crime every couple of weeks. It would be interesting to know what had happened to Kienle, the chief inspector thought. But he didn't know him well enough to ask such a personal question.

By the time the photographer wound on the film in his Leica and climbed out of the ditch, Dönnecke and his team had already disappeared in a Mercedes blowing out a cloud of smoke. He hadn't even interviewed the *Trümmerfrauen,* it dawned on Stave.

'Dönnecke will wait for my photos, then he'll put them in the file and close it once and for all. A few more pictures nobody will ever look at.'

'You'd like to be on the cover of a newspaper again?'

'There are times when I'm nostalgic for the good old days.'

'I'll show your pictures around. They might provoke some interest.'

'Editors?' Kienle tried to sound sarcastic, but Stave thought he could hear just the tiniest trace of hope.

He shook his head sympathetically. 'No, but art experts,' he replied. 'I'd like to know what we've actually found here.'

Kienle nodded towards the bronze head of the woman. 'I've seen that lady somewhere or other.'

'Where?'

'No idea. I can't remember. But it wasn't in a gallery or a museum. It was more like…' He hesitated. 'What I mean is that I've seen the head before, but it was smaller, if you know what I mean. I don't recall it being life-size.'

'A smaller copy? A model of some sort?'

'No. Rather, as if I'd seen this work of art in a photo. When I was with the press I didn't just take photographs myself. I've no idea how many photos I've seen: shots taken by my colleagues, huge piles of photos lying around on tables in the editorial. There must have been thousands. And this head was in one of them. I just have no idea who could have taken it. Or when.'

'If you remember, come and see me. My office is one floor lower.'

'I won't get lost. Things are pretty quiet at present in Department S.'

Stave remained standing in the ditch, watching as Rambohr packed up the artworks in a case, not exactly with the greatest of care. He didn't have to wait next to him, but he wanted to remain in the ruined house until Dr Czrisini had finished his initial inspection of the body, and the bearers had taken it away on a black stretcher.

'Is it one of the many bombing victims?' he asked the pathologist finally, hoping he sounded casual.

'You can't give up, can you? Take my advice: murders are good for your mental health.'

'I'm just curious.'

'More than that – you're suspicious.'

The chief inspector smiled. 'You should be a psychiatrist. But isn't it a surprise that the body still has traces of clothing on it?'

'Not many people die naked.'

'This place was hit by incendiary bombs.' Stave continued, not to be distracted. 'I spotted the weights they attached to the bottom of incendiary bombs. And a few melted coins. I recall – it must have been in the autumn of 1943 – I was called out with a couple of colleagues to the cellar of a bombed house. We searched the shelves for stolen goods but all we found were dozens of jars of homemade jam. But even though the last bombing raid had been a day or two earlier, the jam in the jars was still boiling away. It must have been unimaginably hot in this house.'

'Boiling jam and melted money,' Czrisini repeated, 'but our corpse still has clothing on. No heat. Or at least not enough to burn the shirt off his back.'

'And the artworks aren't melted either. There must have been flames blazing in the attic and upper storey. The objects must have already been here on the ground floor, or maybe the first floor, and only fell through into the cellar when the whole building collapsed. But that must have been hours after the bombs hit, when the worst of the heat had died down.'

'And you think our friend here must have been in the lower part of the Reimershof?'

'Not far from the artworks. Incendiary bombs are treacherous but their explosive force is fairly limited and they aren't particularly heavy. They set the attic on fire, but anyone who had been on the lower floors would have had time enough to escape from the house. Czrisini, you know yourself that back then people actually ran up into the attics to throw the bombs out of the building with their bare hands or pour sand over them. It usually worked too.'

'Usually isn't the same as always.'

'Yes, but if our unknown corpse had just been unlucky, he would have been burned. And he wasn't.'

'No. A fractured skull. His top storey was smashed too, but not by one of the Tommies' incendiary bombs. There's a hole right in the *sutura sagittalis*, the part at the top of the skull where it joins together. A hole with a quite noticeable irregular shape.'

'Could beams or concrete blocks in a collapsing house have caused a wound of that sort?'

'No. Given the size of the fracture, I would be more inclined to say it was a small hammer. The irregular shape however suggests otherwise. A stone? I found nothing inside the skull: a stone could either have got stuck in the bone or would be lying inside the head.'

'As if someone pulled it out again after the deed?'

'Like I said, you can't give up. It might have been a stone, or it might have been a paperweight or an inkwell. This was an office building, after all. It didn't fall on his head by accident.' Czrisini laughed but it turned into another coughing fit.

'Have you thought about Switzerland?' Stave asked.

'I don't need a magic mountain. It isn't tuberculosis. You should worry more about yourself.'

'What was Dönnecke's response to all these indications?'

'He didn't notice the remains of clothing: either he didn't understand the implication or couldn't care less. As for the fracture, he put it down to a "typical shrapnel wound". Shrapnel from a bomb that had exploded near the house was blown through the windows and killed him.'

'Did you tell him what you just told me?'

'Of course. Dönnecke just replied that in the bombing raids shrapnel flew in every possible direction, hitting people.'

'Hitting them in the forehead, maybe, the back of the head, the face, but not in the middle of the top of the skull. If something comes flying through the window it hits people from the side, whether they're sitting or standing, but not from above.'

'In that case he must have been lying with his head facing the window.'

'Anyone lying on a bed or a sofa would be below the level of the window. The shrapnel wouldn't have hit them at all.'

'Maybe he was lying on his desk.'

'With his head facing the window, during a bombing raid?' The chief inspector could hardly bring himself to conceal his anger. Dönnecke was a sloppy investigator whose only interest was to close the file as soon as possible. But this wasn't some traffic accident with a dented bodywork: this was a dead man, damn it.

'It's not your case, Stave,' the pathologist replied, sticking another Woodbine between his lips to replace the last. 'But as you're so curious, you may come and see me at the institute this evening. You never know what you're going to discover on the autopsy table.'

'I ought not to do that,' the chief inspector replied. 'If Dönnecke finds out there'll be trouble.'

'See you later, then,' Czrisini said, holding up a hand in farewell.

A little later Stave was standing in front of a group of twenty women, who had found shelter from the rain under the concrete roof of another almost completely destroyed building nearby. Most of them were wearing old blouses or smocks in faded colours, heavy shoes and had tied scarves around their head to protect them from the dust. A few of them were wearing leather workers' gloves and many of them had protective glasses that had once been worn by Wehrmacht despatch riders, pushed up on to their foreheads in this forced pause in their work schedule. When they were working the glasses would have protected their eyes from the biting stone dust.

One of them, whose age the CID man put at about forty, came up and shook his hand. Her skin was raw, and, despite the damp, floury grey dust had become entrenched in her eyebrows.

'Karla Riel,' she said. 'When can we get back to work?'

'I'm sorry you've had to wait. And also that you had to see the dead body.'

'I've seen more dead bodies than you have,' the woman replied casually. 'And we've found bodies in the rubble that looked a lot worse than that guy.'

'Worst of all are the bodies of children,' another of the women added. The others just stared at him – Stave didn't know whether they were scornful or warning him off.

'I'm interested in the artworks.'

'They send a cop here specially for that?' Karla Riel looked at him in surprise and slightly suspiciously. 'You don't want to know anything about the corpse?'

'My colleague's working on that.'

'Not exactly working overtime, is he? Are those things valuable?'

'Why do you ask?'

'Why are you asking us about them then? We don't normally see a sergeant turn up when we pull a stovepipe or an electricity meter out of the rubble.'

'I suspect they're worth more than a stovepipe.'

'Looked pretty grim, that metal head lying in the dirt.' Karla Riel gave a nervous laugh. 'Somehow it was even more shocking than a real skull would have been. Strange, isn't it?'

Stave asked another couple of questions. *Trümmerfrauen* dragged countless cubic metres of rubble out of the devastated city with their bare hands. Without them getting rid of the rubbish, Hamburg would suffocate beneath its own ruins – and without the bricks that they carefully piled up, and without the piping they reclaimed, the cables, the doors and windows, there wouldn't be enough to rebuild a single house. He took care not to be too severe in his questioning of Karla Riel and her colleagues. He remained polite and before long he was fairly certain that the *Trümmerfrauen* weren't keeping anything back: there was no other bronze that one of them was trying to smuggle out under her smock. Nor had they any idea who the owner might have been, they hadn't found a briefcase, or any other clue that might have helped with the case. He took note of their names and nodded. 'The Reimershof is all yours again. But please ring the police if you find any other artworks.'

'I certainly wouldn't have one of those on my sideboard at home,' Karla Riel replied, tightening the knot in her headscarf.

# In the pathology lab

That evening Stave strolled over to the Institute for Pathology and Forensic Science in Neue Rabenstrasse. The rain had become a fine mist. The CID man felt as if he was walking through soft, cool silk handkerchiefs. The damp slowly penetrated the thin soles of his shoes, and his feet turned clammy, as if he was hiking through mud-flats. Czrisini's empire consisted of an old villa with a few boarded-up windows and plasterwork that in the damp air had turned the yellowish colour of cheap paper.

'So where is the object of my curiosity?' the chief inspector asked.

'In the cooler. I've had less free time than I expected. I had to stand in for a sick colleague and show a few students a trick or two.' He nodded towards a skull, the knitted bones of which had come apart. Stave walked over to it curiously. 'You've put peas in it?' he said, in surprise.

'You put dried peas into the skull from below, then pour water over them. The peas swell up and all of a sudden, "knack", all the fontanels spring open. Very instructive.'

'Very rich in calories. When I think how few rations I have on my card per week, I need the peas more than this skeleton.'

'You also needed well-trained doctors, not that long ago.'

'Okay, so you were busy with your students and their peas. Would it be better if I came back tomorrow?'

'I still managed to find out a few things about our friend. Chief Inspector Dönnecke insisted on a report.'

'He's keen to close the file.'

'He didn't find it necessary to tell me why he was so eager to have the report urgently. I took a quick look at the body and scribbled down a few lines. Then I set the body aside for later.'

'Might it be possible you have a summary of your report.'

'I do, but it's not for you. Don't get me wrong, but I wouldn't like our esteemed colleague to come across a document in your hands that shouldn't be in your hands.'

'I get it,' Stave said, and pulled out his tattered notebook.

Czrisini smiled. 'The victim had been dead for a long time. How long is hard to say. The Reimershof was destroyed some five years ago. That could fit with the verdict, hypothetically at least: dead for five years, but it's only the vaguest of guesses.

'Cause of death: skull injury trauma. Of course I can't rule out any other possibilities if the unknown victim did die in the bombing raid – the air pressure could have destroyed his lungs and he suffocated. Things like that. But there is no doubt that he had a serious injury to the head. It would seem he was hit from above with an L-shaped object.'

'A bit of rubble from the collapsing house?'

'I doubt it. Blocks of cement or beams do a lot more damage; the skull is often smashed to pieces. This would appear to be a single blow with a hard object. Not a hammer, not a piece of piping, not a truncheon, in all of which cases the damage would have been different. And there's nothing inside the skull that could relate to the injury, nothing such as shrapnel from a bomb or anything like that. It would appear to be an external blow from an object that left no trace within the skull.'

'A murder committed with an L-shaped object?' the chief inspector asked.

'If the body had been found anywhere else, that is what I would have said straight away. But in a bombed ruin...' Czrisini fell into a coughing fit that made his whole body shake like a sheet in the wind. 'In the ruins of a bombing raid I cannot exclude that his death was the result of the explosion. How many of us really know what happens when a building we are in collapses?'

Stave thought of his wife Margarethe. He had to hold on to the table, as inconspicuously as possible, until he no longer felt faint. 'Are there photographs?' he asked. His voice sounded somehow hollow, even to himself.

The pathologist didn't seem to notice. He was staring out of the window into the darkness – for so long that the CID man thought he had forgotten he was there. 'Yes, well,' Czrisini suddenly muttered, as if he had suddenly found himself back in the real world. 'I don't know if I should let you have a copy.'

'Should it be found in my hands I can blame it on Kienle.'

Czrisini gave a weak smile and delved into a file until he produced an A4 photo from an envelope: skull bones surrounded by decayed skin, an old wound in the centre of skull, an encrusted black hole.

'Look here,' the pathologist said, pointing at the injury.

'It looks as if somebody had stamped an inverted "L",' Stave said.

'A very big "L", stamped very hard,' Czrisini commented. 'If the skin weren't so decayed I would have found traces of massive blood loss.'

'Fatal blood loss?'

'You can bet a few bundles of Reichsmarks on it.'

'Anything else?'

'The facts lead to the following conclusion: the deceased is a man – the shape of the pelvic bone makes that clear, as do the skull, hands, arms, legs. About 1.7 metres tall, slim. From the condition of his teeth and ligaments I would put his age at older than thirty and younger than fifty. He wouldn't have been a soldier in the Wehrmacht.'

'You can tell that from an autopsy?'

'He had a deformity of his left foot,' Czrisini replied drily. 'In simple German, a club foot. Old Adolf wouldn't have taken him.'

'The Führer had a use for at least one club foot,' the chief inspector replied, shifting his weight unconsciously on to his right leg. Absurdly, his wound made him embarrassed when the pathologist had mentioned a club foot.

'There's more,' Czrisini continued, as if he hadn't noticed the CID man's reaction. 'The deceased was wearing good leather shoes, which remained in far better condition than any other remnants of clothing on his body.'

'He must have had them made by a cobbler.'

'In which case we owe thanks to the unknown cobbler.' Czrisini produced a pair of black leather shoes from a cardboard box: the right one looked smart, save for traces of mould on the uppers, the left however looked like a battered bag of coal with laces. The pathologist pointed at the soles: 'Real leather. No rubber. Nice and smooth. But when you walk in those, everything you step on will scratch the surface, even a grain of sand. Over time the heel and ball of the sole will develop a pattern as if somebody had scribbled on them with a hard pencil.'

He picked up a magnifying glass. 'But look here.'

Stave picked up the right shoe and examined it through the glass. Lots of lines on the heel and ball, but also several lines in the hollow where the arch of the foot would be. 'Well I'll be damned,' he said.

Czrisini nodded in approval. 'Classic clue. The man who wore these shoes fell and was lying on the ground. Normally we only get scratches on the soles of our shoes where we tread the heel and ball of the foot. But this man must have been lying on the ground with his feet against a wall, a kerb, something hard or rough, with the result that his shoes have marks where there wouldn't normally be any. If he had stood up again later, the scratch marks in the arches wouldn't have been as fresh as those on the heel and ball of his foot. That means the last movements he made with his foot were probably from a horizontal position and that means…'

'…he was still lying on the ground, or that in his final struggle for life his feet were pressing against something,' Stave concluded. 'A mighty blow to the head, that splits the bones of his skull,' he went on, 'the man falls to the ground, and in his death throes the soles of his feet hammer against a wall, or something similar. End of story.'

'Nice theory.'

'Is all that in your report to Dönnecke?'

'The chief inspector wasn't exactly thrilled. He said that in a collapsing building you find all sorts of marks on a corpse. I should forget all about the damn leather soles.'

Stave was silent for a long while, then at last he asked, 'What do you think you might find if you were to examine the body again?'

Czrisini shrugged. 'I can't really say. All I know is that our anonymous friend deserves a more thorough examination.'

'Now?'

Czrisini shook his head. 'I'm tired. He's not going to run off on me.'

The chief inspector took a close look at him, his shrunken cheeks, his yellowish skin, his hands shaking ever so slightly. In the old days Czrisini would have worked through the night to discover the secret a corpse might be hiding.

'Okay,' he said. 'Thanks for your discretion.'

That evening Stave strolled along the Alster. He was not in a hurry, there was nobody waiting in his apartment for him. If only the Hamburg summer was worthy of the name then at least he might have spent the mild evening hours sitting on his balcony. His dark, damp rooms felt like a prison cell. Stave walked across the Lombardy bridge and decided to take a detour via Mönckebergstrasse. Through the rain he could see the red of the traffic light, one of only two working again in the city. The only traffic was a few cars and a couple of British trucks, but hundreds of pedestrians were standing diligently at the lights waiting for the green light allowing them to cross.

Mönckebergstrasse had once been Hamburg's favourite shopping street. But it had become narrower because of the rubble and collapsed shop fronts on the pavement on either side. Even so, many of the shops had reopened. Stave passed the Levante store, then the massive bulk of C&A, which had once been a Jewish business but by 1938 had become artificially 'Aryanised'. The chief inspector had thought that after May 1945 it would have been given back to its former owners, but it never happened. Maybe the former owners no longer existed.

The CID man looked in the shop windows on either side of the street. His ration card allowed him ten American cigarettes for June. They had gone to his son, along with those for the previous month that he had saved up. He could have turned the little treasures into Reichsmarks on the black market. *That's another nice little bit of business I have to give up now that I work for Department S*, he thought. With a few bundles of Reichsmarks in his hand he felt almost as if it was back in peacetime, but that wouldn't last much longer.

The shop display windows were pathetically empty: here a plate, there a pair of trousers alongside a few thin overcoats. Stave walked into the shop opposite C&A, its doorway guarded by a stone relief of a lion and martial figures.

'Were the Russians here?' he asked a tired-looking young shop assistant. 'The place looks like it's been looted.'

He got a dismissive look in return. 'You just back from a POW camp?'

'You could say that.'

'For weeks nobody's been talking about anything except X-day. That's why there's so little here.'

'This is all down to X-day?'

'Our second surrender. The surrender of the Reichsmark. The day the Yanks give us new money. But nobody knows exactly when the new currency is going to be introduced, or how much of it anyone is going to get. But the fact that we need a new currency is obvious. Nothing works any more.'

'And that's why you're not taking the old money now?'

'We take it for whatever we have in stock, but firms aren't turning stuff out any more. Or if they are, they're hoarding it.'

'Any shirts in my size left?'

'No.' Then the assistant looked around and leaned over conspiratorially. 'Try the Otto Reuter shop.'

Stave gave a gentle smile. Otto Reuter, O.R. *Ohne Rechnung* – 'No Receipt', under-the-counter business. The kid would look pretty stupid if he pulled out his police ID. But on the other hand, maybe they would have a shirt for him.

'What has Otto Reuter got?'

'Just a simple work shirt, pale blue, 22.50 Reichsmarks.'

The chief inspector didn't scowl. Before the war a shirt like that would have cost 3.50 Reichsmarks. But what the heck? If what money he had would soon not be worth anything at all, then any price was a good price. He laid 23 Reichsmarks on the counter.

The assistant disappeared out the back and returned with a shirt wrapped in packing paper. He handed him five ten-pfennig postage stamps as change.

'No coins?'

'People are hoarding coins. There are rumours going around that they will keep their value. And even if they don't, metal is metal. At least you've still got something in your hand.'

'Let's hope X-day comes soon. Or else we won't even be able to send letters any more.' Stave was fairly certain it was illegal to use postage stamps as money. He shoved the stamps into his wallet. 'Any razor blades to be had around here?'

'Three shops further along. Sixteen times the official price. At least that's how it was at lunchtime.'

'Otto Reuter?'

'You really have been gone a long time.'

Late that evening Stave was sitting exhausted in his bare living room, looking out of the window. The window still bore marks made during the firestorm of 1943: little patches of molten glass that resembled amoebae in the yellow moonlight. The rain had stopped, and the blanket of clouds had broken. But the air was still cold, gusting from the north-west. It's just a break, the CID man thought to himself; the whole weekend is going to be foul weather.

His thoughts drifted back to the damaged artworks in the

Reimershof. And the unknown corpse. One of tens of thousands who had died during the war in Hamburg alone. Who cared about his fate nowadays? All anyone was thinking about was the new currency. He suddenly noticed that for several minutes now he had been stroking the scar underneath his heart. I was lucky there again, he told himself. And then he thought of Karl, squatting on his allotment growing tobacco. And Anna, who right now was maybe staring up at the same stars from her damp basement apartment in Altona. Or maybe she was wandering around in the ruins, looking for artworks and antiques. Or maybe then again, she wasn't alone at all, and was laughing… He pushed such thoughts from his mind. Lucky, he realised, wasn't exactly the word to describe his state of affairs.

# Unknown notes

*Monday, 14 June 1948*

Stave was in a pensive mood as he left the house the next morning. He had a neighbour in the basement: Kurt Flasch, some forty years old, small, sullen, the little hair he had left combed over his bald head, perched on his nose a pair of nickel glasses soldered together in the middle through which his dark eyes shone as if through a magnifying glass. His wife was nearly two heads taller than him and weighed at least twice as much. A man whose family gobbled up everything he earned and who lived in perpetual fear of losing his job. A worthy bureaucrat who in March 1933 had speedily signed up as a member of the Nazi Party and in 1945 had just as speedily been cleared by the British in the first round of the denazification process. Someone with whom the chief inspector had never exchanged more than the most basic neighbourly civilities – until that weekend. For Kurt Flasch worked in the Landeszentralbank, Hamburg's regional bank

So that morning the CID man had hung around the doorway to Ahrensburger Strasse 93, knowing that it was about this time Flasch came back from his 'men's morning', an early glass or two in the corner bar, livened up by cheap beer and home-brewed schnapps. He approached him as he arrived back, acting as if it were purely a chance meeting. Stave wasn't much of an actor but then Flasch wasn't exactly sober enough to think anything of it. It was taking him long enough to get his keys out of his trousers pocket.

'It won't be worth anybody's while to lock the door soon,' Stave had said nonchalantly, watching the man's clumsy efforts, and repressing the urge to snatch the keys from his hand and open the door for him. 'We'll all be so broke on X-day that it won't be worth breaking in.'

Flasch had given up struggling with his keys and was holding them like a teacher would his ruler. 'After X-day, we'll all need to buy extra locks!' he said in a slightly slurred voice.

'The new currency won't fill our bellies any more than the old Reichsmark.'

'Stuff and nonsense. Paper money is all about trust. Nobody trusts the old rags any more. But the new currency is being issued by the Americans, and that will be solid. And when people earn real money again, then they will go back to turning out real things and buying real things. Things are getting better. You wait and see. The black marketeers will be scratching at our doors.'

'When?'

By now Flasch had forgotten all about his keys. He glanced around but in the bad weather, Ahrensburger Strasse was almost deserted. 'In May, American freighters docked at a particularly well-guarded quay in Bremershaven. US soldiers unloaded some 23,000 wooden crates. They were immediately loaded on to eight special trains. To Frankfurt!'

Flasch gave him a triumphant look, but then noticed that Stave hadn't understood the significance. 'Frankfurt is home to the Reichsbank headquarters!' he added. 'With the biggest vaults in Germany! What do you think was in those crates? Chocolate?' He laughed.

'Frankfurt is also the American army headquarters,' Stave replied. 'It could equally well have been ammunition. Or bundles of dollars for the soldiers.'

Flasch tapped the side of his nose. 'I've been at the Landeszentralbank long enough. I can smell money, even if it's locked in the vaults in Frankfurt.'

You're very skinny for someone who can smell money, Stave thought to himself, but he didn't say a word beyond wishing his neighbour a good Sunday – and then opened the door for him.

He ran over the conversation again on his way to the office. If the new money was already in Germany, that meant it would be issued soon. How long would something like that take? Another few weeks? Just a few days? Maybe a year? He couldn't see what difference it would make replacing one mark note with another mark note. Why would the new one be worth something and the old one not? On the other hand, when he had joined the police at the age of 19, he had become a billionaire overnight just on the back of the money he had earned himself: in 1923 the mint had been turning out Reichsmarks in washing baskets. First in millions, then billions, then trillions. The noughts became a joke. Whether it was a newspaper or an egg, things that had cost pfennigs a few months ago, suddenly cost so much that you had to count the zeros on your fingers to work out whether it was ten million or already a hundred million. The pride Stave had felt in his wages soon gave way to cynical scorn. Children were making paper dragons out of thousand mark notes glued together, his parents' neighbours had used bundles of marks to fill gaps in the door. Then, overnight, a new mark had been introduced and everything went back to normal. Normal prices, no inflation, as if it all had been just a bad joke. The chief inspector had never understood how it had worked back then. It had taken years for him to shed the temptation to spend all his income immediately unless it lost all its value within a week. If it had happened back in 1923, it could happen again in 1948.

Lost in memories he took long strides as he walked down Ahrensburger Strasse. The rain washed greasy brown rivers out of the ruins and sent them gurgling over the cracked pavement. He took care to avoid them so as not to ruin his shoes. He thought back to the days of the chaotic Weimar Republic, which had never seemed too bad to him. Perhaps because he had been young back then. With Margarethe. And Karl, who had still been a cheerful boy. Inevitably his thoughts eventually turned to the hail of bombs in 1943. To his son's incarceration in a POW camp. To Anna. And eventually it occurred to Stave that the only person he had spoken to that weekend was the drunk little bank clerk he had secretly sought out. He was relieved when he finally passed the bronze elephant in the doorway on Karl-Muck-Platz.

Before he had even reached his office he was accosted by Bahr. 'We need to go see Cuddel Breuer,' the head of Department S told him.

'Is the boss that unhappy with us?'

'If he were he'd be a very unhappy man indeed. He's making every department hop to it.'

Several dozen sleepy officers were already squeezed into the HQ's main conference room. A few of their colleagues had bleary morning eyes, and more than was good in such an airless room stank of sweat or schnapps. But nobody opened a window because the storm was lashing against the glass. Many of them had wet overcoats under their arms, as Stave had, because they hadn't had time to drop them off in their offices.

Cuddel Breuer came in, looking a lot fresher than any of his staff. 'Children,' he called out loud, 'we're going on a trip.'

Half an hour later some one hundred uniformed police and several dozen bad-humoured CID men in wet overcoats were standing around the city hall and the Landeszentralbank. It was a great lump of a building next to the city hall, light grey and as solid as a giant safe. Up in the gable alongside the coat of arms was still the inscription 'Reichsbank', and, as if it were a commemorative coin, the date '1914–1917'. Beneath this were five stone figures staring grimly down on to the square and in their midst a Hansa trader holding a ship.

'There haven't been so many police standing in front of the city hall since the Führer last gave a speech here,' Bahr mumbled, standing next to Stave. Both men had pulled up their overcoat collars and pulled down the brims of their summer hats to cover their foreheads. Even so the chief inspector could feel his head slowly getting damp and moisture penetrating the shoulders of his thin coat.

'Nobody's interested in the city hall,' he replied. 'Cuddel Breuer may not have told us what's going on, but we're here to protect the bank, not the mayor's retreat.'

'X-day getting closer.'

'I just wish I knew how much closer.'

They were standing by a cast-iron water pipe about a hundred metres from the bank building. The wind was blowing the rain across the square. A stench of mud and decay was rising from the Alster and the little rivers that fed into it. A tram rolled up and with screeching wheels came to a halt on the square. Its pale yellow and red paint-work glistened in the damp, the windows were milky opaque. A few dozen men and women jumped out of the doors and with hands holding down their hats and headscarves, hurried across the open space into the shelter of a building. Just like we used to do when there was an air-raid alarm, Stave thought involuntarily. Hardly anybody paid attention to the police in uniform and plain clothes a few metres apart forming a chain across the square.

'Hardly. I hope something's going to happen soon,' Bahr grumbled. 'I'm getting too old to stand out on the streets in damp shoes.'

'We've got a visitor,' Stave said in reply, and put his hand on the gun in his holster.

Two English Jeeps were speeding towards them and with squealing tyres came to a halt on either side of the Landeszentralbank building. British military police with machine guns leapt out and positioned themselves next to the main entrance. Cuddel Breuer walked up to them, spoke briefly with a captain and then came back. His orders were passed down the line of policemen. 'All streets are closed. The trams are stopped. Do not allow anybody on to the square. It's only for a few minutes.'

Eight heavy military trucks rolled up and came to a halt with their engines running. It was impossible to make out what they were carrying behind their tarpaulins. More military police arrived. Stave noticed two uniformed police to his left preventing a group of women from crossing the square. There was nobody near him.

Several bank employees emerged from the building. Stave spotted Flasch among them, despite the dark brown rain cape he had thrown over himself. They went up to the first truck, which had lowered its tailgate, and began dragging wooden cases from the load bed to the bank entrance, now guarded by a cordon of military police holding their machine guns at the ready.

Stave moved closer. The crates were long and narrow, made of rough wood. On the side was stamped CLAY-W-OCF-OFD-279.

'Looks like a code number,' Bahr observed. 'The word "clay" in English could mean our gentlemen bankers are being put on a pottery course?' he laughed.

Stave was watching the skinny shape of Flasch carrying one of the crates along with another employee, apparently effortlessly. 'It doesn't look as if the cargo's very heavy,' he muttered.

'Not coins then,' the head of Department S commented. 'Paper money, in crates. Eight trucks for the whole of Hamburg. I wonder how much that comes to.'

'Hopefully not enough to draw the attention of a few of our usual customers.' The chief inspector glanced around nervously.

In reality it took far longer than the few minutes they had been told it would to unload all the trucks. In the end a few of the military police joined in, apparently fed up waiting. It was only towards the end of the morning that the trucks finally lumbered off. Stave found himself actually thankful that it was raining so hard. On a normal warm summer's day there would have been hundreds of curious onlookers by now, but the bad weather kept the nosy parkers at bay better then the police could have done.

Breuer kept back a few of the younger detectives and twenty of the uniformed police. A few of the British remained posted next to the bank. All the others were finally allowed to leave. Before long the first tram screeched its way to the stop. Figures with caps and umbrellas began scurrying across the square again. All as if nothing had happened.

That afternoon MacDonald came into Stave's office. The chief inspector shook his hand, surprised, pleased – and ever so slightly hesitantly. 'I had more or less persuaded myself that you might not come, not because of any bad feelings, but because you might want to seduce my secretary. But now I no longer have a front office for a secretary to sit in waiting for you.'

'So that just leaves the bad feelings. I'm sorry, old boy. I'm not surprised you changed departments. Sooner or later even the toughest warrior has had enough of bullets and bodies. And as of an hour ago, I'm all the more pleased. The civilian governor wants to cooperate with Department S on, let's say, a sensitive issue.'

'Discreetly, of course.'

'You can tell your boss. But we don't want to see it in tomorrow morning's newspaper.'

'I'm already on a case.'

'All the better. In that case it will be less obvious that you're involved in something else on the side.' MacDonald took a seat and lit up a John Players. He had long since given up offering Stave a cigarette. 'The British administration has a few informants who've been relaying worrying news.'

'Informers, you mean?'

'Let's say attentive observers. One of the gentlemen came to see me an hour ago and handed me this.' The officer took a leather wallet out of his briefcase and pulled two banknotes out of it: one had a greenish-yellow design on it with the number 5 in the middle and the words '*Fünf Pfennig – BANK DEUTSCHER LÄNDER*'. The other note was blue with a different design, a ten-pfennig note, the same issuing bank.

'Somebody sold a bundle of these notes for Reichsmarks on the black market down by Goldbekplatz. At midday today,' MacDonald added. It sounded as if he was just recounting an anecdote but his taut back and clenched jaw muscles betrayed how tense he was.

'I have never seen a note for either five or ten pfennigs. And certainly never with either of those designs or that inscription,' Stave replied with a smile, 'but I can imagine why you're here.'

The lieutenant used his left hand to dispel a cloud of tobacco smoke. 'That's why we make such a good team.'

'For weeks now people have been whispering about X-day and the new money,' the CID man continued. 'This morning my colleagues and I closed off the square in front of the city hall, for hours. Army trucks came up, crates were unloaded into the Landeszentralbank. Not exactly what I would call a secret operation. There are thousands of new rumours doing the rounds.'

'And a clever forger is using that to spread fantasy money around, toy banknotes. But our informer says they're being sold as the "money of tomorrow". Most people dismissed it as nonsense, but a few more credible souls have actually bought these scraps.'

Stave thought back to a case the previous year which the CID team had found as incredible as it was hilarious: a printer in Hamburg had set up his equipment in the cellar to turn out ration coupons for lard and sugar and coloured them in by hand. They weren't exactly first-rate forgeries but they were good enough for him to get hold of 430 kilos of lard and 320 kilos of sugar, a fortune. And he also remembered the lack of small change in the shop on Mönckebergstrasse. 'Not a bad idea, printing pfennig notes,' he muttered. 'A lot more credible than trying to pass off hundred-mark notes.'

'And the more credible this forger is, the more people will buy his rubbish. And what then? Sooner or later they'll realise that these things aren't worth the paper they're printed on. Yet again people will lose their trust in money. The Reichsmark is nothing more than a joke these days. I don't need to tell you how much Germans are hoping for a new currency. And I'm not revealing any of my allies' secrets when I tell you: yes, a new currency is coming at some stage. But what that currency will be and when it will arrive we have to keep a secret. On no account do we want to betray those hopes and destroy trust.'

'Some wily forger could ruin the whole thing for you.'

'In Hamburg and throughout the three western zones. If people get rattled they become suspicious. And when the new currency comes out, they'll be suspicious of that too. And if they don't trust it, then it will turn out to be a failure. You can't have a stable currency without trust.'

'Sounds as if you'd like this forger locked up today rather than tomorrow.'

'Just get the guy, before he ruins everything.'

'I'd like to have a chat with your informer.'

MacDonald gave a thin smile. 'He's waiting in the next room.'

A young man. Early twenties, crew-cut silver-blond hair covering his chapped scalp, horn-rimmed glasses that were too imposing for his haggard face. The man didn't get up when Stave came in and for a moment the chief inspector thought he was being deliberately impolite. Then he spotted that one trouser leg was rolled up and stitched together under his hips, and saw the crutches lying on the floor next to his chair.

'So you're the money collector,' Stave greeted him, sitting down opposite. MacDonald fetched another chair from a room nearby, closed the door and reached to offer the man a cigarette.

'Heinz Suchardt,' he introduced himself, and lit up the John Players. His hands were shaking.

'One of our most trusted friends,' the lieutenant filled in, reassuringly.

'So tell me about it,' Stave said.

'These notes were going around Goldbekplatz towards the end of the morning,' Suchardt told him. He got less and less nervous with every word. Typical informer, Stave thought. 'You can imagine all the black marketeers are worked up. All morning people have been talking about the trucks by the city hall. Nobody has any idea when it's going to kick off. And nobody knows what's going to happen when it does. Will anything change? Or will it mean the end of the black market? Or will it just get bigger? Ask three people and you get four different answers. There are some things you just can't get any more. Sugar, for example. Everybody is hoarding everything. Even stolen goods fences are waiting for the new currency before they start selling. The price for one American cigarette has gone up overnight from eight Reichsmarks to twelve. People are frittering their money away as if they couldn't care less if they had none left tomorrow. Everybody is nervous.

'And now these bits of paper turn up. Somebody whispers, "That's the Allies' new money!" Somebody buys it. Then he begins to think he's been done over, and sold worthless scraps of paper. So he sells it on. Not bad business in times when the fewer goods there are to buy, the faster prices rise. Then the next person sells them on again. And again. Eventually these two notes ended up in my hands. And they were expensive.' Suchardt gave Stave a meaningful look.

'You'll get paid,' the chief inspector assured him. 'So who started circulating these notes?'

'No idea. I bought them third or fourth hand.'

Stave had been on the point of telling Suchardt to come with him into the office where the CID kept their index of usual suspects, but right at the last moment he remembered the man's amputated leg. 'I'll fetch our index cards,' he said.

A few minutes later he came back with a wooden drawer filled with hundreds of identification documents, the pride and joy of the Hamburg police since 1894, including every known hoodlum in the city, everyone who had ever been sought by the police, all in black and white on a sheet of paper. Photos taken face-on and from the side, fingerprints, last known address, any other identifying characteristics.

'Take your time,' he said.

'Where am I supposed to start?' Suchardt replied, clearly puzzled. 'I don't even know who started spreading these things on Goldbekplatz.'

'See if you get a stroke of inspiration,' the chief inspector reassured him, leaning back in his chair.

He sat there for half an hour while Suchardt slowly worked his way through the cards, until eventually the informer's hand did alight on one of the cards. He pulled it out: 'I don't know whether or not he had anything to do with these fake notes,' he said hesitantly, 'but he hangs around the black market sites and the regulars know he's a bad'un. He's dealt in forged currency before.'

Stave took the card from him, and MacDonald too leaned over to look. 'Toni Weber,' he muttered. Born in Berlin 1903. The police photos showed a thin man with short hair, not looking at the camera angrily or obdurately as most criminals did, but as if in shock. 'An artist by trade,' the CID man read aloud. 'A painter, sculptor, graphic artist. Been in Hamburg since 1945, last known address one of the Ley huts, the emergency accommodation shelters on Langenhorner Chaussee. Fined towards the end of 1945 as a *Hundertfünfund siebziger*.'

'That's not a word I learned in my German classes,' the lieutenant said.

'One-seven-five – "Paragraph 175" of the penal code made homosexuality punishable by fine,' the chief inspector explained. 'Dates back to the Kaiser's days. The Nazis upped the punishment and it's still in force today.' He gave a knowledgeable whistle. 'Then Weber spent half a year behind bars in 1946, not for making eyes at a pretty boy but for forging food ration cards from edition 40. Using a paintbrush and ink.'

'Not the same technique used on these notes,' MacDonald commented.

'Even so, somebody worth talking to,' Stave replied.

'Do I get my money now?' Suchardt asked.

The chief inspector vanished into Bahr's office. For the past few months Department S had been allowed to pay informers in confiscated goods. Stave gave his boss the details.

'Give the lad a pound of butter from our hoard of confiscated goods,' he told him. 'If it's really as important as your English officer friend says.'

'Very generous. It would take a worker six weeks to earn enough for a pound of butter.'

'We have hardly any informers left. As they say, nobody takes us seriously any more. We can afford to be generous. What do you plan to do next?'

'I'm going to spread butter all over one happy informer and send him home. Then I'm going to take a walk down by Goldbekplatz.'

An hour later the chief inspector was sitting by the Goldbek canal in Winterhude in miserable drizzle. The square was shaped like a trapezium with five- and six-storey, colourfully plastered buildings from the late nineteenth century on two sides, and facing them were buildings of the same height, but cheap brick-faced rental blocks. On the western side of the space stood the abandoned Schülke und Mayr chemicals factory: all damp-marked bricks, missing windows, kicked-in doors, a fallen chimney and collapsed roofs. A good place, Stave thought to himself, for smugglers or black marketeers to hide things in the event of a raid. It was easy to recognise the professional dealers, the ones the press referred to as 'food robbers', by their good quality raincoats and expensive leather shoes. Apart from them there were children, housewives, office workers, perfectly normal everyday Hamburg folk. Stave had dealt with the black market for so long, both as a policeman and a customer, that he reckoned he knew the way things worked, even if previously he had only been familiar with the bigger illegal markets on the Hansaplatz and the Reeperbahn.

But something seemed to be different now, and it took him a few seconds to realise what it was. Things happened quicker. There was no longer the old pretence of strolling around aimlessly, half-discreet conversations, haggling behind umbrellas or shiny capes, no overcoats quickly opened and closed, no contraband goods quickly transferred by nimble fingers from one briefcase to another. People were walking back and forth briskly. There was a nervous energy hanging over the square, like the electricity in the air before a storm.

The chief inspector mingled in the crowd. It didn't take long to realise why everyone was so worked up: there were a lot of would-be buyers, but not much for sale. The coffee beans that a week earlier would have cost 300 Reichsmarks a kilo, fifty times what they had cost before the war, had simply vanished, the Allies' penicillin was gone too, as was the smuggled Sunlight soap.

Everything the dealers had to offer was either very expensive or very cheap, or very illegal. A young man tugged Stave's sleeve and opened his coat to reveal a dozen electric bulbs, tucked into specially sewn internal pockets. The CID man couldn't help recalling the robbery down at Hamburg's main post office the week before last, when the labourers who were supposed to load mailbags on to trucks overnight had unscrewed two thirds of the light bulbs in the hall where they were working and sold them off. He could arrest the guy, but it would draw too much attention.

He came across a typewriter going for 2,000 Reichsmarks. An elderly woman whom Stave reckoned to be a war widow was selling a Leica for 40,000 Reichsmarks. 'My husband was such a keen photographer, he always took good care of his camera,' she was telling someone in a low voice. A beginner. What would Kienle do if he saw that? Pounce and buy it? A black marketeer pulled a thick bundle of notes from his hip bag and handed the women a few tattered notes. It might well be that she had just sold her last memento of her husband for a few pieces of worthless paper.

A boy was selling strips of asphalt that he had scraped off a road somewhere: 'For the roof,' he said earnestly when a puzzled Stave asked him about them. 'You can heat them over fire and then stretch them out on top of cardboard. That'll stop the rain coming in.'

The CID man turned away. He was looking for Toni Weber, the artist with his particular speciality. He had brought the index file with him and from time to time compared the face of a man in the crowd with the photographs. No match. He looked around to see if he could find any forged banknotes or ration cards. In vain.

His only surprise was when he was standing near a worker selling bottles of a yellow liquid he claimed was cooking oil, and he almost bumped into Kurt Flasch, his neighbour in Ahrensburger Strasse. He was always bumping into neighbours or even work colleagues on the black market. And it was always an awkward situation, a bit like two acquaintances running into one another in a brothel.

'I thought you had enough to do in the Landeszentralbank,' Stave whispered in amazement.

'And I hardly expected to see a chief inspector dealing on the black market,' Flasch replied in a similarly low voice.

'Is the load from the lorries safely stowed away?'

'Keep your voice down, Chief Inspector!' Flasch glanced around nervously, even though Stave had whispered. 'The load is where it ought to be. I honestly can't say any more, not even to you. They're all going crazy here.'

'And they're dealing in five- and ten-pfennig notes that nobody has seen before.'

Flasch seemed to relax a little. 'Ah, that's why you're here? Me too, as it happens. The bank chairman sent me and a couple of my colleagues out. He heard the rumours…'

'You're supposed to find out if a few notes escaped from the crates and found their way to Goldbekplatz?'

'I really can't tell you what is in the crates. But we are here to look for banknotes.'

'And?'

'Nothing. Seems to have been a false alarm.'

'I'm afraid not.' The chief inspector pulled the two notes from his wallet and held them under Flasch's nose.

He went pale. 'Those are obvious forgeries,' he stammered.

'Well at least that's something,' the CID man said, putting the notes away again. 'How many of your colleagues from the bank are out here? Who knows about all this?'

Flasch shrugged his shoulders. 'About twenty at most.'

Stave wiped raindrops from his forehead, took a look around and wondered how many people had heard of the forged notes, and how many had seen them. He reckoned there were at lease two hundred people on Goldbekplatz. Twenty of them were from the bank, a couple more from CID, God knows how many English. Enough to spread the news throughout the city that these strange notes were forgeries. If that got about fast enough then they would be taken for what they were: scraps of paper. In which case nobody would try to sell these pfennig notes any more and confidence in the new currency wouldn't be dented. At least, that was what he hoped.

'Tell your boss,' he whispered to Flasch, 'that there are laughable forgeries being passed around on Goldbekplatz. Tell your colleagues too. The more people who know about these fake notes, the fewer will fall for them.'

'And you will find the forger?'

'That's my job.'

Flasch looked relieved. 'That'll make the bank chairman happy.'

'Maybe I should splash out on a bottle of cooking oil,' the chief inspector said, a bit more loudly.

His neighbour shook his head gently. 'The most you could do with that is to use it on your bicycle,' he replied, his voice still low. 'That's torpedo oil, from the U-boat wharf at Blohm and Voss. Bone oil with chemicals added to keep it liquid at any temperature. Put that in your frying pan and you won't be able to move your legs after you've eaten. Or you'll have problems up top,' he tapped his forehead.

'Thanks for the advice,' Stave murmured, making a mental note to set one of his colleagues in Department S on to the 'cooking oil' seller. That was if he could find someone in headquarters willing to take on such a task.

As it happened there was an officer back at HQ waiting to speak to him – Constable Ruge. 'My colleagues here are going to be amazed to find a uniformed policeman hanging around my office.'

'What colleagues?'

'Fair point. But the fact you're here means there's a new case. What is it?'

'It's your case, Chief Inspector,' Ruge told him excitedly. For a moment the CID man was astounded that news of the fake currency notes had already got through to the ordinary uniformed police. 'The artworks in the ruins,' Ruge continued, not noticing that Stave had breathed a sigh of relief. 'I found out who had been renting the rooms in the Reimershof back in 1943.'

'Was that part of your work in the constabulary? How did you even find about it?'

'There were a few of us uniformed police there, at the Reimershof, Chief Inspector. We quite often find dead bodies in the ruins, but we don't often come across treasure.'

'It wasn't treasure, just works of art.'

'That's what I mean. There was talk about that, but also about…' Ruge searched for the right word, '…your change of direction,' he added rather lamely.

'Your colleagues are all gossiping like fishwives just because I no longer work for Homicide?'

'You could put it like that.'

'So why were you asking questions about the tenants in the Reimershof without being asked to? It's my case.'

The constable coughed. 'I want to move over to CID, Chief Inspector. And seeing as it's summer and there's not much going on streetwise, I thought I might make a few preliminary enquiries.' Ruge took a piece of paper from the pocket of his uniform and carefully unfolded it. 'I tracked down the former tenant,' he explained. 'And then I pulled up the list of active businesses there in 1943. The top two floors were taken up by a river boat chandler's. Nearly all the other floors below were occupied by a coffee import-export firm, except for the ground floor which was occupied by a banker.'

'The top two floors were destroyed by the firebomb. The artworks weren't there. From 1939 on, business had been bad for the coffee import-export firm.' The chief inspector recalled that right from the beginning of the war coffee had been rationed.

'In any case we couldn't ask any questions of the owner. He died in the famine winter of 46–47,' Ruge went on.

'That left the ground floor. Was there a bank branch there?' The chief inspector suddenly saw himself having to send out a hundred uniformed police to secure the ruins against looters if that got around.

'No. It was just a banker who had rented the rooms, not an actual bank.'

'Privately?'

'Maybe.'

'When?'

'From the autumn of 1937.'

'Right in the middle of the "brown years". And in the ruins we come across works of art that would certainly not have fitted the Nazis' taste. Sounds too good to be an accident.'

Ruge smiled proudly. 'The tenant is still alive. Dr Alfred Schramm. Lives at Fährstrasse 80, in Uhlenhorst.'

Stave nodded respectfully. 'Nice part of town. Right next to the area around the Alster commandeered by the English. It would appear Dr Schramm came out of the war well.'

'His private bank has reopened.'

'That means the English cleared him. He came through the denazification process untouched, or else he wouldn't have got a licence.'

'From what the landlord of the Reimershof told me, it would appear Schramm had more to fear from the Nazis than from the English.'

'He can't have been a Jew though, or his bank would have been taken over and Aryanised.'

'He's from an old Hamburg banking family. It would seem he just didn't like the brownshirts.'

The chief inspector ran a hand thoughtfully across his mouth. 'A respectable man,' he muttered.

'And possibly an art connoisseur,' Ruge added.

'Possibly someone who valued precisely those works of art that the Führer and club-foot Goebbels dismissed. Someone willing to hide away artworks to stop them falling into the hands of the propaganda ministry henchmen. Who kept them in an inconspicuous room in an office building, and might well be glad to get back a few that survived.'

'Should we drive over to Fährstrasse?'

Stave glanced at his watch. 'I have to talk to the public prosecutor about the case first. Dr Ehrlich often works late, but I don't want to push my luck. We'll visit the banker tomorrow, you and I.'

The constable clicked his heels and turned to leave.

'Ruge? Did anyone else ask questions of the Reimershof landlord?'

'Such as who?'

'Anyone from Homicide? Maybe Dönnecke himself?'

'Nobody, Chief Inspector. The landlord didn't even know that a body had been found in the remains of his building.'

'You didn't by any chance ask him about the body?'

'Should I?'

'I'll see you tomorrow.'

Even for the short walk to the public prosecutor's office, Stave had to throw on his raincoat. There'll be moss growing on my hat soon, he told himself gloomily. The grey summer sapped the will to live, even the simplest courtesies eroded by the perpetual rain. Murderous weather. At least that's no longer my problem, he thought.

Dr Albert Ehrlich took a long hard look at him over the horn-rimmed frames of his spectacles. 'You've got thinner, Chief Inspector. Thinner than you were.' The public prosecutor rubbed his right hand over his own stomach, which hung over his belt. 'A good bourgeois belly is the mark of a well-to-do man. English pastries are getting me back to the shape I was in before the war.'

'Thanks at least for not starting by asking me about my change of job.'

'You should write your answer to that one down on a piece of cardboard and have it ready when necessary. It'll save your vocal cords. So, why did you get fed up with murderers? We made a good team.'

'I hope we still are. Or do you now specialise exclusively in murderers and Nazis?'

'The latter are a sub-group of the former, rather a large sub-group.

Indeed I rather leave the fences and black marketeers to the summary courts run by my English colleagues.'

'I have two cases,' Stave said. 'One of them is of interest to the English, our mutual "patrons", shall we say. The other one is of interest to you.'

'Personally?'

'It has to do with art.'

Ehrlich spun round in his chair to look at the lithograph by Ernst Barlach on his wall. *Der Totentanz* – the Dance of the Dead. One of the few pieces of his expressionist art collection plundered by the Nazis that he had got back. 'Maybe a bit of a change would do me good. Tell me about it.'

But Stave told him first about the curious notes that had cropped up on the black market at Goldbekplatz, and showed him the examples. Ehrlich just glanced at them and shook his head. 'I can understand why our mutual friend MacDonald is worried. Green-yellow five-pfennig notes – not just cheeky, it's pathetic. Even the most minimally self-respecting forger turns out tens or hundreds. It's almost ridiculing the efforts of the occupying forces.'

'You think somebody's having a laugh at the British by distributing grotesque money? Sabotage of sorts?'

'What else? A single cigarette costs several Reichsmarks on the black market. Why would anyone take the trouble to create pfennig notes? What does he think these notes can buy? A few strands of tobacco?'

'Somebody is taking the effort to print those and undergoing the risk of getting caught just to discomfort the English?'

'It's worked with MacDonald anyway. You too.' Ehrlich raised his hands in a gesture of acceptance. 'If you catch him, I'll take the case and find charges to bring against him.'

'That will make the lieutenant happy – and his superiors.'

'I'm doing you and him the favour, primarily because I want to deal with the other case.'

The chief inspector gave a thin smile and showed him some of

Kienle's photos. 'These works of art were found by some *Trümmer-frauen* working on the bombed Reimershof.'

'Near the skeleton Dönnecke is hanging on to? I heard about that.'

Ehrlich leaned over to study the black-and-white photographs with eyes that looked as big as an owl's behind his thick glasses. Kienle's images were sharp, but the photos were small, to save on the paper and chemicals.

'They don't belong to you, by any chance?' Stave tried to be as jokey as possible, although deep down he was hoping that Ehrlich would tell him something about Anna's attempts to track down his stolen pictures. But the man opposite him just shook his head.

'Unfortunately not,' he mumbled, 'though they would have fitted in well in my collection. I don't recognise the pieces, even though they do seem vaguely familiar. As if I've seen them somewhere, not the original but either a sketch in a catalogue, or maybe a photo. They look like expressionist sculpture. Not absolute top quality, but solid middle-of-the-road stuff, if you know what I mean. The sort of things a museum might buy but wouldn't put at the heart of a display.'

'The sort of things a visitor would notice walking past on their way to see a masterpiece?'

'Exactly. The sort of sculptures a collector on a civil servant's salary might buy.'

'And a banker?'

Ehrlich looked up in surprise. 'Any banker worthy of the name earns enough to buy the very best. If he's an expressionist fan he'd buy something by the Blauer Reiter movement or Die Brücke. Why do you ask?'

'Does the name Alfred Schramm mean anything to you?'

'Privately, yes, professionally no. A Hamburg banker and patron of art and artists, very open to new things. If you're interested in art, particularly modern tendencies, the world is very open. I know Schramm is a collector and that he also supports one or two artists financially. I haven't actually come across him, either in museums or galleries, or in court. He has an immaculate reputation.'

'Not a Nazi then? Not even one with his sheet washed clean, a "Persil paper"?'

'He always considered the brownshirts to be common as muck. My information is only second hand of course…'

Stave, who knew Ehrlich had close relations with British officers from the time he was forced to spend in exile in England, nodded understandingly.

'But,' the public prosecutor continued, 'Schramm detested Hitler's henchmen as if he'd been vaccinated against them, long before 1933. A fourth-generation banker, conservative, nationalist even up to a point, cultivated and socially aware.'

'Arrogant?'

'Sometimes a trace of arrogance can save someone from making the worst mistakes. Schramm had a lot of influence in Hamburg, had the best overseas business contacts and was at least as "Aryan" as any SS-Standartenführer. After 1933 obviously his business didn't do as well as it had done before, but the Nazis didn't dare lay a hand on him. There were, however, rumours that the Gestapo had taken an interest in him and had files on him. But whatever existed had disappeared. Those gentlemen did a thorough spring-cleaning in early 1945, before the English tanks rolled in. But right up to the end of the war Schramm remained a respectable money man. And now he is once again. Even more so than before.'

'A man I shouldn't make an enemy of during my investigations?'

'What could Schramm have had to do with the things found in the Reimershof?'

'Schramm had rented a floor in the Reimershof. Privately, not for his bank. It is possible, although we can't prove it, that he used it to store the artworks.'

'In which case he'll be happy, and be your friend rather than your enemy.'

'It's just that there's something wrong with the story. If Schramm continued to collect art even after '33, then why wouldn't he hide it in his home. He owns a villa on the Alster. The ideal place to hide things in a vault or even just an inconspicuous cupboard. Why would he instead store them on one floor of a relatively small office building, where he had a lot less room? Where as a tenant he wouldn't be able to build a safe into the walls? And on top of that in an area that was regularly bombed by the British and Americans?'

'Perhaps precisely that made it the perfect hiding place? Who would think of looking there?'

'Yes, that is possible. But when a hiding place is discovered, the person who used it is rarely pleased. That's why I'm checking up in advance on Herr Dr Schramm's influence.'

'It sounds as if I might be interested in this case too. If it even is a case, that is. Up to now all you have are a couple of damaged artworks found among the ruins. That sounds more like a matter for someone working in the "lost and found" office rather than CID.'

'I'll know more tomorrow.'

'Maybe even this evening.' Ehrlich laughed mischievously. 'You're not a great lover of modern art, Chief Inspector?'

'In that respect, I'm still back in the nineteenth century.'

'Then perhaps you could do with a bit of help. This evening the auctioneer Herbert Nattenheimer is holding a sale of old and modern art as well as sought-after antiquities in the Winterhude Fährhaus. You'll see more on display there than in any museum. And would-be buyers who adore stuff like that. You'll also see what sort of prices they fetch.'

'The city is in ruins, people manage to survive from day to day on one thousand calories – and somebody's holding an auction of fine art?'

'It happens regularly, Chief Inspector. Nattenheimer's auctions are a social event and a lot more entertaining than many variety shows. This is your new hunting ground, Chief Inspector. The hammer falls at 8 p.m.'

'I'm dressed too shabbily.'

'You don't have to join in the bidding. Just join the crowd of spectators. You won't stand out. Nattenheimer always draws the crowds.'

'Will I see you there?'

The public prosecutor tapped a file. 'Unfortunately I have an
appointment in court early tomorrow morning. But I will have eyes
and ears in Winterhude. Should any piece from my stolen collection
turn up, I will be informed straight away. Frau von Veckinhausen is
still doing research on my behalf.'

He was hungry and tired, his damp clothes stuck to his skin. He
would have liked a warm meal and a hot bath. Another time. If he
was to turn up on time at the Winterhude Fährhaus, he would have
to hurry. The chief inspector could go part of the way on the tram,
but after that he had to hurry along on foot. He didn't care right now
if people noticed his limp. He glanced at his watch. On his way he
passed through Goldbekplatz; now, at suppertime and in the rain, it
was almost deserted. The only people on the square were three girls,
two of them holding a skipping rope for the third who was singing
a song as she jumped, a song the Nazi League of German Girls used
to sing on their street parades. He continued down Sierichstrasse,
passed under a bridge of the elevated railway held up by rusty steel
beams. It looked as if the whole construction could fall down as soon
as the first train passed over it. It actually dated from the Kaiser's day
and Stave wondered, not for the first time, how it was that massive
buildings had simply collapsed in the hail of bombs, while a few
more fragile things had remained untouched. Things like trees, or
statutes. Or artworks in a ruined building.

The Winterhude Fährhaus was a destination bar and restaurant on
the chestnut tree-lined Hudtwalckerstrasse, right on the shore of the
Alster, built in art nouveau style, with a little tower at one corner and
a glass-fronted café along the pavement. It was lit up like a pleasure
steamer, with shadows visible behind steamy windows. There had to
be hundreds of people inside, the chief inspector was amazed to see.

He pushed his way through the doors, at exactly five minutes to eight. The air was stuffy, from dozens of damp overcoats hanging to dry on the cloakroom hooks. His heart was hammering in his chest. He scoured the room. Anna. She was sitting in the last of the twenty rows set out in front of a podium draped in white velvet. There was a murmur of voices, clouds of smoke, and the scent of perfume. The atmosphere was as electric as at a theatre premiere. She hadn't seen him yet. She was on her own, the seat next to her still free. Stave dashed over before somebody else got there first.

'You?' she exclaimed. For a moment her dark, almond-shaped eyes opened wide in shock, then they lit up. I just hope she's pleased to see me, Stave thought. How beautiful she was. That slim body he used to embrace. How long ago was it now? Her soft black hair, shimmering like velvet. She had put her hair up, but it seemed even longer than ever to Stave. He wondered whether, let down, it would reach her hips. He was so beside himself that all he could say was, 'Your hair's got longer.'

She smiled in confusion. 'No hairdressers are working in Hamburg any more, unless you have cigarettes to push across the table. Nattenheimer here is the only one still taking banknotes. But what are you doing here? Are you trying to turn the remains of your savings into something silver?'

What are you doing here, the chief inspector nearly asked in reply. He was painfully jealous of Ehrlich. Just don't start playing the policeman, he reminded himself. 'I'm educating myself,' he managed to say instead, and in a few brief sentences explained to her about the artworks from the Reimershof.

'Are you no longer with Homicide?' she interrupted.

'It just wasn't for me any more.' Should he mention his gunshot wound? The weeks he'd spent in hospital? His doubts? It would sound too dramatic. He was embarrassed in her presence. And so he left it at that.

'Good,' she said. Just that single word. No smile. But Stave took a deep breath and leaned back. This isn't going to be a bad evening, he said to himself.

There was a growing murmuring across the room, rising in waves along the rows and then dying away to an expectant silence.

'Nattenheimer,' Anna whispered, as if that would explain everything. 'Just pay attention. We can talk later.' She had pulled a notebook out of a small, elegant, leather handbag Stave hadn't seen before. Also a typed list. Ehrlich's inventory of his stolen collection, the chief inspector assumed. But he did as he had been told and kept silent.

A man leapt up to the podium with a lively step. In his early thirties, with an elegant suit. 'A hearty welcome also to our guests from the other occupation zones.' It was the pleasantly sonorous voice of an experienced speaker. 'However, I have to inform you that anyone planning to journey abroad is barred from the auction, on the instructions of the military government.'

He held up the first piece of jewellery. 'A good, flawless piece,' he announced. Stave stared in amazement at the necklace in Nattenheimer's hand, wondering how such things could still exist in the ruins of Germany. 'Twenty-five gemstones, one point five carats, gold,' the auctioneer continued in a seductive voice. 'Offers?'

There was silence for a moment. Nobody wanted to be the first. Eventually a bored-looking young man in the front row held up his hand. 'Ten thousand!' he declared, in an almost indifferent voice. Stave would have had to work another seven or eight years to earn that much. Where had the guy got the money from?

Nattenheimer just gave a weary smile. 'No jokes, please!' he responded. There were a few laughs from the audience. And some muttering.

'Eleven thousand!' someone called.

'Twelve grand.'

'Thirteen.'

The hammer finally fell at nineteen. Nattenheimer had only taken two minutes to boost the price of the necklace. Now he held up the next lot on the podium. One after another, like numbers performed by a variety artist: seventeen thousand for a gold ring, twenty-eight thousand for a large diamond. The expensive jewellery always attracted the same six or seven well-dressed young men with hard faces and calm voices throwing thousands about. After half an hour – the chief inspector had long since stopped adding up in his head how much money there had to be in this one room – Natten- heimer had flogged off his supplies of gold and gemstones.

Now he brought out the silverware, a canteen of silver cutlery one minute, the next a single dessert spoon. All of a sudden there were other bidders: elderly men, fathers, younger men in less expensive suits. The sums offered dropped to about a single thousand, some- times into the hundreds – until eventually a butter knife went for half a pound of butter.

'That is worth a hundred and twenty Reichsmarks,' Nattenheimer grinned. 'Anybody offer more?' The hammer fell.

Next he turned to paintings. Kitsch in oil with gold frames, expressionist drawings, Romantic watercolours, two marble heads of young girls, dating from the nineteenth century – everything went, every style, any age. Anna studied every piece closely but in the end just shook her head almost imperceptibly, as an exhausted Natten- heimer finally abandoned the podium.

'None of Ehrlich's treasures?' Stave asked.

'This was Nattenheimer's fifteenth auction. They have become a sort of popular spectacle. No fence in his right mind would try to sell off stolen goods here. It would be too noticeable. And in any case three quarters of those who come are just here to watch, beginners. But you can't rule out the possibility of one of them trying to sell something of interest to the public prosecutor.'

'Have you found anything for Ehrlich yet?'

'Two sketches by Nolde. On the black market down by Nobistor.'

'Does Ehrlich pay well for things like that?'

'With his useful connections.' A smile flitted across her face. 'Very useful in my business.'

Salvaging artworks and antiquities from the ruins, restoring them and selling them on to black marketeers or the British. Highly illegal.

If Anna von Veckinhausen were to be picked up, an English summary court magistrate could sentence her to a year in jail. Unless a German public prosecutor were to put in a good word for her.

'What about you?' she asked. 'Was this evening professionally useful for you?'

'I've also salvaged a couple of pieces of art from the ruins,' he replied. 'But none of them seemed as *recherché* as what Nattenheimer just showed us.'

'The man is a born artist. Did you know that he's a trained opera singer? Bass baritone. The auction house belonged to his father up until 1935. Then the Nazis closed it down for "racial reasons". Somehow or other the Nattenheimers survived. After the war he couldn't make much money singing, so he had a go at his father's business. And as you can see: trade is booming.'

'People were throwing banknotes at him as if they were worthless scraps of paper.'

'They are scraps of paper. People would do better to invest in gold and diamonds. And if they can't afford that, then silver cutlery.'

'Or just butter knives. I keep asking myself where people have got so much money from. In some cases, I can imagine.' The chief inspector nodded towards two young men chatting with Nattenheimer behind the podium, clearly settling formalities. 'The kings of the black market. But what about the others?'

'The kings of the Nazi era,' Anna laughed bitterly. 'There were people who didn't do badly out of it, providing they knew the right people.'

'Or were themselves the right people.'

'There was probably a thousand years' worth of Nazi Party membership sitting on the chairs here tonight. Not all the savings stockings were burnt in the bombing. There are still more than enough Reichsmarks lying around, waiting to be turned into real valuables.'

'Something solid,' muttered Stave. 'And so easy to vanish without trace. A canteen of silver cutlery complete with a receipt from an auctioneer and a note from the finance ministry certifying that the

15 per cent tax has been paid honestly. And all of a sudden there is no longer any link to Reichsmarks, or the question of how you might have earned them.'

'But you're not here looking for old Reichsmark notes?'

'Old artworks. Or rather not really old artworks, more artworks with no owners. Let's have a cup of coffee here. We can talk about my case.' And hopefully about us too, he hoped, though he didn't dare even hint as much.'

They strolled into the room next door and found one of the few free tables. There were lots of people who had been at the auction, Stave noticed, but not one of the well-dressed gentlemen who had bought gold or gemstones.

'A coffee, please,' Anna said to the thin, sweaty waitress.

'Ersatz or real coffee?'

'Ersatz coffee.' She smiled at her companion. 'Unless you've had a pay rise.'

'Two ersatz coffees,' Stave said. He pulled out the photos from the Reimershof and briefly explained what he had found out.

'I would like to have found those,' Anna murmured, studying the pictures closely.

'You recognise them?' he asked hopefully.

'No, not so far. But they're expressionist pieces, probably from the twenties. Solid. Not something English officers would pay a lot for. Nor any of my black market customers. But there are connoisseurs who would be interested.'

'Valuable pieces?'

'Who can say for sure nowadays? You just saw someone pay more than a month's salary for a butter knife. But when we get proper money again, the game may be up – who would give valuable cash for a damaged concrete head? In the Weimar Republic sculptures like that would have cost a few hundred Reichsmarks, maybe a thousand.'

'And afterwards?'

She frowned. 'Not even you are quite that naïve. As far as the

Nazis were concerned that was "non-Aryan art". Unsellable, except abroad.'

'Abroad?'

'The Nazis sold off lots of pieces they had looted from museums or had stolen from collectors in galleries in London, Paris or Switzerland. They plundered as comprehensively as the Red Army would do later.'

The chief inspector sipped at his coffee. It had little taste, but at least it was hot. The Reimershof stood directly on one of the little rivers from which an inconspicuous barge could reach the harbour. The banker had certainly had better connections abroad, one of the reasons why the Gestapo had left him alone. Had he perhaps been planning a bit of smuggling, only to have the plan ruined by a couple of firebombs? Works that all of a sudden had become unsellable in Germany, but would fetch good prices overseas? Perhaps a little bit of a payback for the decline in his financial business since 1933? But how had Schramm come across these pieces of exotica? It might have been that these pieces didn't actually belong to Schramm, but rather to museums or collectors. People who might now be asking themselves how their treasures had come to end up in the ruins of the Reimershof. Stave thought of Ehrlich's stubbornness, his genial implacability. The public prosecutor had built up his collection together with his wife, a wife who had later been driven to suicide by the Nazis. For Ehrlich it wasn't about money, it was about memories. And he was the merciless enemy of whoever had stolen them from him. It will be interesting to interview the banker tomorrow, he told himself.

'Do you know a Dr Alfred Schramm?'

Anna shook her head. 'A suspect? Or a victim?'

'The one doesn't exclude the other.' He told her what he had found out about the banker.

'May I keep the photos?'

He handed her one of the few prints he had. She put it into her elegant handbag.

'A new acquisition?' Stave asked, nodding towards the handbag.

For a second or two she blushed like a young girl who'd been caught out. 'On the contrary,' she admitted, stroking the soft brown leather. 'I've had it for years. It was more or less the only thing I managed to save when I fled west. It's amazing what useless things we drag around with us, isn't it?'

Stave glanced at the handbag and stopped. Anna von Veckinhausen. There was a monogram in gold on it: 'A.v.G.'. He felt faint. If this had been an interrogation, he would have asked her then and there about the 'G'. As it was he just sat there, as if somebody had slapped him in the face.

'I'll ask around a bit,' Anna went on, not having noticed his confusion. 'Somebody must have seen these busts somewhere.'

Stave's heart was hammering in his chest. He tried hard to keep the disappointment out of his voice. Disappointment that she had told him so little about her past. Fear, Jealousy. And then a wild irrepressible hope. 'So we'll meet again?'

'I'll tell you what I've found out. In the Fiedler. Let's say five o'clock? Could you accompany me home now? It's curfew soon and I'm too tired to run.'

The rain had died down. The walls of the bombed-out houses still shone damp, and the air was cool and heavy, the evening sky a dark violet between the empty window frames. Anna didn't take his arm as she would once have done, but strolled alongside him at arm's length under the darkening sky. But Stave was happy just to inhale her perfume. When they passed through the glow from one of the few functioning streetlights, her hair shone.

They exchanged only a few words. Not one word about their time together, or about his son, Karl. He made a point of not asking her questions, trying not to act like a policeman, which he so often did: What are you doing these days? Do you see Ehrlich often? Or have you found someone else? What does the 'G' stand for? He didn't mention it, even though it was torturing him. Just concentrate on being a man walking through the city at night with a pretty woman at his side.

An hour and a half later they were standing outside the door to her basement apartment in Röperstrasse in Altona. The Elbe was glistening like a strand of silver beyond the end of the street. A fishing boat was steaming slowly upstream to the moorings by the Altona warehouses, the bitter smoke from its funnel reaching as far as the building where they stood.

'Thank you for accompanying me,' she said.

'Anna…' but suddenly Stave couldn't find anything sensible to say.

She smiled, bent towards him and kissed him on the cheek. 'You should spend your wages on razor blades,' she whispered. 'Before the money become worthless.'

'It already is.' He held the door open for her, and stale air met them.

'I'll be in touch,' she said.

'Today is my lucky day,' Stave replied, closing the door gently behind her, to prevent it slamming shut and waking the neighbours. 'I'm being serious,' he added, but she could no longer hear him.

# Signs of recognition

On his way back home Stave had the feeling, simultaneously uncomfortable and yet strangely pleasant, that he was somehow detached from the world around him. The partial façades on either side of the street felt like a gloomy set for some experimental piece of theatre, where the main roles were played by Death and Destruction. Yet he wanted to whistle a tune and dance just like the stars had done in the musicals of the thirties.

He wasn't paying attention to where he was going. At one point he was stopped by a British patrol, two soldiers in a Jeep, who let him go when he showed them his police ID, even giving him a friendly salute. The days were long gone when the slightest sound among the ruins had the British brandishing their machine guns.

After three quarters of an hour the CID man found himself back in Neue Rabentstrasse, not even halfway back from Anna's place to his own apartment. He hurried along, pulling his overcoat collar up against the drizzle that had resumed, then suddenly stopped and turned around.

There was a light on in the pathology building, a warm yellow square in the façade of the badly maintained former villa. Behind the window lay Czrisini's office.

Too worked up and too hungry to be tired, Stave tried the handle on the door on impulse. Unlocked. Who was going to break into a morgue, after all? He felt his way along the dark corridors until he found the door to Czrisini's office, knocked and walked in.

'You scared me to death,' the pathologist exclaimed.

'I assume that doesn't happen often in your job.' Then he paused. Czrisini was in the process of packing books and files into a chest.

His office, which normally looked like a shambolic museum storage room, now looked like the storehouse of a company that had gone bankrupt. 'What are you up to?'

'I'm tidying up. What are you doing here?'

'I was out walking. It's pure chance. I saw the light was on. Is everything okay?'

'Because I'm tidying up?' Czrisini smiled. 'Even old dogs can learn new tricks. I'm learning to be tidy. Or at least trying to.'

For some reason or other, Stave felt uncomfortable without knowing why. 'When you've learned, you won't be able to drop by and see me any more,' he said, and tapped his forehead with his right hand in farewell.

'Wait a minute,' the pathologist called after him. 'I have something to show you, if you're not too tired yet.'

'The Reimershof corpse? That would wake me up.'

Czrisini smiled and walked off. He's shuffling, Stave thought. Normally the pathologist was first to turn up when a body was found, as agile as an excited bloodhound. Czrisini flicked a light switch and led him along a few corridors to the autopsy ward in the basement. He pulled a box out of a shelf and opened it.

'Be careful. The fabric is fragile after so many years in the dirt and rubble.'

'The dead man's clothing?'

'What remains of it. Or at least what we could remove from the skeleton. The corpse was on its back. The shreds of clothing were just those in front of his ribs, the pelvis and the legs, plus the special leather on the shoes, which you already know about. No wallet, no documents, no coins or keys in the pockets.'

'The bombing raid took place in the summer of 1945, a warm day if I remember rightly.'

'It got a lot hotter when the firestorm broke out,' Czrisini's voice faded. But you're right: at the time of his death the man was probably wearing light summer clothes. Summer slacks without a belt, a light shirt and a blue jacket.'

'Dönnecke won't get anywhere much with that.'

'He knows nothing about it.'

'Why did you keep your mouth shut?'

'I didn't keep my mouth shut – our colleague kept his ears shut. The chief inspector wasn't very interested in what I had found. He wanted to relegate the case to the filing cabinet as quickly as possible. One way or another he fobbed me off. Of course it's all in my report, but I doubt it will ever be read. Including this interesting clue I found at breast level on the corpse, between his shirt and jacket.' With a tweezers the pathologist held up a ragged scrap of cloth that lay beneath the other bits of clothing in the box. Yellow, with a black mark.

'I recognise that,' Stave mumbled. 'It's a Jewish star.'

After he had said farewell to Czrisini, the chief inspector walked the rest of the lengthy trek to Ahrensburger Strasse, his head filled with his thoughts. From the first of September 1941, all the Jews in the Reich were obliged to wear the yellow six-pointed star. He remembered it well because their bosses ordered the enforcing of the rule 'under penalty of severe punishment' and every Jew known to the police who did not follow the regulation was to be arrested. It had seemed sordid to him to patrol Mönckebergstrasse to enforce the rule. And indeed he had come across a Jew, an ENT doctor Karl had gone to see when he was little. Those were the days when Jews were still allowed to treat non-Jews. The man had been walking down Hamburg's most prestigious shopping street without the star. It was as if he was challenging the law. Stave neither arrested him nor even spoke to him, just pretended not to know him. Afterwards he had worried for days someone might have noticed and denounced him for dereliction of duty. But nothing happened. He never saw the doctor again.

By the summer of 1943 everyone wearing a yellow star had vanished from the streets of Hamburg. The few citizens who referred to them merely said, 'They've been resettled in the east.' If the dead man found in the Reimershof really had been a Jew, then by summer 1943, he was definitely somewhere he should no longer have been. A Jew who'd gone into hiding and was holed up in an unused office? An office where somebody who didn't dare venture out into the street was killed by a bomb?

It was Dönnecke's case, he reminded himself. But his former colleague wasn't interested. And even if he had known about the Jewish star: after millions of Jews had died, Dönnecke above all people wouldn't bother to look into the fate or even the name of a single dead Jew.

Maybe I should have stayed in Homicide, after all, Stave thought. Aren't people and their fate more important than things, even works of art? But then he thought of Anna's remark when she had found out he had changed department. 'Good.' She had hated Homicide as if it were a rival: all his cases had stolen Stave's time, evenings, weekends, nights. And anyone who dedicated his life to deaths and murders would find in the end their soul poisoned by permanent suspicion, perpetual questions. That – and the look on Karl's face when he came back from the war and found Anna instead of his mother by his father's side.

Back home he found there was still a piece of bread in the fridge. The damp air meant a white mould had grown on the upper side of the loaf. He cut it away carefully, making sure he was wasting as little as possible. Then he cut it into slices and chewed each one individually and thoroughly. Washed down with water from the tap and his last pickled gherkin. He also had a few rubber potatoes but he was all of a sudden too tired to cook them on his old iron stove. Maybe tomorrow.

When he finally fell into bed, the short summer night already giving way to a grey mist, he fell straight into a dream: Anna and the skeleton dancing in the Winterhude Fährhaus, a mad dance to shrill music played by his son Karl on a violin. Nattenheimer, the auctioneer, was swinging his hammer like a conductor's baton and telling jokes. Dr Czrisini, a Woodbine in either side of his mouth, was piling the spectators' chairs into giant crates. But what about me, Stave asked himself in his dream. I can recognise everybody, but where am I? He couldn't see either his hands or feet, he opened his mouth but no sound passed his lips. As if he were a ghost, floating through the room, invisible to everyone else.

# An artist's life

*Tuesday, 15 June 1948*

There was one person who wasn't in his dream – the person he went to see the next morning, as early as he politely could: Public Prosecutor Ehrlich

'We need to talk about the corpse.'

'That's no longer your business, Chief Inspector.'

'It's Dönnecke's business.'

'But you have something to tell me about the Reimershof corpse? What's the problem?'

'Dönnecke's the problem. He's not taking the case seriously.'

'One of innumerable corpses in an innumerable number of bombed buildings. I have no intention of supporting your colleague's lack of engagement. But I have a certain understanding in that he has other murder cases to deal with. He is currently also working on two others.'

'The dead man in the Reimershof was a Jew. The Reimershof was destroyed in 1943. It doesn't take forty years working in Homicide to see that there's something that doesn't fit there,' Stave replied.

The public prosecutor leaned back in his chair. 'That wasn't mentioned in the report Dönnecke gave me. Tell me more.'

The chief inspector told him about his visit to Dr Czrisini and the remnant of the yellow star that the pathologist had found hidden under the corpse's clothing. And the scratches on his leather soles. And his club foot.

When he had finished Ehrlich beat a tattoo with his fingers on his desk. It was only then that Stave realised how exhausted he looked.

'Have you heard the expression "drawing a line"?' the prosecutor asked.

'You're laughing at me.'

'It's very fashionable nowadays. "We need to draw a line." You hear it everywhere. Time to move on, time to put the past behind us, time to start over. It's better to look towards the future than back to the past.'

'In my opinion the unidentified dead man is a murder victim. Even if the murder happened a few years ago.'

'The act of Navy Captain Rudolf Petersen also took place a couple of years ago. His story might be a lesson to you, as it was to me. He was a commodore of the German fast attack boat fleet. He had three deserter sailors shot – on the tenth of May 1945, after the German unconditional surrender. I took him to court.'

'The old Aryans are afraid of you.'

'Maybe not for much longer. I lost the case yesterday. He was set free. Obviously I am going to appeal. But if a similar case comes up I'm not going to be so over-optimistic, to put it mildly.'

'You aren't going to ask Dönnecke to revisit the case?'

'Petersen had three men shot in public after the end of the war. There are witnesses, documents, the man himself doesn't even deny it. And even so I didn't have him locked up for even a single day. And the evidence you're presenting me with is a few patches of yellow cloth and scratches on old leather soles.'

'It's not enough to charge somebody,' Stave admitted, 'but it is enough to pursue an investigation.'

'For Homicide but not for Department S.' Ehrlich looked at the man sitting opposite him, with the sad expression of an old owl. 'What a shame you switched departments,' he muttered eventually. 'I could confront Dönnecke with what I know about the Jewish star. I could put pressure on him. I could force him to revisit the investigation.'

'But you can't set me on Dönnecke's heels. You're the public prosecutor. But our old colleague is the one who has to produce results.

If he can't be bothered to get his fat backside off his office chair, then you won't get any evidence with which to press charges.'

'So what do you suggest?'

'I could investigate it. Secretly.' Then quickly added, 'Discreetly.'

'That was just the answer I was waiting for,' the prosecutor said, with a thin smile. 'I'm not a man to draw red lines. Ever. Ask about, Chief Inspector, discreetly, that's obvious. Use the artworks case as camouflage. It might be that they have something to do with the dead man? Give the man his name back. Give me proof that it really is a murder case. Then I will open formal charges, in the first place against person or persons unknown. And afterwards, if maybe you find out more, who knows?'

'If anybody finds out I'm secretly interfering in Homicide matters, I'm screwed,' Stave muttered. 'Dönnecke will want my head on a plate. And Cuddel Breuer won't lift a finger to help me. He's got me down as a quitter.'

'There couldn't be better cover for what you have in mind. And don't forget me,' the public prosecutor assured him.

'I'll keep you posted. Discreetly,' Stave said, and got up off his seat. He was wondering if it was really a good idea to suggest this secret collaboration with the public prosecutor. But he had got his old adrenalin back: the joy of the hunt.

'By the way, Stave,' Ehrlich held up his right hand in a sort of greeting as the chief inspector put his hand on the door handle, 'welcome back on board!'

An hour later Stave and Ruge were trundling along the streets in an old patrol car. The chief inspector was filled with the seduction of power given him by the fact he had a secret he couldn't share with any of his colleagues. He felt like a secret agent. MacDonald would slap me on the back and laugh, if he knew about it. The rubber on the windscreen washers had gone weeks ago and they were leaving semi-circular streaks on the glass. Not even the police could get their hands on replacements; there were no more pre-war supplies in the warehouses, and making new ones wasn't exactly one of the priorities of German industry right now. The chief inspector drove more slowly than he would have liked to, straining to peer out through the smeared and fogged-up windscreen.

'Be careful on the narrow streets,' the young constable warned him. 'There's hardly any tread left on the tyres.'

'I drove a panzer on the eastern front.'

When he saw Ruge open his eyes wide and stare at him, he made a face: 'That was a joke.' He slowed down further.

'Is Dr Schramm expecting us?'

'I didn't call him. I thought it might be better to surprise him. That has its advantages when you're interviewing someone.'

'Even if he's not in?'

'There'll be somebody who can tell us where he is. Even if it means we have to spend half the day rattling around the streets in this old bath tub.'

Stave drove the awkward old banger over Lombardbrücke bridge and turned left. To their right was the white fairy palace of the Hotel Atlantic, to the left the Alster, grey under a layer of cloud. There was a solitary rower forcing his boat through the waves. Stave watched him, then suddenly turned the wheel and nearly crashed into the kerb. A big black car squeezed past them drenching them in a shower of water, dirt and the stench of exhaust fumes.

'A Mercedes 170 V,' Ruge called out, recognising it. 'Should we pull him over?'

The chief inspector grabbed the steering wheel more tightly and forced himself to breathe calmly again. 'We'll get that blind driver another day, there aren't that many new cars driving around Hamburg.'

Within a few seconds they had caught up with the black car because there was a British lorry grinding along the street and even the impatient driver did not dare overtake that. Stave stared at the curved wing, the chrome bumper and the perfect lacquer bodywork, as if it was an expensive piano. For a second he was almost tempted to shunt the old patrol car into the rear of the shiny bodywork, and had to pull back a bit in order not to get hit by the spray of the Mercedes.

'That thing'll do over a hundred kph,' Ruge mused. 'One-point-seven litre litre engine, thirty-eight horsepower, at least as good as the pre-war model.'

'You're in the wrong job to get your hands on a car like that.'

The policeman laughed. 'Cars are my passion. Even as a child I knew all about them. For 170,000 Reichsmark cash, Mercedes will deliver a 170 V to your door. At least that was the case but the word is now that there are none in stock.'

'Mercedes also waiting for X-day?'

'Delivery issues is the official explanation. Whatever that means.'

They crossed the bridge by Schwanenwik and down Adolfstrasse towards Uhlenhorst: white villas, trees, hedges, almost no bomb damage. Nobody on the pavements.

'Our racing driver is taking the same route as us,' Stave observed as he saw the black limousine turn left into Fährstrasse. Beech trees and lindens on either side of the road, their branches dark and wet from the rain. White and ochre-coloured villas behind them and at the end of the narrow street a view of the Alster.

The black 170 V turned into the gravelled drive of a three-storeyed, bright yellow residence resembling a villa in Tuscany.

'Number 80,' Stave noted. 'Nice house for a racing driver.' He turned into the drive behind the Mercedes, parking the old patrol car diagonal so that he blocked the way.

A man in his mid-sixties with a large angular head, thick white hair, blue eyes and a cigar in the corner of his mouth climbed out of the Mercedes. A Prussian blue wool overcoat protected his massive body from the rain. The chief inspector recognised the brown and yellow checked lining: a Burberry, he reckoned, that had been the uniform of the Hamburg well-to-do before the war. The man was limping, his left hand leaning on a dark wooden walking stick with a heavy silver handle.

'He's not happy that we're parked in his entranceway,' Ruge whispered.

'Next to that villa our patrol car looks like an outsize ashtray,' Stave replied as he opened the driver's door and stepped out. 'We'll give the gentleman something else to think about.' He pulled out his ID card and announced 'CID' in a voice loud enough to be heard up and down the quiet street.

The elderly man stopped suddenly as if Stave had slapped him in the face. 'Please come along.' His voice was deep and used to giving orders. He turned round rapidly and, as fast as his limp would allow, walked past the Mercedes towards the house.

'Dr Schramm?' Stave asked when they reached the porch to the villa's entrance, protected from the drizzle. He introduced Ruge and himself.

'What do you want of me?'

'I have a few questions relating to the Reimershof. I have reason to believe you know the building?'

'It was hit by a bomb. 1943. Totally destroyed.'

'Not totally,' the chief inspector replied, with a narrow smile. 'May we come in?'

Schramm fumbled a large key into the lock. Arthritis in his hands, Stave thought. Before the banker had fully turned the key in the lock it was opened from inside. A housemaid opened the door to them, a young woman in a white bonnet and black dress. The last time the chief inspector had seen a servant like that had been in the cinema, before the war.

'Herr Direktor,' she stammered.

'It's alright, Elfriede,' Schramm reassured her, took off his coat as if it was the most normal thing in the world and handed it to her. He placed his walking stick in a wicker basket next to the door, more carefully than the way he had handed the maid his coat. 'These gentlemen and I are going into the piano room. We won't be needing you.'

The maid vanished like a shadow: Stave thought he could almost smell her sense of relief. The banker took them into a room illuminated by a grey light through the multi-paned windows. Beyond them Stave made out a well-kept garden. His eyes wandered back to the room they were in to the Bechstein grand piano, to the heating stove with silver-framed sepia photographs on its shelves. The one in the middle showed a group of people posing together in an impressive room: Schramm, younger than now, a wizened woman in a wheelchair, a few much younger men and women dressed in the style of the 1930s. None of them was smiling. Rays of sunlight fell through the windows behind them, similar to those here in the piano room. The walls were covered with bookshelves. In front of them stood sculptures, vases with sumptuous flower arrangements and framed certificates behind glass.

'My wife's last birthday,' Schramm said, having noticed his visitor's gaze. 'Christmas, 1938.'

'She was poorly?' Stave hinted that Ruge, who was clearly uncomfortable, should take a look. Maybe the uniformed officer would spot something.

'Anaemia. The doctors tried everything, but nothing helped. She died in 1939, on the first of September. I don't believe that was a coincidence.'

'My condolences, though I realise it's far too late.' The chief inspector turned away from the photo and turned to the elderly banker. 'I was called to the Reimershof yesterday. Or rather to what remains of it. You had been a tenant there?'

'One of many.'

'In the clearing-up process the *Trümmerfrauen* came across some noteworthy objects.' Stave took the pictures of the sculptures out of his coat pocket. 'Do you recognise these?'

'No.'

Stave looked at Schramm in surprise. 'Take your time. Have a good look.'

'I have no problems with my vision or my artistic appreciation or my memory. These are not from my collection.'

'Have you an idea why I have come to you with these photos?'

Schramm sighed. 'I am passionate about art. My wife was too. You could say it was the greatest passion we shared.' He cleared his throat.

'You were also a patron of contemporary artists.'

'And I still am. Insofar as there still are talented young people around after twelve years of barbarism. It is easier to earn money than it is to create art, believe me.'

Stave, thinking of his own petty paycheque, didn't agree, but nodded all the same. 'That is why, among all the tenants in the Reimershof, we came to you first.'

'Why would I keep works of art in an office? I had taken a few rooms there, two for files and one with a desk and a telephone. Somewhere to retreat to, to get away from the hectic day-to-day at my bank. A place to…' he hesitated briefly, 'to deal with certain more confidential bits of business. So confidential that I, shall we say, didn't want to deal with them within the official remit of my bank business.'

'What sort of business?'

'That falls within banking secrecy laws, but nothing illegal if that reassures you.'

'Yes, of course,' the chief inspector replied, in a tone that made clear it certainly didn't reassure him at all. 'And this business didn't involve art?'

Schramm used his arthritic right hand to make an impatient gesture. 'I have my art collection here. Who keeps things like that in the office? Especially modern sculptures like those? In the brown years?' He nodded towards an oil painting near the heating stove, of a plane about to crash from a sky as black as night on to an uninhabited city. 'It's by Radziwill. My wife loved it, especially after her diagnosis. She also like Seurat, who painted in a completely different style. I have two or three Liebermanns in the salon next door, a few from the New Objectivity movement, a couple of Fauves. Expressionists, too,' he added, after a short hesitation. 'But mostly drawings and oil paintings, no statuary.' He nodded at the photos in Stave's hand. 'Those are expressionist pieces. Solid work as far as I can tell from a police photo. Good, but not so good that you would have found them in the Galerie Flechtheim in Berlin back in the twenties. And of course after the twenties you wouldn't have found them anywhere at all.'

'So you've never seen these pieces?'

'Not in any museum or gallery where I was a client, not in any of the studios of the artists directly supported.'

'Who shared your offices in the Reimershof?'

'Nobody. It was my refuge.'

The chief inspector thought back to the dead man. 'You didn't have a secretary? Not even a messenger, or a caretaker?'

'A cleaning lady came by once a week. I can't imagine what she might have had to do with the works of art you found in the ruins.'

'Nothing, I imagine. Dr Schramm, in the ruins of the Reimershof we also found the corpse of a man.'

'That's very sad, but in this case you're not asking the right man. There were other tenants there, but I hardly knew any of them.' Schramm didn't exactly seem to be shaken by the news.

Stave handed the banker a card with his telephone number. Early that morning he had typed out his name, rank and number for his new department on several pieces of cardboard. It looked shabby, but that was hardly his chief priority at the moment. 'Please get in touch if anything should occur to you,' he said. 'It's also possible I might have to talk to you again about this.'

Schramm pulled out a leather wallet. For a moment the chief inspector thought his was going to be presented in turn with an undoubtedly much finer visiting card. But instead the banker took out a piece of paper that had been folded over several times. At the top of the yellow sheet it read, 'The State Commissioner of the Hansestadt Hamburg for Denazification and Classification', and typed beneath the banker's name. It was a discharge sheet, a clean bill of political health, nicknamed a 'Persil note' on the black market. Forgeries went for a fortune on the black market, passed from hand to hand. But this one looked like the real thing, Stave thought.

'I've been cleared,' Schramm said, his voice shaking with barely suppressed agitation. 'I have the best of relations with the British occupation forces, and the mayor. For years I was interrogated again and again by those Gestapo thugs. They made an invalid of my wife and I had to sit and watch how those "gentlemen" just stared coldly. They almost certainly opened a file on her illness. But those times have gone. And you're not going to bring them back. Or should I say "carry on". I am a busy man. I'm not going to have you turn up here every day, parking your patrol car in full visibility on my drive, in order to ask me absurd questions in my own house about obscure works of art. You'll need a good reason before you turn up here again, a very good reason. Have I made myself clear?'

'Thank you for speaking so freely,' Stave replied, and reached for his hat.

A minute later he was sitting next to Ruge in the patrol car, turning the ignition key on the rattling eight-cylinder motor.

'I wouldn't like to have him for an enemy!' the constable exclaimed, whistling between his teeth. He hadn't dared even speak until they were a bit down the road.

'Too late. You already have him as an enemy, but with a bit of luck he won't have noticed either your name or your face.'

'But you gave him your card.'

'Didn't you notice anything unusual?'

'Apart from the huge villa, the expensive Mercedes, the well-maintained garden, the thick carpets, the oil paintings on the wall, the grand piano, the heating stove, and the tasty housemaid?' The constable shook his head. 'Nope, otherwise I didn't notice anything. Joe Soap, just like you and me.'

'What about the photo on the stove ledge?'

'The woman in the wheelchair? Dreadful business.'

'Forget about the poor dear.'

'The men and women standing next to them? They didn't exactly look happy either. Is one of them in our card index? I could take a more detailed look.'

'The room, Ruge!' Stave sighed. 'Did you take a good look at the room where the photo was taken?'

'Bigger than anything I have, that's for sure.'

'And better furnished.'

'Indeed, paintings and bookshelves and…' All of a sudden his voice died away and he went pale.

'…and sculptures on the shelf.' As he turned right on to the street that bordered the Alster, Stave pulled one of Kienle's police photos out of his overcoat.

'The bronze bust of a woman that was in the Reimershof,' Ruge whispered.

'Which Schramm insisted he had never seen before, even though until at least the end of 1938 it had been in his own villa, as evidenced by the photo with his unfortunate wife and the gloomy relatives. Behind the cosy family group that bust was standing on the shelf. I'd like to know what lies behind this strange gap in our banker's memory.'

'Could that be a reason for asking him a few more questions?'

'A very good reason.'

Back in his office Stave's confidence evaporated. It was silent, and the drizzle soaking the window fell in such microscopic droplets that it had the chief inspector yearning for a proper rain shower so that at least he could hear the pattering. There was a stench of foul air, bitter cleaning fluid and damp carpets. He had to admit to himself that he had nothing against Schramm. The banker hadn't told him the truth about the bronze bust. What of it? A lie, but one that was to no one's loss but his own. Schramm was rejecting a piece of art that had once belonged to him. Hardly a crime. And that was all Stave had. No motive, not even the slightest suspicion why the old man might have lied to him. Ehrlich wouldn't open a case against such an influential man, one who had even been persecuted by the Nazi regime. It was a bagatelle. A case to be closed and filed.

Yet even so, Stave was not happy with the idea that it should be just left to gather dust. That would never have happened in Homicide. At least not if he was in charge. No reason to start behaving like that just because he had moved to Department S. After all, this was the body that Dönnecke was doing nothing about. Schramm had rented two rooms, he had said so himself. The corpse had been lying in the pile of rubble that the chief inspector had surmised were the ruins of the room where the artworks had been kept. Was it Schramm's second office? Or was it just a coincidence? Was it the room of a different firm? If Stave had been in charge of that case he would have asked the old man about the corpse, and waited to see what reaction he got: embarrassment, shame, fear, just the tiniest hesitation, a flicker of the eyelids... But as things stood he would have to approach it via the artworks. The CID man sighed and at the same time laughed at himself for such a theatrical gesture. He had a few talents but it had been a long time since acting had been one of them. Maybe it was time to have a go.

He put the narrow ring-folder in his filing cabinet, the first file in his new office. Slowly he began to make himself at home. He took an empty grey cardboard casebook out of his desk drawer and opened his second file: 'Currency forger, Goldbekplatz.' If he didn't get any further with one case, he could always tuck into the second.

A quarter of an hour later Stave found himself gradually coming to understand why his colleagues had nicknamed Department S, Department Deadend. It was cursed. His second case too had run into a brick wall. He had sent a few uniformed police down to Goldbekplatz, and others out to the Ley huts in Fuhlsbüttel. Nothing. Toni Weber, the artist and convicted forger, had disappeared into the drizzle. Maybe he was with one of his 'Paragraph 175' friends? He would have to ask his colleagues in Vice. Their relevant files had survived the surrender. But the chief inspector was reluctant to snuffle around in things like that. He thought it was nothing to do with a judge or a policeman who an adult human being shared his or her bed with.

But what had happened to him? Was he still living in Hamburg? Had he anything at all to do with the forged notes? He had nothing more than a vague allegation against him.

It's time for me to find out more about the guy, Stave decided, getting to his feet. Half an hour later he came back to his office with another file: the old investigation into Toni Weber's case. First of all, an anonymous allegation against him. The Vice Squad's investigation, a testimony by a rent boy. Then a charge of breaching Paragraph 175 and a fine. But no more. Earlier, Stave reflected, it had been punishable by several years in jail, or being sent to a concentration camp and forced to wear a pink triangle, being beaten up or even a miserable death being hung by piano wire.

The second part of the file consisted of a couple of typed reports, bad photos of forged documents laid out on a table, copies of the charge and conviction for forgery. Apart from such sparse information as his date of birth and address, there was nothing personal. No name other than that of the rent boy mentioned in the first case, but in the second there was one more: Paul Michel.

The chief inspector flicked through the interrogation notes. Even through the bureaucratic language you could feel the fear that Michel must have experienced. He was brought in as a witness, but he had known he could face charges too. On at least one occasion Michel had taken forgeries from Weber's printer down to the Goldbekplatz – concealed in his steel leg. A disabled war veteran, Stave guessed, an old friend of Weber's, maybe a 'special friend', although if so, that had been of little interest to his questioner because Stave could find no precise mention of such a relationship anywhere, just here and there vague references in the witness's statement which were probably quite harmless but which anyone who had been so minded could have considered improper.

Michel had insisted he didn't know he was carrying forgeries: he had thought the ration cards were the real thing. A poor lie, not least because trading even in real ration cards was illegal. And also because he didn't have an answer when asked by the CID man why, if he considered them to be genuine, he had concealed them in his prosthetic leg.

Nonetheless Stave could find no other reference to Michel in the file. No charges, and therefore obviously no conviction. They had just let him walk. Maybe Michel had just been too small a fish. Maybe somebody had been sympathetic because he had only one leg. Stave didn't like the idea of turning up in front of the man like a ghost from his past. But for now he constituted the only lead he had. He took down the man's address and set off.

Lerchenstrasse was narrow, little more than an alleyway near Heiligengeistfeld in St Pauli. It wasn't very far from the CID headquarters but Stave was soaked to the skin by the time he got there. He glanced briefly at the Schiller Theatre on Lerchenstrasse, a round building like a circus tent which up until 1945 had hosted crude comedies and operettas. He had been there once with Margarethe, 1938 or 1939, he didn't remember exactly. Now the gutted building was used to house refugees and the homeless. Three teenagers were leaning against the outside wall, flat caps pulled down over their foreheads, hands in their trouser pockets, cigarettes between narrow lips. He could feel them watching him as he strode along the pavement.

At Lerchenstrasse 23 there was an apartment block that had been virtually decapitated: a ground floor with fire-blackened brick walls, above it blown open, inaccessible apartments with drenched ceilings and floors, walls askew, plumbing pipes, remnants of heating-stove chimneys. All that remained of the roof was a charred beam standing out against the sky like a fallen tombstone cross. Somebody had scribbled the name 'Michel' on the blackened door in chalk. Nice handwriting, Stave thought.

The man who opened the door to him was skeletal, bald and with skin as chapped as someone of venerable age, his dark eyes sunk deep into his skull, the scrawny left hand clutching a walking stick. Yet despite all that, the chief inspector reckoned he was only in his late forties. He glanced down briefly. The right foot of the man opposite was in an old slipper, but below his left trouser leg a leather shoe sat on the end of a leather frame.

'Herr Michel? I need to talk to you,' he said, and took out his police ID.

The man went pale. 'Not that old story?'

'Up to a point. But it's nothing to do with you,' the CID man said reassuringly. 'May I come in?'

'At your own risk. But take shallow breaths until you've got used to the smell.' The stench of filth and faeces overwhelmed Stave like poison.

'It comes from the drains sometimes,' the one-legged man said. 'There's nothing to be done about it.'

Two bare rooms. A heating stove with an enamel plaque: 'What stops you getting cold is every bit as good as gold.' There were cracks in the walls, filled in with brown clay and old newspapers. Michel noticed Stave looking at them and raised his hands apologetically. 'The cracks keep getting bigger. We fill them with whatever we have to hand, to stop the draughts.'

'It's not making the walls any more stable.'

'I know. Every storm makes the whole place sway as if you were on a ship. Sometimes when a door slams it sounds like an explosion and we all run out, just like we did back in '43, in case the building really does collapse. Only now instead of running down into the cellar, we run out into the open air. These days the cellar belongs to the rats. Sometimes we get clouds of stone dust and we have to wrap damp cloths over our faces to stop from suffocating. One day the ruins above our heads will simply come tumbling down.'

'You don't live here on your own?'

'With the wife and five children. They're out fetching rations.'

Michel led him over to two chairs next to a wooden oil paint-lacquered table with an open packet sitting on it. Stave stared at the yellow cardboard carton with the words in black 'CARE U.S.A.' He was staring enviously at the tin cans inside, meat and margarine in boxes, sugar, honey, bacon, raisins, chocolate, and above all, two pounds of genuine coffee. The chief inspector didn't know what to make of the aid parcels that kept arriving in ever-greater numbers, sent to Germany by charitable organisations overseas. He longed for such delicacies he had been deprived of for so long, but on the other hand he also felt a vague sense of humiliation looking at such generous gifts. Not that he himself had been tempted to accept such a token of sympathy: he knew nobody in America and was not on any distribution list run by Caritas or the Red Cross.

'I just picked that up from the post office,' said Michel, following his guest's gaze. 'Cost me more than 44 Reichsmarks in duty and carriage costs.'

'A small price for such a treasure trove of conserves.'

'I have friends over there, who think about me. In Hollywood.'

'Yes, my friend Charlie Chaplin sends me postcards now and again.'

'I'm not joking. I was in charge of supplies at UFA film studios. A lot of our colleagues in the industry got homesick in 1943 and left for California. I kept in contact with them, at least as long as that was still allowed. But they never forgot me over there.' He tapped the cardboard box. 'I'd pack up my bags and leave this hole for California straight away if the *Amis* would let me in. But they're not taking any German immigrants at the moment, least of all cripples like me.'

'So far you've not been convicted of anything though,' Stave growled, and noticed Michel's face muscles twitch. 'And if you answer a few of my questions, you'll never see me again.'

The one-legged man let himself down on one seat and offered his guest the other. 'Don't get me wrong, Chief Inspector. I've had assurances before from the cops that I'd be left alone, but here you are. The next time it'll be a different one of your colleagues, and you will still be able to say you kept your promise that you personally wouldn't turn up again. But what good's that to me?'

Stave ignored the comment, pulling out a battered notebook. 'What do you know about Toni Weber?'

Michel just closed his eyes and sighed – rather too theatrically, the CID man thought. 'Toni has a talent, a habit of doing favours for the wrong people. It's his only failing. He's a good man. And a very good artist. If we didn't live in such barbaric times, you wouldn't have to come to a tip like this to find out about him. You'd be reading his name in the newspapers.'

'But we do live in barbaric times.'

'Which is why you're here. Toni Weber is no friend of mine, but he is a professional colleague. He was an independent artist in the Weimar Republic, a sculptor, graphic artist, did a bit of oil painting. When the economy started to go downhill in 1929, he caught the wind and became a prop supplier for UFA.'

'He moved into film?'

'It was a wise move. The more miserable people become, the more they go to the cinema. Apart from anything else, that was when "talkies" were first coming in. Those were gold rush days. The studios in Berlin needed people who were good with their hands to build the sets: castles, magnificent interiors, factories, costumes from all down the years, copies of works of art to decorate the set. Weapons of all sorts, chandeliers, ships, strange cars. You can't imagine what we concocted from chipboard and plaster.'

'And you two met up at UFA?'

'Two failed artists on a pleasure steamer, yep. There was no way our works were going to end up in galleries any more, but we still brought a wage packet home every week. I started a family. Weber was a good colleague, if a little taciturn.'

'Taciturn?'

'Particularly after '33. His private life was…' Michel hesitated, 'somewhat unconventional. And the art he had produced in the Weimar years wasn't exactly the sort that Adolf would have featured in his planned museum in Linz.'

'Degenerate art?'

'Things wouldn't have gone well for him after '33 if he hadn't moved into film. The movies were the great passion of old

"Hopalong". Goebbels was in love with the studios, as long as they produced what the gentlemen in the propaganda ministry wanted to see. We turned out movies, Goebbels was happy, nobody asked what we had done before '33. No visit from the Gestapo, no call-up to the front.'

He pulled a face. 'But in the end I'm afraid the front came to us. We were still shooting movies when the Ivans were already in the Berlin suburbs. While fighting our way back from a movie shoot, we got shot at with bullets! A few of the survivors said it was a low-flying Soviet plane. Others said it was a T-34 tank. The argument between them was heated and totally irrelevant.' He tapped his prosthesis. The iron sounded hollow.

'Did you and Weber come to Hamburg together?'

'No, I was in the field hospital for a long time. My wife and the kids were somewhere in Berlin when the Russians marched in.' He fell silent, staring at the ceiling. 'Well, anyhow we found our way back to one another and made our way here by the end of '45. She didn't want to live anywhere there were Russians. I only came across Weber again here. I had thought he had been killed in that attack, but he had escaped. We met up again by chance at a meeting of the Artists' Economic Community.'

'Sounds like something bureaucratic.'

'Actually, it was a self-help organisation. Members got ten sheets of watercolour canvas a month at a fixed price. Not much, but better than nothing. A simple hairbrush that I would once upon a time have picked up for eighty pfennigs was now costing twelve Reichsmarks on the black market. I made my own canvases. Jute sacks, picked up for fifty Reichsmarks a load, treated with lime and chalk. That way a finished painting would last long enough to still be hanging in some museum in five hundred years' time. But that was hardly my biggest concern.'

'Is it still even possible to sell paintings?'

Michel gave a bitter laugh, and nodded at the cracked walls of the room. 'Not for me. It would seem I lost my talent at some stage while working for UFA. When I was young I was quite a decent sculptor and woodworker.'

'How about Toni Weber?'

'His talent was undiminished, to say the least. In both fields. He got back into the movie business. Worked with Helmut Käutner, on the production of *In jenen Tagen*. Put the props together. And at the same time he was doing watercolours. Portraits.'

'Of living people.'

'Who else? There are a few Hamburgers who came through the whole mess just fine. The most successful painter in town is Ivo Hauptmann, the son of the famous author. It'd cost you three thousand Reichsmarks to have your wife immortalised. At least Weber would only charge you eight hundred.'

Stave thought back to Schramm, the banker, and nodded: 'A small but lucrative market.'

The one-legged man scratched his head. 'But it's growing. Nobody might know what will happen after X-day, but art is a good investment in uncertain times. The more insecure things get before the new currency comes out, the better things are for artists. For most of them anyhow, not for me. Weber had an exhibition recently at C&A. They had an opening day called "Art Special". In a department store. But it was a success, as far as I heard.'

'If he was so successful, why then was Weber forging ration cards in 1946? The rations cards you had hidden in your prosthesis.'

'Thanks for the reminder. I had almost forgotten,' Michel replied with a sour face. 'Back in 1946 Weber hadn't made his name yet. He was an artist but couldn't sell anything. You have to keep at it. But when he came out of jail he made up his mind not to let anything like that happen to him again. And one way or another he succeeded. When he came out of Fuhlsbüttel, he actually began to sell a few paintings. Then Käutner came along with his movie. And since then things have gone well for him.'

Stave wondered if he should ask Michel about Weber's sexual preferences. About any of the artist's 'special friends'. But maybe he knew no more than he had already alluded to. The chief inspector was well aware that the '175ers' kept their private lives very private. Unsurprisingly. He decided against pursuing the issue.

'Do you know where I might find Weber?'

'In Travemünde.'

The CID man leant back, somewhat pleased at last to have got something to go on, but somewhat disappointed to find out that the man wasn't in Hamburg. 'Why?'

'He met a new client at the C&A exhibition. One of those gentlemen who've come into a large sum of money recently.'

'A black marketeer?'

'You can say something like that out loud; if I was to say it, there'd be a few well-built young men at the door kicking hell out of my one remaining shin bone.'

'But why is Weber in Travemünde?'

'His new client has a holiday home on the Baltic. He's hired Weber to decorate it for him. The client invited him up there. He's been there for a few days now.'

'Do you have a name?'

'Yes, as it happens. Weber was so proud of getting the contract that he told everybody about it.'

Five minutes later the CID man left the apartment, relieved that the ruin hadn't collapsed on his head. He took a deep breath and shook his overcoat in the hope that it might somehow get the stench out of the fabric. He had an address in Travemünde in his notebook and a bad feeling in his gut. Toni Weber was a good businessman, getting a job as a prop assistant for one of the few movie production companies still functioning in Germany. As a painter turning out portraits of the well-to-do for a few hundred Reichsmarks. As the decorator of a house belonging to a black marketeer. Why should someone like him bother to forge a few obscure currency notes? As a repeat offender he would be risking several years behind bars. Stave feared that once again he was heading up a dead-end alley.

It was just before five o'clock. He walked into the Fiedler dance-café, a one-storey flat-roofed building squeezed into a bombed space between two of the six-storey rented apartment blocks. On the shabby white-painted façade beneath the café name, two words had been painted on: 'Hot food'. Stave, who once again had had no lunch was for a moment tempted to grab an early evening meal, but then he remembered Anna's preferences and ordered two cups of ersatz coffee. As he handed the young waitress a single Reichsmark note she dropped her head shyly.

'I can't bring you any change. We haven't got any coins, and no postage stamps either.'

Stave was about to reply that he was happy for her to keep the change, when he realised just in time how absurd an answer like that was nowadays. Was the waitress to cut off a corner of the note? No coins meant no tips. So instead he handed her another Reichsmark note and said, 'That's for you.'

The café was quiet at that time of day. The CID man sat down at a wobbly Formica table by the window, with a view of the door. He wondered fleetingly how Anna knew this place. They had never come here together. Then he remembered the 'G' in the initials on her handbag, and the wedding ring she'd sold to the jeweller. You needn't have worked for years for the CID in order to draw certain conclusions. He was suddenly seized by jealousy and lust. As well as the policeman's natural curiosity. Who was this G? Was it because of him that Anna had withdrawn from their relationship? A husband who had turned up again and his wife discreetly ended an affair? Should Stave use his connections with the police to take a little look into Anna's past? And while he was at it, maybe a little research into her present. Put her under discreet observation, just for a day or two, to find out who she might be meeting up with? Don't do that to her, he told himself! Don't do that to yourself!

Ten minutes later Anna walked in, a little out of breath and her face red. His heart stopped for a moment at the sight of her. He wanted to kiss her, but only awkwardly held out his hand.

'I've got something for you!' she exclaimed, before throwing off her raincoat and sitting down next to him. 'That's why I'm late, bogged down in the art market.'

'Where else?' he replied. The reality was that he was relieved she hadn't been somewhere else. With another man.

She pulled the photo of the bronze female head out of her handbag. 'This is a depiction of the actress Anni Mewes,' she declared triumphantly.

'How do you know that?' Stave asked in amazement.

'One of the female curators at the museum recognised it as Anni Mewes.'

'I've never heard of her.'

'She was a middling-level star in the silent movies of the twenties. When she was a young woman living in Hamburg she played alongside Gründgens. In 1920 she moved to Berlin and appeared on stage alongside Marlene Dietrich. Then she had a few roles in UFA movies, and then a few turns on the stage. But nobody has seen anything of her for years. I'm not even sure she's still alive. But I know who made this bronze sculpture of her.' Anna paused for effect and smiled at him, as happy as a young girl, a sportswoman who's just won a race. Stave thought she looked simply adorable. 'An expressionist from Berlin, called Toni Weber.'

The CID man choked on his ersatz coffee.

'A friend of yours?' asked Anna in surprise.

'He's a man with a lot of friends. But I've only heard the name,' Stave spluttered. 'And not that long ago.' He coughed a few times more and told her, without going into details that MacDonald would have preferred kept secret, about forged notes turning up on Goldbekplatz and that he wanted to question the artist about them. At the same time thoughts were whizzing through his head: expressionist art, degenerate art, portraits of silent movie stars. That would explain how someone like Weber had ended up in the movie business when the financial crisis struck: he had old contacts. It also explained why he had got back into the business after the war. All along he had maintained a certain reputation for painting portraits of the rich and famous.

'Are the other sculptures that were found at the Reimershof also by Weber?'

'The art historian I spoke to doesn't think so. She's known Weber ever since the Weimar era. Did you know that he survived the war and is now living in Hamburg?'

'In a Ley hut on Fuhlsbüttel Strasse. But he's rarely at home. He prefers to spend his time on the Baltic coast.'

She laughed in surprise. 'We complement one another remarkably well!' she exclaimed.

'Indeed,' Stave said pensively and then, before his reaction should become awkward to one or the other of them, abruptly changed the subject. 'Was the banker, Schramm, ever a patron of this Toni Weber? Do they know each other?'

'It's possible but my friend at the museum knew nothing about that.'

The chief inspector leaned back. Weber's artwork had been in Schramm's bombed-out office building, and before that in his villa. Schramm's denial that he recognised the bronze. A dead Jew. Weber as a suspect, or a witness, maybe not at all involved in the forgeries circulating on Goldbekplatz. There was no pattern, he told himself, no pattern at all. Even so, he felt like a hunting dog that had caught the first wind, and at the same time he suddenly felt as if his luck had turned. I'll ask Weber about the mystery of the bronze bust, he thought. That will allow me to get to him without it seeming suspicious. And only afterwards will I confront him with the other case. Normally a suspect guesses why a policeman wants to talk to him, and immediately puts in place a defensive strategy. But not in this case: Weber has to be made to think it's all about his old artwork. He won't be on his guard, and that meant he might be able to take him by surprise and squeeze a few clues about the Goldbekplatz case out of him. That's if he was in any way involved in it.

Stave managed to persuade Anna to have an early evening meal.

That gave him the opportunity not just to sate his own hunger but also to spend another hour with her. The shabby café with its wobbly tables and the rain running down the dirty window had become the most beautiful place in the world. But eventually she got to her feet. 'I have to go,' she said.

'Will we see each other again?'

'Gladly.'

And in that second Stave knew that he wasn't heading down a dead-end alley after all.

# Travemünde

*Wednesday, 16 June 1948*

Stave and MacDonald were travelling in a dark-green British Jeep north-east up the old Reichsstrasse 75. They had left Hamburg half an hour earlier. Fields on either side of the cobbled road, pale yellow flattened ears of corn, fields of potatoes like swamps. A bent-over farmer coaxing a carthorse across a meadow. The storm was blowing rain from the north-west. It must have looked just like this in the Middle Ages, Stave thought. Water was coming in through a rip in the car's canvas roof, which was already so damp that every time the vehicle with its hard suspension hit a bump in the road, the pair inside got a shower. The tiny windscreen wipers flicked back and forth but even so the chief inspector could see no more than a hundred metres ahead. He was glad he wasn't driving.

He had suggested to the British lieutenant first thing in the morning that he might accompany him to Travemünde. He had accepted and, as Stave had secretly hoped, suggested they take a British military vehicle so he wouldn't have to borrow one of the patrol cars and go through the hassle of dealing with paperwork and petrol rations.

For a while they sat behind a dented brown Opel Olympia that dated back to before the war. It had to be a German driving. The car had a number plate with the letter 'BH' followed by four numbers. Up until a few weeks earlier the occupation forces had used number plates beginning with 'HG' for 'Hamburg Government'. Now it was called the 'British Zone Hamburg' – a tiny formality, expressed in just two letters, but nonetheless a sign of decreasing tension and a return towards normality, an abbreviation in one's own language and not that of the foreign soldiers. As they moved out on to the rural roads with less traffic the man in front accelerated away from the Jeep.

'He'll be at the Baltic coast before us,' MacDonald muttered, trying to sound indifferent. But he didn't fool the chief inspector, who could hear in his voice the disappointment of a driver who finds himself left behind.

'I hope this journey isn't for nothing,' Stave said. 'We haven't reported it in advance.' Telephone calls were banned between 7.30 in the evening and 7.30 in the morning to avoid the chance of the decrepit telephone network failing. That very morning the CID man had tried to make a call but the operator had told him he could be waiting up to six hours for a free line. He declined the opportunity to send a telegram via Lübeck: they were often conveyed to their ultimate destination by bicycle or on foot – it would be faster just to take a car.

'Our artist won't run off,' the lieutenant said, clearly happier again. 'Not when there's a bit of business in it for him.'

'I'm not going to order something from him.'

'No, but I am.'

Stave looked at the officer in surprise. 'Are you interested in art?'

'I'm not a barbarian. I quite liked the bronze bust you showed me from the police files. I could do with one like it for my living room back in Scotland at some stage. With Erna's features. And if we can't get hold of the bronze, then he can paint a portrait.'

'Maybe somebody can melt down the shell of a hand grenade and make a piece of art out of it.'

'You're starting to sound like a pacifist. But I would prefer something solid in metal rather than a work on paper. And it would be a suitable reminder of Hamburg for Erna.'

Stave's right hand tightened around the grip on the dashboard. 'You're leaving soon?'

'Later this month. It's breaking Erna's heart. On the one hand she wants out of here, but on the other she's going to have to leave her son behind. He's just eight years old.'

'Is he still living with his father?'

'The court gave him custody. Even though…' the lieutenant hesitated, looking for the right expression, 'he's rather bad-tempered.'

'He hits the boy?'

'The kid can usually dodge out of his way. He has only one leg.'

'Is the guy out of work?'

MacDonald gave a bitter laugh. 'A cripple these days? Of course he's out of work. But he isn't an adulterer. The divorce is Erna's fault, so she loses custody. That's the law. One way or another there's a price to be paid by everyone in this mess.' The lieutenant stared religiously straight ahead.

'What price do you have to pay?'

'Right now, whatever Weber charges me.'

'Art is expensive.'

'All things are relative. Let's see if the artist's eyes light up when instead of Reichsmarks I wave pound notes in front of him. Maybe they'll smell better. When the world's back to normal someone like Weber could become an international star: galleries in London, New York, Paris. I'll resell his work, make a huge profit and quit the service.'

'You'd sell a portrait of Erna?'

MacDonald shook his head. 'You're right. I need to order two things in Travemünde, one sculpture for the living room and another for a safe in the bank.'

'Sounds as if you got the idea from a certain Hamburg banker. And your nice little investment will only pay off if it isn't Weber turning out the forged pfennig notes your superiors are so worried about.'

'If that turns out to be the case, then he'll have more time for painting. In that case, of course, there'll be no trips to art exhibitions abroad.'

'Do you think he is the forger?'

'In the wake of all you've told me about Weber, it sounds absurd. But it does seem to be our only lead in the case.'

'Not just in this case.' The chief inspector told him in detail about Schramm apparently having no recollection of the bronze bust despite it being in his villa in 1938.

'Do you think the two cases could be connected?'

'What could these curious banknotes have to do with a bronze bust's sudden reappearance?'

'Schramm is a banker?'

Stave gave the British soldier a sceptical glance. 'That's a very vague connection. Too vague to present to Cuddel Breuer, or even to Public Prosecutor Ehrlich.'

'But it's crossed your mind, hasn't it?'

'You know me too well,' the chief inspector admitted. 'Art, money, a banker – it all fits together somehow. But I don't have anything more to hand.'

'Not yet, anyhow. We're almost there.'

The Baltic coast was an idyll. It was as if there had never been a war: houses for warm summer days with terraces, colourful window boxes, well-tended front gardens, hotels with rooms with a sea view for five hundred Reichsmarks a night, including breakfast with marmalade and real coffee. The air smelled of salt and grass and the rust from the funnel of a big Swedish ferry anchored in the harbour.

'Glad to see my colleagues in the Royal Air Force at least forgot this town,' the lieutenant said. Stave remained silent. The two of them drove past the casino – an elegant art nouveau building – recently reopened.

'Is it just because of the rain that there's hardly anybody around?' MacDonald asked. 'The casino is empty, the terraces abandoned. Travemünde is supposed to be the paradise of the most successful black marketeers. The casinos and the hotels must have opened for some customers.'

'For the black marketeers from all the occupation zones. You're right. Up until a few weeks ago there were people up here having fun that was worth several thousand years in jail. But the rumours about X-day spoiled their mood. They all want to be at home when the time comes. My boss at Department S has stomach cramps because all the black marketeers, who in a normal summer have fled the city, are now squatting in Hamburg and he has far too few men to deal with their invasion.'

MacDonald pulled up next to a hotel. Stave asked the bored porter for directions to the address Michel had given him. Five minutes later the Jeep came to a halt outside the house Toni Weber was supposed to be decorating: a villa with a square extension reminiscent of a lighthouse. A view of the Baltic. A front garden as big as a marketplace, and behind the house the chief inspector spotted the red earth corner of a tennis court.

'Nice place,' MacDonald commented admiringly.

'It would be a real pity if we have to arrest him in the middle of his work,' Stave said, hauling his bone-shaken body out of the car.

The man who opened the door to them was gaunt and had a stoop that made him look smaller than he was. Brown hair, just slightly too long, big eyes and the brown skin of someone used to working in the open air, unusually powerful hands with long fingers. The chief inspector recognised him from his photo in the police file.

'Herr Weber,' he said, 'we'd like to talk to you.' The man's face displayed naked fear when he looked at the police ID card held up to his face and saw the British uniform and the Jeep drawn up to the door.

'This isn't my house,' he stammered.

'We're not looking to buy it. We just want some information from you.'

'Is this an interrogation?'

'There are no charges against you.'

Weber led them in. Tall windows, bright rooms that gave the impression of being bigger than they actually were, because of a lack of furniture or curtains. Weber walked through the house to the back where a room opened out on to a terrace and the garden. Roses in curved beds, the first blossoms already out: red dots in a world grey with rain. They reminded Stave of drops of blood.

'I need to close the pots quickly to stop the paint drying up,' the artist explained. There was a ladder in the room and newspapers covering the parquet floor. To the rear there was a picture outlined in black on the plaster which Weber had clearly just finished covering with a strong-smelling paint: a Baltic landscape with rolling waves, sailing ships, seagulls, clouds, a lighthouse on a steep slope to the shore and a steamer on the horizon.

'It's what the owner wants,' Weber explained in a tone of voice that made quite clear he wasn't taken by his own work.

'Not exactly expressionist.'

'That's putting it kindly. But these days you take whatever you can get. And it's good exercise for the hand and eye and the feel for colours and proportions. But you haven't come all the way out here from Hamburg to study modern murals.' Weber looked at them nervously.

Stave pulled the police photo of the bronze bust out of his coat pocket. 'Do you recognise this?'

'Anni Mewes,' he exclaimed. All of a sudden his nervous tension disappeared. 'She sat for me as a model, not long after I finished my training in Munich. Must be more than twenty years ago. Where did you find it? It looks in a dreadful state, and all that rubble around it.'

The chief inspector told him about their discovery in the Reimershof, and showed him photos of the other pieces. 'They aren't mine,' Weber replied, 'even though they look somehow familiar. But there were so many expressionist works about then. Before 1933.'

'How could your bronze bust have ended up in the Reimershof?'

A shrug of the shoulders. 'After Hitler seized power it was wiser not to hang around galleries or with artists any more. I got into UFA, which I am sure you know from your police file. I'd done the bust of Anni Mewes long before that for a film fan in Berlin. A rich guy. He might not have been just a film fan but maybe also one of Anni's lovers. But what business of mine was that? I had by then more or less forgotten it – until the summer of '37. My bronze bust ended up in the Degenerate Art exhibition after that.'

'You were in the company of some famous colleagues.'

'As far as Goebbels was concerned we were all enemies of the people. You could read that every day in the newspapers. And in the weekly cinema news there were films saying the same. In one of them where Hitler and his propaganda minister were wandering through the exhibition making jokes, you could see the Anni Mewes on a pedestal in the background. When I saw that in the cinema I crept out while it was still dark. I worried every day that the Gestapo would come knocking on my door.'

'And did they.'

'No. The Degenerate Art exhibition contained hundreds of other pieces. I gradually calmed down. The most famous works were either destroyed by the Nazis or flogged off abroad. The rest ended up in warehouses and were simply forgotten about. My Anni Mewes was in the second group. I came across it later, however. It turned up in a propaganda film.' He laughed. 'The bronze bust of Anni nearly featured in more films than the good lady herself.'

'When was that?'

'Spring of 1938. I don't remember which day exactly.'

Stave did his sums. The bust had been presented in the Degenerate Art exhibition in the autumn of 1937. Most of the works on display had been commandeered. He remembered the police helping, taking down unpopular works from the walls and carrying them off. They emptied whole rooms like that. By then, at the latest, the Anni Mewes bronze must have been taken from whoever had commissioned it. In the spring of 1938, it turns up in some little film – even if just as a prop, a scene setting designed by the ministry for propaganda. In the winter of 1938, however, the bust is suddenly in the private rooms of the Hamburg banker, Dr Alfred Schramm. Had he bought it from the propaganda ministry? A banker who was no friend to the Nazis? It seemed unlikely. Then in the summer of

1943, the bronze ends up in the ruins of an office building in which Schramm had rented rooms. It was an odd odyssey.

'Do you know a Dr Alfred Schramm?'

Weber made a pained expression. 'The banker? A great patron of the arts and artists. And, unlike many such men, he doesn't only favour the works of dead artists, but also contemporary masters during their lifetimes. At least a few of them. If he discovers an artist it's as good as winning the lottery. Unfortunately I wasn't that lucky back in the twenties. And from 1933 on I didn't do anything that anybody would have collected.'

'And since 1945?'

Weber laughed. 'If Schramm were my patron, do you think I'd be pushing my paintbrush around here?' He nodded at the Baltic scene on the wall.

'Have you ever met Schramm personally?'

'Never.'

'Do you know if Schramm – whether through a middleman or a gallery – ever bought one of your works?'

'I've never received money from him. And I doubt he has ever bought any of my works.'

'No money from Schramm? Not even before the war – 1938 for example?'

'Not one pfennig. Never.'

In that case, there we have a motive for Schramm to say he'd never seen the bust, Stave thought to himself. He took a deep breath. The exhausting trip up to Travemünde hadn't been in vain. He briefly wondered if he ought to tell Weber about the photo in Schramm's villa, but decided against it. Nor would he ask Weber about the anonymous corpse found in the Reimershof. He glanced at Mac-Donald. The Brit seemed unhappy. The chief inspector suppressed a smile. The lieutenant had little interest in the circuitous meanderings of the bronze bust. He wanted to know about the forged banknotes.

'There's one other thing,' the chief inspector said, sounding as chatty as possible as he pulled the pfennig notes from a bag.

Weber stared at them as if they were live hand grenades. 'Oh no,' he spluttered, 'I don't do stuff like that any more. The business with ration cards was a mistake. I was hungry. But even so it was stupid.'

'How do you know these are forgeries?' Stave asked softly.

'Pfennig notes in those colours? What else could they be? So that's why you're here. The bronze bust means nothing to you.'

The CID man refused to be drawn. 'Where were you last Monday?'

'In Travemünde. My client has sorted out a room upstairs for as long as I'm working here. I'm leaving tomorrow but I've been here on the Baltic for the last two weeks.'

'Do you have witnesses?'

'The baker down in the village. The cleaning lady who comes by once a week. The neighbour who must have seen me at work through the window. He's…' Weber hesitated, '…a very good friend.'

'We will check those out,' Stave replied, and made a note, angrily underlining the words. If that was true, then Weber hadn't been on Goldbekplatz when the five- and ten-pfennig notes turned up. That would have been too simple.

'Take a closer look at these notes,' he said to Weber. 'You're an artist. Maybe you'll recognise another artist's stylistic signature. Could it be somebody you know who made them?'

'I'm not in that business any more,' Weber protested, but still lifted up the notes, looked at them, held them against the light, and then eventually shook his head. 'I couldn't have done these even if I'd wanted to. Nor could anyone else I know. When I forged the ration tokens, it was on cardboard, using a pen and Chinese ink. These have been printed on special paper.'

'With a mint machine?' Stave asked.

'Maybe. Maybe not. In either case they're from a professional printer. Look here.' He held up the ten-pfennig note to the light and pointed to the edge. 'That isn't quite right. The colour and the lines are separated by a millimetre or two, the pattern overlaps the blue colour ever so slightly. It's either a print mistake or an imperfect forgery. But it hardly matters as the note itself is just ridiculous.'

'Why?'

'Because ink and paper are hard enough to get in the occupied zones, as any artist will confirm,' Weber replied despairingly. 'Any forger would confirm it too. This scrap of paper and the blue colour on their own are worth more than ten pfennigs. Who's going to print banknotes that cost more to produce than they're worth? Who would print banknotes if it would make him poor? Back then I spent a lot on the materials for the ration cards: pens, ink, the cardboard. But in the end I got more for them than it cost to make them.'

'Not counting the six months in jail,' Stave interjected.

'If you're having a go at banknotes,' Weber continued calmly, 'then maybe ten-mark notes might be worthwhile, hundred better still. But pfennigs? In notes that nobody will recognise? Forgers can do their sums.'

The chief inspector thought back to when MacDonald first presented him with the notes and said that their sudden appearance could undermine confidence in the new currency. Maybe that wasn't a side effect these odd notes might have, but actually their primary purpose? Maybe whoever turned them out wasn't interested in profit but in creating uncertainty and chaos? The CID man was beginning to feel as if he'd been looking in completely the wrong direction.

'You've been of help to us,' Stave said, folding the two notes again. All of a sudden he felt tired.

MacDonald had listened to the interview in silence. Now he looked out of the window and took a deep breath. He was clearly disappointed too, though he forced a charming expression on to his face.

'I have one other matter,' he began.

Over the next quarter of an hour, he discussed rates with Weber for a portrait of Erna Berg. The artist became more friendly, excited even, and began gesticulating and walking up and down the empty room. A bronze bust? Impossible! There wasn't enough metal available in the whole occupation zone, even if it was a British officer asking. A painting?

'If the lady is willing to sit for me,' Weber said.

'Not enough time for that,' MacDonald replied. Yet again Stave was taken aback. They're leaving that soon, he thought to himself.

'But I don't even know the lady,' the artist protested.

'I have a photo here. From a studio.' The lieutenant pulled out of his uniform pocket a sepia-brown photograph wrapped in grease-proof paper and handed it over to Weber as if it were a treasure.

'To paint a portrait in oil based on a photographic print is about as artistically challenging as that Baltic landscape on the wall,' the artist exclaimed.

'I'll pay you ten pounds for it,' MacDonald promised.

'I won't even try to convert that sum into Reichsmarks,' the artist exclaimed, puzzled. 'But I'm your man. I'll have to borrow the photo for a while. A week?'

'One week,' MacDonald said, holding out his hand and shaking Weber's hand to seal the deal.

One week, Stave thought. He's in Hamburg at least that long.

When they said goodbye a few minutes later at the door of the villa, Stave, by then almost at the Jeep, turned back to the artist and said: 'How much are you being paid for the Baltic idyll?'

'Three thousand Reichsmarks cash,' Weber replied, smiling nervously. 'I've heard that may no longer be as much money as I thought when I took the commission. That's why I'm going back to Hamburg tomorrow. I don't want to miss anything. It could be that what I'm involved in here might not just be bad art, but a bad deal too.'

'It would appear you're not the only one doing a bad deal,' the inspector muttered, touching the brim of his rain-soaked hat in farewell.

They hung about in Travemünde for another hour, asking questions of neighbours and local shopkeepers. Weber's story held up, he'd been on the coast for days and nobody had seen him leave, not even for a short walk.

'Our artist has an alibi,' MacDonald said.

'And I have one more problem,' Stave replied. 'Even if I'm not particularly surprised.'

On the long drive back Stave stared silently out of the window at the grey landscape. He reflected on the two cases, dissatisfied with himself. And on the secret investigation which nobody from Homicide dare find out about. I switch from Homicide to Department S, a step backwards in the eyes of most of my colleagues. And the next thing you know I'm dealing with another corpse. And I'm getting nowhere with my first official case. Cuddel Breuer is going to think I never recovered properly from the gunshot wound. That I'm burned out. And maybe he's right. I must have heard something in the interview today, some detail I need to get to grips with.

He was only aroused from his thoughts, rudely, as they were already passing through Ahrensburg and the groaning of the twelve-cylinder motor made a strange sound almost as if the engine had swallowed itself.

'The spark plugs. Or the distributor,' MacDonald speculated breezily. 'Let's hope the old banger doesn't fall to pieces beneath us. Who knows when the next patrol might come by to pick us up.'

The CID man dreaded a long trek on foot in the rain. 'What are our chances?'

'Fifty-fifty. But you live on Ahrensburger Strasse, and that's just an extension of Reichsstrasse 75. With a bit of luck we'll make it that far and I can drop you right outside your front door.'

'You're going to keep on driving?'

'The army has a workshop on Holstenhofweg, just a few hundred yards from your house. Right on our route, even though it would be against the rules. I'll force this old crate right through town to our fleet car park, return it officially, put in a report – and then, provided the engine hasn't completely died, some bad-tempered sergeant will have to take it back to Holstenhofweg.'

'In that case we can pass my house by. I'd also like to go into town.'

'Where to?'

'Grindelallee. The exchange centre.'

'Aye aye, sir.'

And indeed half an hour later the Jeep, rattling and stuttering, was dragging itself down Grindelallee. Stave agreed to meet up with MacDonald the next day to keep him up to date with the progress of his enquiries – provided there was any progress to report. He sprang out of the vehicle with relief as it spluttered its way into the distance.

The exchange centre was a long wall made of wooden boards from old crates by the side of the street, set up by somebody or other and tolerated by both the British occupation forces and the German administration. There were hundreds of notes pinned to the wooden wall, yellowed with age and soaked by the rain, the washed-out ink on many of them almost unreadable. This was where people who didn't want to take the risks of the black market offered things. Every now and then the police sent a patrol car by, because it was illegal to offer things that were rationed – sugar or butter for example. But apart from that these 'barter businesses', as they were described officially by the police, were benignly tolerated because they helped to ease the shortages.

It was a flea market in pieces of paper and even in this weather dozens of men and women were wandering up and down staring at the notices, so intently in places where the writing had been all but washed away by the rain, that they looked like entomologists study-ing a rare species.

Stave joined the line and read: 'Potatoes in exchange for a cycle lamp'; 'Have coat, need shoes'; 'Bedclothes on offer in exchange for rabbit (live)'.

He was looking for a bicycle himself, because three years after the war the main streets were now mostly clear of rubble. And he was tired of having to plod through the streets on foot for hours. His old bike had been in the cellar of the rental building where he had lived until 1943 – it was probably still there, buried under tons of beams and bricks that had collapsed the night the bomb hit it.

Stave came across a note that from its condition didn't look as if it had been there all that long – maybe he wasn't too late. 'Men's bike in exchange for typewriter.'

He had an old black Olympia at home. The typewriter stood on the table of the apartment he had been allocated after the bombing. Even now he had no idea who had lived there before him and what had become of them. He had never used the typewriter, but had been telling himself for years that he ought to hang on to it, to give it back to its former owners one day, should they ever knock on the door. But right now looking at the board with the offer pinned to it, he realised that nobody was ever going to knock on his door and demand the Olympia back. He took down the name and address of the other party. He hadn't a telephone. Obviously.

Stave was about to leave when he spotted another notice. It was the handwriting that drew his attention: blue ink, sloping a bit, uneven, an adult's handwriting, but one that still showed the exaggerated loops of a schoolchild. He recognised it. It was that of his son, Karl.

All of a sudden he was worked up and interested to see what his son had to offer: 'A Persil box full of dry tobacco, for Mommsen's *Roman History*.'

The chief inspector remained there looking at the advert for so long that other people came up and joined him. Karl was growing tobacco on his allotment. Dried leaves cut up small could be rolled in newspaper to make homemade cigarettes people called 'broomsticks'. It was an attractive offer in times like these. But why did his son want a book in return? He tried to remember why the name Mommsen seemed vaguely familiar. Was it a novel? Or non-fiction?

The chief inspector looked around until he spotted an elderly bespectacled gentleman a few metres away, who looked like a retired teacher.

'Excuse me,' he said to him, 'but what is Mommsen's *Roman History*?' and pointed to Karl's advert.

The man looked at him as if he had asked who Kaiser Wilhelm

was, then finally grinned condescendingly. 'Theodor Mommsen was a great scholar at the end of the last century. His speciality was ancient history. His *Roman History* remains the standard work. I myself wouldn't give up my own copy for a cardboard box full of tobacco. But I'm sure he'll find somebody. There were dozens of editions of Mommsen's work. It was on the bookshelves of all the best houses, before times turned so barbaric.' The man snorted and looked down his nose at him.

Stave thanked him and looked back at the notice in confusion: why would his son want a book about the history of ancient Rome?

# Forgotten files

*Thursday, 17 June 1948*

In his office on the quiet floor in CID headquarters Stave sat flicking through his notebook, deciphering his scribbles from the day before. He found nothing that got him any further along.

He looked up surprise when there was a knock on his door: Kienle.

'I remember!' he exclaimed.

'Your real name? You're not Ansgar Kienle, but Martin Bormann, the Führer's vanished secretary. Ought I to arrest you?'

'Maybe your new job should be renamed Department SS, for its bad jokes,' the police photographer replied. 'I remember the bronze bust found in the ruins – the woman.'

'Anni Mewes. A film actress. By artist Toni Weber. I've got further than that.'

His visitor was taken aback. 'Maybe then the rest doesn't matter now, even though it is rather odd,' he murmured.

'Tell me.'

'I saw her in the cinema.'

'She was a movie actress.'

'No, I don't mean the woman. The bronze bust, the sculpture. I saw it in the cinema, must have been the end of the thirties. I just can't remember which film. But I know I was in the Lichtspielhaus cinema and saw the bust really prominently in one scene and remember thinking it was a pity we only saw things like that in the cinema nowadays and no longer in art galleries.'

Stave closed his eyes. 'I'm an idiot,' he mumbled. When Weber had told him about the propaganda films and getting props, he had thought he meant one of the usual things cobbled together for the weekly cinema news. Another broadcast about degenerate art, a few withering words, a couple of clips and then Goebbels or the Führer. For not one second had it occurred to him that he might have meant a feature film. 'You are the best scene of crime expert in the Hamburg police,' the chief inspector said in praise.

'I'm just about the only one,' Kienle reminded him calmly.

Now Stave knew what he really should have asked Toni Weber yesterday. Was there any more he could tell him about this film in which the bronze bust had been used as a prop? The chief inspector had concentrated so much on a possible connection between the artist and Schramm that he had made a note of everything else but not really thought it through.

For the CID man the cinema meant Berlin, UFA, the glitter of the capital. All long gone. Hamburg was the new movie capital, a lot shabbier than the old capital, but even so. People like Weber had come from the Spree to the Elbe after 1945, to escape the Russians. His former colleague Michel said Weber was working in the prop department again, but this time for Käutner in Hamburg.

There had to be more survivors from the UFA days here. If Käutner was able to make movies here then he must have hired experienced people. Who knows: maybe one of them had also worked on the propaganda film in which the bust had featured? Maybe as a prop man? And he had got hold of it and afterwards passed it on to somebody.

Stave stormed out of his tiny office, about to shout out, as he had in the days with Homicide, that he was off on an investigation, when he remembered just in time that Erna Berg was gone and there was no secretary sitting in an anteroom outside his office.

He walked past the closed office doors and down the stairs to the vehicle fleet.

'I need a car,' he called to the mechanic on duty.

'Don't we all?' The man hesitated a second. He wouldn't have done that when I was still with Homicide, the chief inspector thought before swallowing his wounded pride. 'I need to go out to Fuhlsbüttel, to the Ley huts on Langhorner Chaussee.'

'Out to where the scum live? You don't just need a patrol car, you need a couple of cops too.'

'It's broad daylight.'

'All I have is a pre-war Mercedes and we've just taken the radio out of it. Nobody from HQ will be able to get in touch with you.'

'That means nobody will interrupt me en route.'

'But if you have problems?'

'I have my service pistol,' Stave lied. The truth was his FN22 was hanging in its holster in a cupboard in his apartment.

'Don't get any holes in the bodywork.'

'One more or one less wouldn't make much difference to that car.'

Five minutes later Stave roared off behind the wheel of an asthmatic, dark-coloured car on the long road to Hamburg's northern suburbs.

The chief inspector wound his way through Harvesthude and Eppendorf. Now and then he would pass a forest of umbrellas on the pavement. People scurrying here and there. Odd, he thought. He braked and noticed that the passers-by were staring at empty shop windows. Some of them were chatting, others just gesticulating at the desolate display windows in the shops. We're overdue for X-day, Stave thought, or gatherings like this will turn into demonstrations. He thought back to the forged notes found on Goldbekplatz, and suddenly understood rather better why MacDonald was so worried.

A quarter of an hour later and the old Mercedes turned off Alsterkrugchaussee on to Langhorner Chaussee. Stave put his foot down. He had only a few kilometres to go, but the traffic in the northern suburbs was lighter. The Mercedes spluttered. When he got to the Ley huts he braked, parked and made sure both driver and passenger doors were locked. It was safer like that.

Ley huts were like little rabbit hutches for humans: square, about twenty square metres in total, with lean-to roofs, basic flooring, one door, no heating, no bath. They were more like allotment sheds than real houses. Italian prisoners and forced labourers had made them in 1943 out of the cheapest material available, for the tens of thousands of homeless whose houses had been levelled in the bombing. Even after 1945 they had been popularly named after Robert Ley, the head of the German Workers Front, who had organised their construction.

Along Langhorner Chaussee there were dozens of them in several rows, the entrance doorways under the sloping roof facing north, the sides with windows facing south. It was as if these miserable little dwellings made of waste wood had turned their back on the city in shame.

At first they had been inhabited by families who had lost their home in the bombing raids and had nowhere else to live. But in the past two years many of them had moved back into the city to better accommodation. Those who were left were the people who even in the old days had little money – and then came refugees from the east, displaced persons and POWs coming home from the war with no family left. It was a settlement that counted as a impoverished district, even in a city that still lay half in ruins.

Stave wondered why someone like Weber who apparently was earning good money hadn't found somewhere else.

It was midday by now. The chief inspector was hungry but also impatient. He asked two boys playing cowboys and Indians in torn shirts and lederhosen that were too short for them if they knew Toni Weber.

'Have you got a cigarette?' the older one, barely ten years old, asked him cheekily. The younger one made a howling noise, patting his mouth with his hand in what was supposed to be an Apache war cry – or maybe just a scornful laugh in disguise. The CID man wasn't interested in telling him off and just produced a John Players from his coat pocket.

'Weber lives over there. It's by far the warmest hut.' The kid laughed ironically and pointed at the shed that lay furthest from Langhorner Chaussee, almost on the edge of a little copse. It was the only one to have been recently painted, the woodwork blue, the door and window frames white. There was a garden laid out around it with thorny roses next to the windows, their blossoms standing out in the grey drizzle. You could do worse, Stave thought, beginning to understand why somebody might choose to stay here. A little idyll – provided you had the time, the strength and the talent, to keep the cheap accommodation in good condition and close your eyes to the poverty all around.

'He's a pretty boy, that Weber,' the kid added, grinning.

Stave ignored him and walked over to the hut. Before he could knock on the door it opened. 'I happened to see you arrive,' said Weber, looking tired and suspicious. 'I just got back from Travemünde on the train. Late, as always.' He waved him inside. He doesn't like being seen standing outside his hut, Stave thought. You can hardly blame him, though. He walked through a windbreak curtain into a clean, surprising bright room. A shelf, a walled-in hole in the floor to keep sausages and yoghurt cool, two basic chairs, a table made out of an old door, probably salvaged from the ruins. On top of it lay a pile of thin paper with charcoal drawings. To the right, a wall made of thin boards cobbled together separated a second room with a curtain as a door. Stave glanced through and saw a single bed and a commode.

'You live alone here?'

'Yes. I'm better at drawing than I am with women. But that has its advantages these days.' When the CID man gave him a questioning look, Weber shrugged his shoulders. 'I have twenty square metres to myself here. How many people can say that nowadays? This little settlement is better than its reputation. My neighbours are decent people. Most of them don't talk a lot, if you know what I mean.' The chief inspector thought of the two kids, but said nothing. 'And these huts will last for years yet,' the artist added. 'They could be the most solid memento of the Third Reich.'

'The people who put them up weren't exactly experts.'

'But they were conscientious workers. It took a lot longer to build these than expected. After all, the longer they worked here the longer it was before they had to go back to the concentration camps. Did you know that even the deputy head of Nivea lived here? He wasn't a hundred per cent Aryan, as far as I've heard. You just have to keep these places in good condition. The roofing back then was so useless that it's not much better at keeping water out than a torn towel. You have to keep climbing up there and putting down new layers. Then things are fine. But you haven't come out here to see me just for a few DIY tips.'

'I could do with some,' the CID man said, but shook his head. 'It's to do with the bust.'

The artist stared at him in surprise. 'Not the forged notes, then? I thought that was what you were really interested in.'

'Possibly. But it's the bust I want to ask you a few more questions about. You said the last time you saw it was as a prop in a film. Was that in Berlin?'

'Of course.'

'In the cinema?'

'No, when I was working: back in 1938 they were shooting a film for the Berlin film studio UFA at the same time as I was working on another one. I caught a brief glimpse of the bust, being used as an on-set decorative prop. It was some piece of stupid propaganda: they had built on the set a copy of some Jewish villain's house, or something similar. They brought a few pieces from the propaganda ministry's warehouse to Babelsberg and put them on the set. I was seriously shocked when I saw it because I was afraid somebody would recognise it as mine and blow the whistle. But nobody paid much attention to the artworks, they were just props like any other. After shooting was finished they disappeared again, probably back to the warehouse.'

'I assume this propaganda ministry warehouse was in Berlin?'

'Yes, as far as I know. Obviously I didn't ask.'

'But after 1945 a lot of movie companies moved from the capital to the banks of the Elbe. Do you know if anybody who was involved with that movie could be in Hamburg now?'

'Are you joking?' Weber stared at him, then shook his head. 'How could you know that? You never worked for UFA. The director of that film lives in Hamburg. Very nicely, all things considered, at least as far as I know.'

Stave held his breath. 'Who?'

'Veit Harlan.'

The chief inspector turned to look out the window, to hide his surprise. 'The most famous film director of the Third Reich,' he muttered eventually.

'Goebbels's darling. The director of *Süss the Jew*. The husband of actress Kristina Söderbaum. He took off quickly enough in 1945. One day he was shooting a B-movie, the next he vanished from Berlin only to turn up in Hamburg. Last year he was finally cleared by the courts: Category 5, just a "fellow traveller".'

'I recall the scandal. There were articles in the press. And some artists protested about his categorisation.'

'None of which did Veit Harlan any harm. He lives down by the Alster. In a villa. Some people always land on their feet.'

'How many movies did he make under the Third Reich?'

'A dozen? I don't know. Lots.'

'Do you think he might remember some of the props?'

'Maybe you can kickstart Harlan's memory. I would love to know how the guy got hold of my bust of Anni Mewes. But with famous men like him who always have powerful patrons, an ex-convict like me can't simply knock on the door and ask questions about an old prop. I never thought I would say this to a policeman, but I would be grateful if you could pop by and tell me how your conversation with the famous director went. I could sketch you while we talk.' The artist nodded towards the pile of charcoal drawings. 'As a little present for your wife.'

Stave felt a twinge, but he forced himself not to show it. 'I know an art connoisseur who might be interested,' he replied, getting up and plodding towards the door.

With the door handle already in his grip, the chief inspector turned around: something had just occurred to him. Could the corpse in the Reimershof be that of the man who had brought the bronze bust from Berlin to Hamburg? 'Among the people who worked in the prop department for UFA, were there any Jews?'

Weber stared at him for a moment, uncomprehendingly. 'Jews playing with Goebbels's favourite toy? Anyone wearing a yellow star wouldn't even have been allowed to sweep the studio floor.'

Stave nodded. It would have been too easy.

There was a chalk drawing of a naked woman with huge breasts on the hood of the patrol car. The two kids were nowhere to be seen. The chief inspector calmly wiped away the drawing with his handkerchief and regretted for a moment that the car didn't have a radio. A quick call to HQ and he would have had Harlan's address. He could have driven there, knocked on the door – and maybe unleashed a scandal. He thought back to Weber's warning that the director had powerful patrons. And it occurred to him that Harlan's wife, Kristin Söderbaum, even though she had lived in Germany for years, was still a Swede. The British were in charge in Hamburg and they wouldn't be pleased if some pushy German CID man were to launch a complaint against a citizen of a neutral country. I need insurance, Stave told himself. MacDonald will see to it that I can tread on Harlan's toes without taking any risks. I need to talk to the lieutenant.

Even so, Stave was in no rush to take the patrol car back to the police pool. He was going to visit somebody else first. Unannounced.

It was with more than a little *Schadenfreude* that the chief inspector deliberately parked the Mercedes to block the driveway to the villa on Fährstrasse. He handed the housemaid his damp hat and overcoat, and sat down in the salon as if he were at home.

'Your behaviour is impertinent,' Dr Schramm sniffed when he stormed into the room five minutes later dressed in a dark silk housecoat.

Stave stared at him. When had he last heard that adjective? When had he last seen a silk housecoat? He felt as if he had fallen through an invisible tunnel back to pre-war days.

'I've got a new lead,' he replied. A lie. 'About the artworks in your office building.'

'The Reimershof was not my building. I only rented two rooms there.'

The CID man ignored his interjection. 'It's taking me in the direction of the movies. The director Veit Harlan. I thought that you, as an art connoisseur—'

'I've nothing to do with that character,' Dr Schramm forcefully interrupted him. The hand with which he was clasping the damask-covered arm of the chair on which he sat was so tense that the skin had turned white.

'You know him?'

'I know his name, of course. But not personally – even if he is almost a neighbour. I wonder why the British let him off the hook, and allowed him to live in one of the best areas.'

'One of the objects from the Reimershof was for a certain time, how shall I put it, in Herr Harlan's possession. The bronze bust of a woman.'

'How very nice for him,' the banker replied in a curt voice. He leaned forward. 'I need to explain one or two things to you, Chief Inspector. While that man was directing *Süss the Jew*, I held on to my Jewish employees. My most trusted senior official was called Rosenthal. Just having that name on my list of salaried employees was enough to earn me a visit from certain gentlemen in leather coats. So even if Veit Harlan and I are interested in the same modern art, something that surprises me somewhat, it is still no reason for me to be linked to him. Not back then and certainly not now.'

'The bronze bust by Toni Weber was confiscated by the Nazis sometime after 1933 as degenerate art, and displayed in the infamous exhibition of such in 1937. In the spring of 1938 it was used by Veit Harlan as a prop in one of his films – one that was shot in Berlin,'

Stave said calmly. 'But by 1943 at the latest, the piece was being kept in an office building in Hamburg. How did it get there? Who stored it there? When I find out, then I'll know who it belongs to. I could give it back to the legal owner. My case would be solved.'

The chief inspector wondered if he should mention to Schramm the photo with the bust in it – proof that in late 1938 the sculpture was already in Hamburg, in fact in precisely the villa where he was now sitting opposite the banker. Everything suggested that Schramm at some later stage had hidden the object in his private office rooms in the Reimershof – perhaps because the visits from the Gestapo were threatening enough for him to decide not to keep degenerate art in his home any longer. Then it fell victim to the bombing raids of 1943. Schramm only needed to confirm the story, and the bronze bust and probably the other works of art, even still worth several thousand Reichsmarks, would be returned to him, and no policeman would worry about the whole business ever again.

Don't start imagining things, the CID man told himself. Why had Toni Weber, who had made the bronze, never mentioned a word about Schramm? And how and why would a work of art leave the hands of a Nazi film director for those of a man under suspicion by the regime? And what had the corpse, found in the ruins next to the artworks, to do with all this? Something about the story didn't make sense – and if Schramm acknowledged the piece as his, then I would keep on his heels, keep digging, not giving him any peace. He'd already had enough to do with hard-nosed policemen of the most dangerous sort. He's not going to tell me anything.

'There are so many unsolved cases,' Schramm replied, 'from 1945 onwards. This really isn't one of the most important to scratch one's head over, I imagine. Put it in the files and give the artworks to the city of Hamburg. They'll end up in a museum, which is where they belong.'

'Thanks for the advice.'

'You should take it to heart,' the banker replied. It sounded like a threat.

Stave drove to Police Station 31, in Barmbek, only a few hundred metres away. Jewish staff, he thought to himself. Schramm had had Jewish staff, even after 1933. That was something in itself. If this had been an official enquiry he would have got access to lists of staff. Personnel files, things like that. Instead he would have to go around the houses.

The Barmbek police station had a telephone. He grabbed the receiver, worked the dial and in a few minutes found out where Mac-Donald was: in the British officers' club in Volksdorf. The sergeant he had on the line spoke English to him. Slowly and loudly, as if he were speaking to a stupid child. Even so, the CID man had to ask three times before working out where the club was: Ohlendorff'sche Villa. He had heard of the place before the war, but never been there. He studied the city map in the police station and eventually found his destination right at the edge.

'You have to say one thing for the English,' an older cop said to him. 'They know how to find the nicest houses, even if they are out in the sticks.'

'You know the house?'

'Volksdorf was part of my old beat. The Ohlendorffs used to be the most important family there. Junior princes. They made their money in business: guano dung from Peru. It's amazing how and where people can make money. And how they can lose it again. Things started to go downhill for them even before '33, and not just in business. The youngest one was more interested in music. And he was also a freemason. The Gestapo almost certainly had a file on him. The fact that the Tommies commandeered the Ohlendorff villa was just the kiss of death for them.'

'How long is it going to take me to get up there?'

'Volksdorf was barely damaged. The roads are clear. Less than half an hour – always assuming that old Mercedes gets that far.'

'I'll get another thousand kilometres out of it.' Stave muttered, gave the constable a nod of thanks and picked up the telephone receiver again to call MacDonald.

'Old boy, I'll invite you to lunch.'

'Sounds like an offer I can't refuse,' the chief inspector replied.

The villa was a two-storey, salmon-pink lump sitting on a hill in parkland with exotic trees Stave couldn't name. There was an archway above the door, like the entrance to a Romanesque church. To one side was a small semi-circular extension almost like a chapel. The exterior was plain, with a glass-walled salon to one side, which appeared to be the restaurant dining room. All in all, the house was the expression of a spirit that longed for the levity of the south but was born of Hanseatic sobriety. Money from bird shit. As the chief inspector walked across the parkland he passed a couple of gravestones. He assumed they were those of past owners of the house, until he read the name: it was the Ohlendorffs' dog cemetery.

English military police, uniformed German servants, sweet cigarette smoke, ice cubes tinkling in heavy glasses. As soon as he entered the officers' club Stave felt he had wandered on to the set of one of those adventure films set in exotic lands that had been popular before 1939. MacDonald folded up a copy of the *Manchester Guardian* weekly he had been reading and made a gesture to the sergeant who wasn't going to let the German pass. The he led Stave over to a pair of broad leather armchairs with a view out on to the park. The chief inspector leaned back. There was a scent of old leather and printer's ink. A servant, a gaunt elderly man, set a glass of lemonade on the table in front of him unasked. He avoided looking at Stave. He probably regards me as a collaborator, the CID man suddenly thought.

'Have you got the forger?' the lieutenant whispered hopefully.

'What I have got is a lot of questions.'

'That's a shame. But if it had been an easy case, then an amateur like me could have solved it on my own.' MacDonald smiled, but didn't completely manage to hide his disappointment.

The chief inspector, who knew his British friend was with the secret service, glanced indulgently out of the window at the word 'amateur'. 'I've put a couple of Department S colleagues on to it,' he said, 'without spelling things out too clearly, of course. They're looking through the department's usual suspects who have access to printers. If Toni Weber's right, the things were turned out on a printer, and a banknote printer can't be kept upstairs – the things are too heavy. They need a large space either in a hallway, an apartment or a workshop. But living space is scarce, paper is scarce and ink is scarce. If somebody has a big piece of equipment like that set up somewhere, then sooner or later it's going to be noticed. If somebody really is using one to turn out fake banknotes then it's only a matter of time before we find the press.'

'We might not have that much time.'

Stave looked at the man opposite him. 'What's forcing our hand? X-day and the new currency? Or your transfer?'

'X-day. Did you know that the majority of German company bosses have already paid their workers half a month's wages? Because they believe that the new currency will be introduced before the end of this month. People are hoarding goods. Shops have less in them than they had in the winter when they came close to starvation, because now salespeople are hiding their goods in the hope they'll soon fetch a better price. And because nobody wants to keep the old Reichsmarks in their tills. We Allies have more or less become prisoners of you Germans: we have no option but to introduce the new currency as soon as possible. The business is slipping out of our control, we have to bring it in now.'

'Whether there are forgeries out on the black market or not?'

'If we can't get our hands on the forger before X-day, we'll have to do it afterwards. But quickly.'

'It is, of course, a possibility that the printing press we're looking for isn't even in Hamburg.'

'We're searching everywhere throughout the British zone.'

'What if,' Stave hesitated for a moment, 'the Russians have it? The Soviet zone begins just a few kilometres beyond Hamburg. It would be easy to smuggle a few forged notes across the Elbe.'

'In that case we'll have to bomb Moscow,' the lieutenant replied calmly, so that Stave wasn't sure whether or not it was a joke. The chief inspector downed his lemonade in one, because all of a sudden his throat had gone dry. 'Is X-day tomorrow?'

'It's not far off. I honestly can't tell you any more,' MacDonald replied, getting up from the armchair. 'Come along. I've got a table reserved for us. An English lunch is better than people think. While we eat you can tell me about your other case, and – like any new father – I'll tell you a few soppy stories about my daughter.'

Ten minutes later Stave was dubiously poking around a plate of lamb with mint sauce while recounting the saga of the bronze bust.

'I want to be sure of what I'm doing before I knock on Harlan's door,' he said in conclusion.

'I'll ask about it in London,' MacDonald promised. 'From what I know the Swedes are very embarrassed at having Kristin Söderbaum as one of theirs. The less the public read about her in the press, the more they like it. If you could keep any interview with her as discreet as possible, Stockholm's ambassador would be very satisfied.'

'Do you want to come with me?'

'That too is a question for my superiors. I'd be interested to meet a guy like Harlan, but as I said, discretion is the main thing that matters. I need to see if I can get permission.'

MacDonald pulled out a handful of photos from his shirt pocket: rumpled and pale around the edges from having been handled so much. Erna, smiling with a baby in her arms; Erna by the shores of the Alster, a baby on a blanket; Erna with MacDonald and a large pram between trees, maybe taken on a timer; Erna in a summer dress that made her look coquettish.

'Little Iris is a ray of sunshine,' Stave said. 'And Erna looks great.' And indeed she had put on a bit more weight than he remembered and her hair had grown. In a few of the photos it even looked as if she was wearing lipstick, something you never saw any more on German women. She looked buxom, strong, full of the joys of life. But yet he thought there was something sad in her face. Thinking of the son she no longer had custody of.

'She's going to enchant my family back home in Lockerbie,' the lieutenant replied, although his voice didn't sound completely convinced. He smiled briefly, shuffled the photos together and put them back in his shirt pocket. He seemed to have something more to say, but couldn't quite manage it.

Noise. Shouting. Clatter. The ground quaking. Stave and MacDonald spun round. The chief inspector automatically reached for his gun before remembering at the last moment that he had no authority in a British officers' club, and that in any case he wasn't carrying the weapon; he took a deep breath. A young captain had come into the glass-doored room from the park, on horseback. Somehow or other he had ridden the damp black steed through the double doors until he was among the tables, posing like a living statue, threateningly imposing in a room that was glassed in on all sides. His comrades cheered him and somebody handed him a whiskey glass. His steed snorted nervously and shook its head, stinking of sweat and pawing the ground with its right rear hoof.

'Cheers!' the captain called out, throwing the empty glass to one of his comrades. Then he tugged carefully on the reins, and slowly, bent low over the horse's neck, rode back out the door. It was like a scene from some crazy dream.

His comrades cheered noisily and shouted things in English that Stave didn't understand. He glanced at the elderly uniformed servant, who simply stared down at the floor. The horse's hooves had left deep scratches on the ancient parquet, and there was a steaming pile of dung between two tables. The chief inspector watched the captain out in the park using his spurs to drive the horse to gallop away. He tried not to show any emotion.

'The captain's name is as long a cavalryman's sword. Old aristocracy. Great sportsman, the usual stuff.' MacDonald said by way of explanation.

'There's something I want to discuss. Something you certainly won't get the permission of your superiors to look into,' Stave said, changing the subject and dropping his voice.

'I'm on for it.'

'You haven't heard what I'm asking.'

'If it's forbidden it's fun. Some of my comrades trudge through ruined houses. I prefer to investigate what's not allowed in the company of a German policeman.'

'I want to break into a colleague's.'

MacDonald lowered his fork. 'His office at CID HQ or his house?'

'CID HQ. His office. At night.' Stave cleared his throat. 'I did something similar last year. Nearly got found out. It would be good this time around if I had somebody to cover for me.'

'Doesn't exactly sound like something an officer and a gentleman should do,' the lieutenant replied with a smile. 'When do we start?'

'Midnight.'

'Perfect. Who is it we're going to drop in on?'

'Chief Inspector Cäsar Dönnecke of Homicide.'

MacDonald leaned back in his chair. 'A man known to my service.'

'People allude to Gestapo connections, but nobody has ever been able to prove anything.'

'Something you want to change?'

'No. All I want to know is what my colleague has found out in his current case. Or why he has done next to nothing.' Stave put MacDonald in the picture concerning his third, secret, case.

'Schramm the banker protected Jews. He says so himself, and Public Prosecutor Ehrlich backs him up. In those days Schramm was renting a floor in the office building. Might it have been possible for a Jew to have hidden there? Apart from anything, one of the works of art found next to the dead Jew's body had been one of the props used by a director who turned out propaganda films. Veit Harlan might have been one of the last people in the Third Reich to have entertained relations with a Jew, however obscure the connection might have been. I think that my colleague Dönnecke's official report is wrong: the deceased is no accidental victim of a bombing raid, but had something to do with the artwork. And I'd like to know whether Dönnecke – let's say unofficially – found out anything about him. Or if there was nothing about him to find out – and if that was the case, why?'

'Sounds a good enough reason to risk a career by staging a break-in,' MacDonald replied.

Late that afternoon, Stave returned to his office. He had pointed out to MacDonald a particular window to the rear of the CID where the lieutenant should wait for him. Stave waited on the fifth floor until late. Eventually Wilhelm Bahr, the head of Department S, left for home. All of the other staff had left long ago. He could hear no doors banging on other floors, no loud voices, no clatter of foot-steps on the linoleum. The great slab of a building was sunk in a sea of silence, the abandoned corridors lit only by the glimmer of emergency lighting. Stave tiptoed down the stairs carefully, feeling as if he were creeping through a labyrinthine witch's castle. From the bottom of the staircase he took a careful glance into the anteroom: an elderly uniformed duty officer flicking through a copy of *Die Welt*, an ancient 'people's radio' next to him, its valves glowing as it poured out the gentle music of NWDR's evening programme. The man was hard of hearing. All the better.

Stave crept down the ground floor corridor to the lavatory, the window of which he had indicated to MacDonald. He went into a cubicle, locked the door and pushed open the window.

'Easier than I thought,' MacDonald whispered, pulling himself up and through the opening. He was out of uniform, in dark trousers and a similarly dark old shirt. 'Maybe I should change jobs.'

'If they get you, you'll end up in jail.'

'If they get you as a soldier, you end up in a hero's grave, and that's clearly not the better alternative. Breaking and entering – the longer I work with you the more criminal experience I acquire!'

'Follow me,' the CID man said in a low voice, closing the window. 'Have you got a torch?'

'This isn't the first time I've done this,' Stave reminded him. He turned on the little torch and a yellow light danced around the washroom. 'We need to get up to the sixth floor,' he whispered.

Dönnecke's office wasn't locked. There was a stench of cigar smoke and sweaty clothing in the air. On his desk several sets of documents and files were piled up askew, while several of the doors and drawers of the cupboards were part open, the office of a man who felt sure nobody would dare snuffle around in it.

MacDonald took a quick glance around. 'I'll leave this mess to you,' he whispered. 'I wouldn't know where to start and haven't a clue what I'm looking for.'

'Nor do I,' Stave admitted. 'Keep watch at the end of the corridor, where you can keep an eye on both this office and the stairwell. If the duty officer should decide to do his round, warn me.'

The chief inspector carefully thumbed his way through the documents, taking care not to let any of them slip out of position. For the most part the files covered cases long closed. What did Dönnecke actually do? Eventually, almost hidden between two towers of paper, he found a thin folder with a badly typed label that read, 'Unidentified body, Reimershof, 11 June 1948'.

Stave grabbed the folder, sat down and flicked through the contents quickly: Kienle's official photos, a very brief record of an interview with the *Trümmerfrauen*, carried out by a very young officer and only days after the body and artworks had been discovered. Czrisini's autopsy report – with the reference to the Jewish star the pathologist had found among the remnants of clothing. No note next to it, no follow-up investigation, at least none that could be found in the files. The chief inspector asked himself if his colleague had even bothered to read the autopsy report. No more interviews with any other potential sources. Not even a Red Cross missing persons search. Dönnecke's final report, barely one page. The conclusion read: 'No evidence to suggest either murder or suicide. Probably a victim of the 1943 bombing raids. Unidentified. First name: Rolf (see attachment).'

The CID man blinked, and flicked through the rest of the documents. A handwritten comment, probably by one of Dönnecke's underlings, along with another official photo showing crushed together scraps of leather found underneath the corpse when it was lifted up. Maybe the remains of a briefcase, disintegrated in the rainwater and bodily fluids. No coins, no keys, no photos. But a remnant of paper, grey cardboard, maybe the membership card for a club or a library or something of the sort. The ink on the scrap was smeared with only one word, barely legible: 'Rolf.' The cardholder's forename? Or that of whoever had issued the card? One way or the other, no matter how vague, it was the only reference that they had to a name connected with the deceased.

Stave could feel his heart beating faster. That was what had kept him in CID all those years: the fever of the hunt. He could see no trace of that in the other paperwork in front of him. Sober words, no suggestions, no speculations. If nobody else had noticed the fragment of paper with the name on it, Stave suspected Dönnecke would simply have ignored it.

He closed the folder. What had he expected?

More out of disappointment at this meagre discovery, and in genuine hope of finding anything else, he pulled open the desk drawer: a pair of glasses, two cigars, a couple of pencils and a single piece of paper, a page from a notebook, scribbled in Dönnecke's stiff, pedantic handwriting, the heading underlined twice: 'Memo re: Stave.'

The CID man leaned back in his chair and took a deep breath. His hands were shaking. He recalled the rumour that Dönnecke had had something to do with the Gestapo. Their headquarters in Hamburg had been the Stadthaus, and old Dönnecke had never worked there. As far as anyone knew?

'Stave is investigating the "artworks" case,' he read.

This guy was running a dossier on me, he realised in amazement.

'Stave no comrade: politically and professionally unreliable. Contacts

*with the English. Unstable since the death of his wife in 1943, condi-*
*tion aggravated by bullet wound this past summer. Left Homicide, just*
*working for Department S.*

*His artworks investigations have led him to Schramm! Schramm's*
*Gestapo file – vanished. Burnt? Check out.*

*If Stave makes difficulties, exert pressure: son returned POW, divorce*
*(A.v.G. alias A.v.V.)'*

Stave felt so faint he was almost sick. It was clear that Dönnecke felt threatened by the investigations. Something to do with
Schramm, the bronze bust and the Gestapo. Something I'm not supposed to find out. And if I do find it out, he'll interview Karl. Or...
he closed his eyes in exhaustion. 'Divorce,' he thought, and 'A.v.G.
alias A.v.V.' Anna. The guy somehow or other knows we had a relationship. He knows I'm a widower. Divorce – that has to mean that
Anna was married. That it would be Dönnecke of all people who
would remove his final doubt. That damned 'G'.

He felt like ripping the office to pieces, smashing everything, big
and small, recklessly, rushing out into the city by night, kicking in
the door of Dönnecke's apartment and... Get a hold of yourself.
He sat on Dönnecke's chair and took a deep breath. It was more
than just recognising his own fury that somebody had been snuffling around in his private affairs. Anna was married. He glanced
out of the window, the drops of drizzle running down it shining like
diamonds in the light of a streetlamp.

Diamonds. The thought took him back to last summer when he
had watched Anna going into a jeweller's in the colonnade to buy
something: an old wedding ring. I'm an idiot, he told himself, idiot,
idiot, idiot. Dönnecke's right. Pathetic.

He jumped with shock when suddenly the office door opened.
'Have you found anything?' MacDonald appeared like a worried
ghost in the torchlight.

'More than I wanted to,' Stave answered wearily.

'The case is closed?'

'No, but a few jigsaw pieces have turned up and might be forming a picture. The body found in the Reimershof may have had the fore-name Rolf. There may have been a Gestapo file on Dr Schramm that Dönnecke is determined shouldn't fall into my hands. That may be why he dragged his feet on the investigation.'

'So our adventure has paid off.'

'More than I imagined.' Stave got to his feet. He wished he had never set foot in Dönnecke's office. But there are things you can't tell even to a friend. 'Let's get out of here, before somebody sees us.'

# The Gestapo legacy

*Friday, 18 June 1948*

The sun hadn't yet risen by the time Stave re-entered the CID head-quarters. He hadn't even bothered to get into bed overnight. His apartment stank of mould and damp. He had left the windows open for hours. Hopefully it would dry out at some stage. His mind was full of thoughts – some of them ideas that led him down a blind alley, but also others he was afraid to think through. So he sat there shivering at the kitchen table before damp sheets of paper, on which he wrote two letters: one to Anna, the other to a former Gestapo agent.

He needed to see Anna again, to talk to her, to somehow come on to the subject of her past. He hadn't mentioned anything about Dönnecke's snuffling around, let alone what his colleague had found out. He didn't mention the ring. Or 'G'. He had just asked to meet up and suggested the only restaurant in the vicinity of her flat. 'Let's meet up tomorrow and eat at Sellmers Kellerwirtschaft.' He wanted to add, 'Call me at the office if you can.' But he was afraid to speak to her without being able to look her in the eye. So instead he just ended with, 'If I don't hear from you, I'll assume you're coming.'

Stave had pushed the letter through the cap beneath the door or her basement apartment. He had walked to Röperstrasse along empty streets as it was still curfew. Layers of mist were rising from the Elbe, the walls of the houses glistening with damp. Her flat was in darkness. Hopefully she was still asleep, he thought, rather than the darkness meant she was somewhere else.

The other letter was also a request for a lunchtime meeting

– though not one for which the chief inspector intended to pay the bill for two. During the 'brown years' Stave had tried to keep out of the way of the Gestapo – which wasn't easy given that in Hamburg alone there were at least two hundred men working for the political police. People referred to their headquarters in the Stadhaus in whispers, or better not at all. Already by the April of 1933 the first prisoner there had died – or rather the first that Stave had heard of. The dockworker Gustav Schönherr had been tortured, and following this 'in-depth' interrogation had managed to 'fall' out of a window in broad daylight. It was not just among his colleagues that it was said one or another officer might have helped him plunge to his death. The whole city knew – and was meant to know: the more the Gestapo were feared, the more successful their investigations.

Nonetheless in the autumn of 1938, the morning after the *Reichskristallnacht,* a Gestapo man had turned up in Stave's office. Just why he had done so, the chief inspector never found out, because this Philip Greiner was so drunk he could hardly walk and clearly couldn't string two words together. He was puffy-faced from tears and had soiled himself. Precisely at that moment a furious senior SS officer turned up, complaining that the tyres of his Mercedes had been slit during the night. Stave managed to move the tottering Gestapo man into a next-door room and then take down the details of the incandescent officer's complaint. If the SS man had seen the drunkard he would have exploded with rage. Stave had done Greiner a favour that day, a favour he had never called in. Until now.

Greiner had been sacked by the British in 1945 like all the other Gestapo. Stave had lost touch with him, but it hadn't been hard to find out his address: there were still members of the CID who went out to play cards in the evening with former Gestapo agents. He told Greiner in a few brief lines that he wanted the information the Gestapo had held on Dr Schramm and on Dönnecke. He had invited him to lunch in the Winterhude Fährhaus – big, unobtrusive and far enough from the CID headquarters to make it unlikely they would bump into a colleague. Then he had called Constable

Heinrich Ruge to his office and told him to make sure he handed the letter to Greiner in person. 'And don't mention this to anyone!' It was vital that Dönnecke did not find out that Stave was suddenly getting in touch with a former Gestapo officer.

The young policeman had by now given up clicking his heels together militarily when he was given an order. Instead he just nodded and smiled conspiratorially. 'What am I to do if he refuses to accept the letter?'

'Tell him I'll come and remind him about November 1938.'

The ring of his telephone made him start. It had been days since he'd heard a phone ring in Department S.

'Old boy,' said MacDonald. The line was bad even though it was a local call. 'Can we meet at midday at the workshop on Holsten-hofweg. I have no time to meet earlier. But I can pick up the Jeep there, then we can arrange our meeting with the movie mogul for one of the coming days. I should have got permission to meet him by then.'

'Gladly, as long as you drop me at Winterhude afterwards.'

'In my next life I'm going to be a taxi driver. Make it 11.30.'

Stave heard a click, then the hum of the unused line. He stared out of the window lost in thought. The music hall across the way was veiled by a thin mist as if covered in sheets of thin, dirty gauze. His office stank of old cleaning fluid. The chief inspector's head was still filled with swirling thoughts. Anna. MacDonald working for the British secret service. Suddenly it occurred to him that the lieutenant might be able to find out something about Anna von Veckinhausen. If a Gestapo man had noticed her, surely a British agent might do the same? Might there be a British file on her as well as a German one? Lying in an office somewhere? And if there is do I really want to know?

Don't kid yourself, there was no way he was going to be satisfied until he knew everything. Once a policeman, always a policeman. I'll ask MacDonald. He glanced at the clock on the wall and counted the minutes until their meeting at the workshop, at the same time dreading it.

Given that he was still holding the telephone receiver in his right hand, he used his left to flick thorough his notebook and then dialled a number. The Landeszentralbank.

A few minutes later he had Kurt Flasch on the line.

'I really don't have the time, Chief Inspector.' Flash sounded more stressed than ever.

Good opening line, Stave thought. He would just lean back now and ask as many searching questions as he wanted. But he liked his neighbour, who seemed always to be struggling against drowning in his vast family.

'X-day getting close?' he replied understandingly.

'That's hardly a secret by now.'

'You've been particularly busy since this morning?'

'A few colleagues and I had to work through the night.'

'So it's all ready to go?'

'This might sound ridiculous, Chief Inspector, but I really can't tell you that. Rules are rules.'

'What colour will the new notes be?'

There was a silence on the other end of the line. 'I really don't know if…'

'Blue, salmon-pink. And green in all variations: yellowish green, bright green, turquoise.'

'Why do you ask?'

'Printed on banknote presses?'

'Obviously. But that…'

'In Germany?'

Silence again. Stave thought he could hear strained breathing over the crackle of the line. 'No. The notes are being printed in one of the Allies' countries.'

'Would it be possible to print notes like that in Germany?'

'Not yet anyway. There are still printing presses and material in Frankfurt, but they were hit by bombs, which will hardly surprise you. But when they're repaired and set up again, yes, of course. But that is going to take time.'

The CID man sat upright in his chair, surprised and suddenly attentive. 'You mean to say that right now there isn't a printing facility in all four occupation zones that could turn out the new banknotes? Not even a private one?'

Flasch laughed. 'That would be forbidden. And it wouldn't be possible even if somebody wanted to. Too complicated, too expensive. The old Reichsmark rags are still being knocked out in Frankfurt. But the new notes? Nowhere.'

'I won't take up more of your time,' Stave replied, and hung up.

The business of the pfennig notes on Goldbekplatz was becoming more and more curious. Weber had already told him it would be complicated to turn out such notes. And now Flasch had emphasised it was so complicated that nobody in the occupation zones could do it. No surprise then that nobody in Department S had been able to find a print works. If nobody in Germany has the capacity to produce notes like this, then it can only mean one thing: the notes are being printed abroad. I wonder what MacDonald will make of that.

He flinched when his boss pushed open the door to his office without knocking. His flabby cheeks were bright red and he was breathing heavily.

'Stave, you must be the only one here who hasn't been listening to the radio?'

'We started shooting back at 5.45 this morning?'

'Don't try any jokes that'll make me nervous. It's official: we're getting new money. Mayor Brauer has just announced it on NWDR. They've been making an important speech on the radio since early morning. Don't you keep up?'

'I've been working,' the chief inspector replied brusquely. 'When does it start?'

'The day after tomorrow.'

Stave gasped for breath. No wonder Flasch had been working

through the night. 'They're going to distribute the money on a Sunday? I would have thought the mayor might have given us a bit more warning to prepare for a new currency.'

'They don't want to give speculators any opportunities. In any case all the shops are closing. It's chaos at the stations with everyone trying to get home. You've got the day off too. We've no interest in the black market today.'

'So what exactly is happening?'

'Brauer said the Allies will be distributing new banknotes. "Deutschmarks". We'll have to get used to the name. All across the city on Sunday there'll be exchange offices set up. Every German will get forty marks per head, and another twenty in August.'

'Doesn't exactly sound like a fortune.'

'Have you saved up a lot of money? Put aside a few notes or more?'

Over the previous few years the chief inspector had spent most of his meagre income on coffee or cigarettes to swap down at the station for any news of his son who had gone missing in Russia. Ever since Karl had come back home he had been helping him out in one way or another. 'I'm as good as bust,' he admitted.

'Congratulations. The right strategy. Money in the bank will be converted at the rate of ten to one. The outlook is even grimmer for cash held at home. A one hundred Reichsmark note will get you five Deutschmarks. One thing's for sure: you're not going to get rich at that rate.'

Stave closed his eyes and thought of Toni Weber. The artist had been paid 3,000 Reichsmarks for his work up at Travemünde. Work he had spent several weeks on. And the day after tomorrow it would be worth just 150 Deutschmarks. How many people would be in a similar situation? How many will find out their work has been worth next to nothing. How many black marketeers, fences and smugglers will be panicking? They never paid their money into the bank. They had crates full of banknotes that would now be worth only one twentieth the value printed on them. And no way of spending them or exchanging them anywhere before Sunday.

'Business on the black market will be hectic today and tomorrow,' he muttered.

'Maybe, maybe not,' Bahr responded. 'Nobody has any idea what's going to happen after X-day. Just because you've got new money doesn't mean you can buy anything with it. It could be that the black market will take off again on Monday. If you ask me, the Allies are behaving like rash gamblers at a roulette table, wagering everything on a single number. If it works, then we can all sit back. If not, we have a problem.'

Something occurred to Stave: 'Will there be notes issued in pfennigs?'

'Fives and tens, but I have really no idea what they might look like.'

'Blue and green with a diamond pattern,' Stave replied, suddenly impatient. 'I need to talk to the British straight away.'

He left the CID headquarters along with dozens of other colleagues. Busy bees swarming out of the hive after the death of the queen, the chief inspector mused. He squeezed into a crammed tram. The pavements were crowded with office workers, housewives, children, war-wounded, bustling in all directions with small speedy steps. An organ grinder playing the tune to which a sea of people danced like waves. Empty shop windows, the doors locked and bolted. Hand-written notices in sheets of rain: 'Closed for renovation'; 'Stocktaking'. Stave wondered if any of these shops would open up again on Monday. Or whether X-day would be a colossal mistake, a bullet in the head of a reeling economy.

It took him nearly a quarter of an hour to cross the station. Crowds on the platforms, in the passageways, on the iron walkways above the tracks. Piles of suitcases. Shouts, crying children. Loud whistles from old locomotives. The nervous tension of thousands crackled beneath the high vaulted roof.

Just behind Wandbek market, barely two kilometres from his destination, uniformed police were blocking Ahrensburger Strasse. The chief inspector showed them his ID card.

'Sorry,' said a sweaty young corporal. 'An unexploded bomb found next to the pavement. Nobody gets through until the fireworks guys have done their stuff. You can get around the area using the side streets.' He nodded towards the villas down Marienthal and began giving him directions. But Stave waved a hand dismissively. 'I live locally.'

The chief inspector set off. Trees, well-tended front gardens, two Opels parked on the kerb. But even here, behind the curtained villa windows, twitching even though the rain was falling straight down, the CID man felt a hint of unrest. As if a revolution were about to erupt. Angst about the money that from Sunday on would simply vanish, to be replaced by another.

Stave reached the railway lines, and walked along the tracks away from the city centre until eventually he got where he wanted to be. Jenfelder Strasse crossed the tracks via a level-crossing barely 300 metres from his apartment, though he hardly ever came this way. Why would he? There was a dilapidated white shed next to the rails, the remnants of a long since vanished factory. Next to it was a square with a wall around it, waist-high bright green grass and trees with widely spread branches, an iron gate. The CID man was about to hurry on his way when he suddenly came to a halt. Gravestones, most of them half-sunk into the soft earth. He took a closer look. Hebrew characters. An ancient Jewish cemetery.

How could this cemetery have withstood the maelstrom? It was probably so old and hidden away that even the Nazis at the height of their rage had forgotten about it. It was undamaged, no bombs, but also, as far as he could see from the iron gate, there also hadn't been any burials here for a long time. Nobody came to tend the graves. Nobody at all to visit this abandoned bit of land. He thought back to the new money and the nervousness about its introduction, and the dead Jews now forgotten – and felt somehow both ridiculous and guilty at the same time. He hurried on his way, only a few metres now.

Number 49, Holstenweg, was the workshop on the left-hand side of the street, a grubby but nonetheless intact building in a part of the city that was almost totally undamaged, with warehouses, little factories, and a print works. On the parking lot stood a British lorry and two Jeeps. There was another Jeep on the hydraulic ramp. Several British soldiers covered in oil were standing under it having a genial conversation.

'Welcome to Rolls-Royce army-style!' MacDonald called out, emerging from the shadow of an awning, and carelessly flicking away a half-smoked John Players that fizzled out in a puddle. 'We've just had to let our German mechanics go. They were too edgy. Now our recruits have to do the work on their own. I fear we'll have to switch to using horses soon.'

'Is that your Jeep on the ramp?'

'No, I'm glad to say that belongs to a colonel. Mine is parked outside. They finished working on it just in time, before your mayor gave his speech and our mechanics' hands began to shake.'

'My hands were shaking too – but for different reasons. You knew all along that those weren't forgeries, but genuine notes, brand new ones. They were notes from the Allies' print house. Notes that had been delivered in crates, taken into the Landeszentralbank under strict security. I stood there and watched them myself. Notes that aren't due to be distributed until this coming Sunday but were found in the wrong hands only hours after the last English lorries had driven off, and then suddenly turned up on the black market.'

'I told my superiors you would find out where the notes really came from.'

'You've been having fun with me!' Stave didn't know whether he should be angry or just laugh off the whole grotesque investigation. 'The story about the fake notes and the forger was made up. I could have spared myself the visit to the one-legged guy's hovel just like we could have spared the effort of the trip up to Travemünde!'

'The Baltic coast is pretty.' The lieutenant held up his hands apologetically. 'But I wasn't allowed to say anything, not even to friends. Orders from on high. You can imagine the uproar in our HQ: here we are bringing over a new currency from America under conditions of extreme secrecy and security – and a few notes turn up on the Goldbekplatz in Hamburg while we're still piling them high in the treasury.'

'You've got a leak in your security.'

'And very close to the source. Luckily it was only trickling out.'

'In any case it's no longer that important to find the culprit. From Sunday everybody will have their hands on these bits of paper. A few pfennig notes won't damage confidence in the new currency.'

'From Sunday on, it won't be noticed whether our security breach led to a trickle or a flood. Every German citizen will get a pro capita handout of forty marks. What's going to happen if all of a sudden four hundred turn up on the Goldbekplatz? Or four thousand?'

'The new bits of paper will be worth no more than the old bits of paper.'

'I need to get this guy in custody.'

'And all this time I was looking for a forger, a printer or an artist. When in fact it might be an English military policeman.'

'An Englishman, even in plain clothes, would be as conspicuous on Goldbekplatz as a Sherman tank in the car park at Royal Ascot. Our man is German.'

'Let's assume we're dealing with a local. What next?'

'Do you have a suspect?'

Stave shook his head wearily. 'No, no suspect.'

'But have you a potential lead? Is there anything you can tell me?'

'Afraid not. Orders from on high.'

For a moment MacDonald gave him a puzzled look, then laughed out loud and clapped him on the back. 'Serves me right. But keep me in the loop.'

'In any case, without you I'm up the creek without a paddle,' the chief inspector reminded him.

'Right. Now, the Harlan business. Your other case. You can interview him tomorrow. Or to be more precise, we can interview him. A British officer has to be present. Frau Söderbaum insisted.'

'You mean Harlan and his wife already know I want to question him?'

'It was unavoidable. But they have no idea why a chief inspector from CID is interested in them. I can imagine that's making them nervous.'

'If I had Harlan's past, I'd be nervous too.'

A few minutes later the Jeep was trundling along the roughly repaired streets towards Winterhude. For the first time Stave noticed how many of the ruins had in the meantime been patched up with flat roofs.'

'It's coming on,' MacDonald said jovially, noticing the direction of the chief inspector's gave. 'Now there's the new money – give it ten years and you Germans will be ready for the next round.'

'Maybe we'll be fighting shoulder to shoulder on the same side instead of against one another, just for a change.'

'Indeed – against Uncle Joe. The road to Moscow. I believe our comrades in the US Army are prepared to exchange some of their Indian scouts for a few of your squaddies: at least they already know the way.'

'The way there, and the way back.' Stave was thinking of his son who had wasted the best years of his youth on the Eastern Front. In ten years' time, he thought silently to himself, Karl would just be thirty, still young enough to go through the whole bloody idiocy again. Would it never stop?

He jolted himself out of it. 'There's something else I want to ask you. Something personal,' he began.

The lieutenant was concentrating on staring through the wet windscreen as if he was driving through the hectic traffic of Piccadilly Circus, rather than the abandoned streets of a city in ruins. 'As long as you don't want to ask how to get Erna Berg back from me, I'll answer any question.'

'Actually, it does concern a woman. Anna von Veckinhausen.'

The CID man held his breath after mentioning her name. He had never spoken about her to the lieutenant and didn't even know if he knew anything about their relationship.

'Your girlfriend,' MacDonald said bluntly.

'It's a complicated story.'

'All proper stories about women are complicated.'

'Is Anna…' Stave searched for the right word, '*known* to the British?'

MacDonald allowed himself a boyish smile. 'Don't worry,' he said. 'The entire garrison knows that this lady sells antiques to our officers. And even the most stupid recruit can imagine where she finds her treasures – and that it's best to leave the matter alone unless you want to get into trouble with a few art-loving captains and colonels.'

'I was thinking rather of Frau von Veckinhausen's personal connections.'

The lieutenant gave him a brief, inquisitive look. 'Are these really personal questions – not a police investigation?'

Stave's heart stopped beating for a moment. 'Yes. But should I be interested, as a policeman, I mean.'

'Regrettably, yes, although it's really a matter for my colleagues.' MacDonald changed up a gear with a jerky, almost angry, movement. As though he hated what he had to do. 'The lady we're speaking of has reverted to her maiden name, ever since she arrived in Hamburg as a refugee from the east. Strictly speaking, that's not quite legal. To do that you have to have gone through a proper divorce in a court.'

'Who's her husband?' Stave asked, realising his voice sounded as if somebody had winded him with a blow to the stomach.

'Klaus von Gudow. This is where my comrades come into play. We'd like to ask this Klaus von Godow a few questions. Or better still put him on trial. And best of all, hang him.'

'He's a war criminal?' Stave felt faint.

'He's not exactly on the first page of our list of wanted criminals, but he's quite high up on the second. The second tier of the Nazi regime, the ones who carried out the deed.'

'The deed?'

'The murder of the Jews.'

Stave closed his eyes. 'Feel free to go ahead and tell me everything,' he muttered.

'I'm sorry, old boy. I would have spared you the whole story, but it was you that brought up the topic…'

'By chance I saw Anna's old handbag, with her initials: A.v.G. It set me thinking.' Stave refrained from mentioning the pawned wedding ring and Dönnecke's notes.

The lieutenant resumed in a calm voice. 'Klaus von Gudow is a stereotypical *Junker* from east of the Elbe: family pedigree going back to the Middle Ages. One or other of his great grandparents had fought Bismarck in a student duelling competition. His father was a personal friend of Hindenburg. Gudow himself is a lawyer with top qualifications and an impressive career in the diplomatic service. He was a card-carrying member of the right party.'

'Before 1933?'

'Long before. Anyway, his relentless climb took him to the Foreign Office in Wilhelmstrasse, as a diplomatic legate and head of Department D, known internally as the "Jews' Office".'

'But he escaped your clutches in 1945.'

'Unfortunately. Vanished during the Battle of Berlin. There have been rumours about a Klaus von Gudow in Austria, in Italy, in Argentina, in Paraguay. But never any proof. When his wife turned up in Hamburg, obviously our people found it interesting. Maybe her husband was holed up somewhere in Hamburg? We had her followed for a while. That, and the change of name, suggest that she is quite determined to forget Klaus von Gudow.'

Stave thought once more of the ring Anna had bought back from the jeweller. That suggested the exact opposite of trying to forget him. 'Did Anna von Veckinhausen have…' he hesitated, 'anything to do with her husband's "business"?'

'She was never investigated. She never held any office and was not even a party member. She was the lady of the house, hostess of a very-well-thought-of salon in Berlin, if I'm not mistaken. Very cultured.

You know most of the people on our wanted list are thugs and sadists. Nutcase characters who joined the SA and then later got the chance to indulge themselves in a concentration camp or a ghetto. The other half, however, come from another planet: perfect family men, loving husbands, caring fathers, songs around the Christmas tree and summer vacations on the Baltic. Men you would like to have as your neighbours, colleagues, maybe even friends. You didn't have to be a Nazi to live happily enough alongside these people. Provided, of course, you weren't a Jew or a communist. We're here.'

MacDonald braked outside the Winterhude Fährhaus. Stave hadn't been paying attention to the road. He felt as if he had been beaten up. Clumsily, he hauled his legs from the footwell and, holding on to the bodywork, pushed himself out of his seat.

'I would have preferred to tell you more pleasant things. But forgive me for getting involved in things that don't concern me. After this dreadful business,' – with a vague gesture the lieutenant indicated the ruins all around them – 'people have a right to have a second chance in life.' He paused, then touched the rim of his cap with his right hand. 'But don't forget our appointment tomorrow with Veit Harlan.' And with that he roared off.

A second chance, Stave thought. He would have liked to have thought it all over, there and then. But he didn't have enough time. He pulled up his coat collar, because raindrops were falling from the sorry-looking chestnut trees as if from a saturated sponge, took the dozen steps to the entrance of the Winterhude Fährhaus and turned the door handle. He had already spotted Philip Greiner – at the furthest table in the darkest corner of the room, with a view of the door. The former Gestapo man had seen him too and nodded nervously. Mid-thirties, slim, his blond hair combed straight back, watery blue eyes, with a persistent twitch under the left lid. The chief inspector had to suppress the urge not to stare at it.

'Nice to see you're punctual,' Stave said to him.

'It might be nice for you,' Greiner replied, pulling a John Players out of the packet, tapping it on the table and laboriously lighting up. 'Coming here for me is about as pleasant as a dentist's appointment,' he muttered through the blue cloud of smoke emerging from between his thin, colourless lips. It made Stave think of the smoking ruins the morning after the nights of bombing. Pull yourself together. He noticed there was a small black briefcase next to Greiner's left foot. A good sign.

'Let's eat something,' the chief inspector suggested. 'At least that'll differentiate our meeting from a visit to the dentist.' He waved the head waiter over. Given that three years after the end of the war food was still rationed, it was not easy to order a meal, even in a restaurant. At least not legally. In the meantime a new habit had evolved, one which Stave hated as he hated all the tricks that were used to get round sensible regulations. But today he was going to use it himself, because he thought the former Gestapo man might be more loquacious on a full stomach.

'Unfortunately I seem to have forgotten my food ration card,' he told the head waiter with a regretful smile, hating himself for doing so.

The man nodded understandingly. 'I could lend you mine,' he said. 'Against 30 Reichsmarks deposit.'

Greiner glanced quickly from Stave to the waiter and back, before realising that he hadn't got his ration card either. The waiter disappeared, with 60 Reichsmarks in his pocket and an order for potato salad and bread in his notebook.

'You surprise me,' Greiner admitted when the waiter was out of earshot.

'I'm hungry,' the chief inspector replied, and it wasn't a lie.

A bottle of Rhine wine was being nonchalantly uncorked at a nearby table and there was the seductive smell of mocha coffee in the air. 'There are hundreds of Reichsmarks being wolfed down here,' Greiner mumbled sourly.

'This time next week all you'll be able to do is use them to light cigarettes.'

'I don't have enough money for those any more.'

'You're finding things hard?'

'Who would take me on? My old job clings to me like leprosy. And I'm at risk of facing trial. Even though I was only doing my duty.'

'Who's accusing you?'

'Public Prosecutor Ehrlich. A Jew. Typical.'

Pour sod, thought Stave, without an ounce of pity. Aloud he said, 'Maybe you'll get off scot free. There are others who've had a soft landing.'

He nodded with his chin towards the thin man in the long woollen coat who'd just walked in, his hair parted neatly, with a cravat, a hat and a serous expression on his face. He was greeted effusively, the waiter bowing and leading him to a free place at a well-lit table. The sound of glasses being clinked. Carl Vincent Krogmann, a businessman, a National Socialist – and up until 1945 chief mayor of Hamburg. He sat down along with some other distinguished gentleman amid jovial chatter.

Greiner regarded him, white with fury, his lips trembling and his eyelid flickering.

'Fresh from the internment camp in Bielefeld,' Stave whispered. 'Nothing much more will trouble him.'

'The little guys get hanged, while the big shots live the good life,' Greiner whispered, a murderous look in his eyes.

Stave wondered what it would have been like to be sitting in a Gestapo cell in the Stadthaus when the door flung open and you found yourself staring into those eyes.

'Sometimes the big shots come a cropper too,' he said, attempting a sardonic smile.

The Gestapo man nodded, pulled up the black briefcase and thumped it down on the table: 'So, what do you want to know?'

'Do you have the file on Schramm?'

Greiner shook his head. 'You do ask naïve questions.'

'Never lose hope.' It was clear to the chief inspector that in April 1945, when the British had already taken nearby Lüneburg, the

Gestapo in the Stadthaus, in the jail out at Fuhlsbüttel and the Neu-engamme concentration camp had destroyed all their traces: burned documents, executed prisoners. No witnesses, no evidence. Probably the reason the man sitting opposite him was still walking around free, despite all the efforts of Public Prosecutor Ehrlich.

Greiner pulled out a grey cardboard file. 'An index file,' he whispered, smiling almost nostalgically. 'We had two million of them: Jews, communists, homosexuals, bible bashers, incorrigible thieves, backstreet abortionists. We've got them all in here. Enemies of the Reich, military morale poisoners. Fall into the hands of the Gestapo anywhere in the Reich – and your name's on the index forever. People believed that spies were everywhere. Or that we beat everything they knew out of prisoners.'

'And you didn't?'

'Of course we did. But first you have to have a prisoner. And this,' Greiner stroked the box lovingly, 'was our memory. Names, names, names. In the end, aren't we all hunter-gatherers, just like our cavemen ancestors? The hunter is the hero. But the gatherer is the one who provides for hard times. We burned the detailed files under the noses of the Tommies. But these, at least a few of them, I held on to. In case times change.'

Stave wondered if there wasn't a card index somewhere with his name meticulously written on it. He took the piece of cardboard from Greiner's reluctant grip.

'Schramm, Dr Alfred,' he read, with the address he already knew written below. 'Banker, foreign contacts.' Comments that Schramm was suspected of channelling money abroad 'to support' the Jews. A list of several interrogations and searches of his property. But no indication of a single judgement against him. No reference to degenerate art. No names of anyone who might have been a suspected accomplice, helper or sympathiser. It would have been too much to expect to find some reference to expressionist art in the Gestapo's files, the chief inspector thought, or to come across a man with the forename 'Rolf'.

'Was he part of your business?'

Greiner shook his head, 'I never had anything to do with him. I just kept his index card because he has remained an influential man. And you never know…'

Stave turned the index card over. The name of the police officials responsible for looking after the card. Two names that were barely legible and meant nothing to Stave. But right at the bottom: 'Cäsar Dönnecke, K.z.b.V.'

The abbreviation stood for *Kommando zure besonderen Verwendung* – 'Special Purpose Detachment' – an elite unit in Hamburg, feared in all the police stations. 'Dönnecke did the right thing,' Greiner grumbled, following the chief inspector's eyes. 'Never moved over to the Gestapo. Stood his ground by CID. The Tommies let him walk free.'

'I know,' Stave muttered grimly. All of a sudden he understood why Dönnecke wanted the case of the dead body found in the Reimershof to be swept silently under the carpet. He was afraid that the Reimershof would lead somebody to Schramm – and that the mention of Schramm would lead them to the connection with Dönnecke. And nowadays Schramm was once more a powerful man. If the banker were to find out that one of those who once made his life a misery was still with the police and sniffing around in his former business, he would move heaven and hell to ruin Dönnecke.

'Back then Dönnecke and the K.z.b.V. worked with us,' Greiner went on, having failed to notice Stave's anger. 'A real tough customer. In February 1945 he ran over two workmen who had found ration cards in a bombed factory and snaffled them. Both had been storm troopers from the beginning. Not that it did them any good.' He formed an imaginary noose with his hands and placed it around his throat.

Stave looked at the index card and put it in his pocket. He didn't even consider asking permission. When the head waiter came over with the potato salad, Greiner rubbed his fingers together in embarrassment, waited until the waiter had gone again, then glanced around, before lowering his head confidentially over the table. 'When SS-Sonderführer Heissmeyer, who had been carrying out tuberculosis experiments in the Neuhausen concentration camp, suddenly got cold feet, Dönnecke had twenty infected children taken to a school on Bullenhauser Damm. The children were given morphine in the cellar, and then when they were unconscious a few men hung them.'

Stave looked at the potato salad, then out of the window. His stomach felt as if he had just swallowed acid. 'Proof?' he spluttered.

'I could find some. Have you something against your colleague Dönnecke?'

'You never know,' Stave mumbled. If I make a fuss or just get up and go, then this guy will never trust me again, he thought to himself. And it could be that I will need him again. He put the first spoonful of potato salad into his mouth and forced himself to swallow the gloopy mush.

'In the Führer's day you could drive to the sea for thirty Reichsmarks,' Greiner said, 'and a salad like that wouldn't even be served to a Jew.' But he nonetheless wolfed his down with remarkable speed.

'Times change,' Stave replied, wishing he was long gone.

# A vanished husband

Stave was grateful for the rain that night, if only because the rain-drops beating against his window cancelled out the oppressive silence in his apartment. The empty half of his double bed. The room he had made up for Karl, which his son hadn't set foot in for over a year. The big kitchen, where for years there had been no smell of coffee or fresh bread wafting in the air.

He would have liked to read – it would have given his restless brain something to concentrate on – but he needed to keep his electricity bill low and his last candle had burned down weeks ago. So he just lay there, listening to the rain and his thoughts.

I don't understand anything, he told himself. Neither my work, nor the woman I love, nor my son. Dönnecke is a swine and a child murderer. But he's right: I've lost it.

He swung out of bed and felt his way into the living room. Since just a few weeks ago a glow from the first street light outside had been coming through the window. He got down on the floor and began stretching exercises. Press-ups until his upper arms shook and his upper body collapsed on to the linoleum with a dull thud. Knee bends: sweat rolled down into his eyes and there was a taste of iron in his mouth. He was down to his underwear. His heart was racing. He counted aloud, each number an exhausted sigh between tortured breaths. The he stood on his left leg only, spread his arms out wide and tried to keep his balance. Up on to his tiptoes, down again until his heels almost touched the floor. Up again. Down again. Each time he rose up his damaged ankle felt as if somebody was hitting it with a hammer from the inside.

It was not even 5 a.m. by the time grey dawn began to creep in. Stave stood in the living room, his body a slippery puddle of sweat. The scar on his chest hurt. He swayed into the bathroom and threw up into the toilet from exhaustion, then with his last ounce of strength climbed into the old enamel bathtub. No warm water, not that it mattered. He stretched out under the cold water, shimmering with a reddish tint of rust, scrubbed his skin down with hard soap, then forced himself under the water again.

Eventually he got out and lay on the tiled floor between the bath and the toilet, shivering, his feet and hands blue, the latter too weak to grab the towel hanging on a hook on the door. But for a brief moment a wave of relief swept over him, happiness almost: his head was finally empty, his brain had capitulated to pain and exhaustion.

Much later he sat at the table with a steaming cup of ersatz coffee clasped in his hands. Damp brown bread with ersatz honey, a spread that looked like warm wallpaper paste, tough and yellowish white, and didn't taste any better. He felt as if he was returning to his own body after a long absence, partly wary, partly surprised, as if coming back to his own apartment after a journey round the world.

An unexpected loud knocking on his door – it wasn't half past seven yet and his visitor probably thought they were waking him – surprised Stave and had him jump to his feet even though a warm pain flowed through every muscle in his body, his chest was heaving and his left ankle was swollen.

It was Constable Ruge. 'You're up already?' he exclaimed, staring at him with a look that made Stave realise even cold water hadn't erased all traces of his night-time exercises. I probably look as if I've been beaten up, he thought to himself, forcing a smile. 'Early morning exercises,' he explained. 'Has anything new turned up?' he asked hopefully.

'Only new orders.' The young policeman held up his hands

apologetically. 'We're being sent out by Cuddel Breuer to tell eve-ryone in CID there's a special detail being held tomorrow and all officers are to be at headquarters by 8 a.m.'

'A special detail? Sounds like something from Adolf's days.'

'Am I to take that as a compliment?'

'Single officers are being told first, Cuddel Breuer said. We're to let married men sleep a little longer,' Ruge said offhandedly, raising his right hand to the tip of his cap.

Stave pulled on his best shirt, his best dark trousers, a light summer coat that was hardly good enough for the endless drizzle but none-theless looked better than anything else he had to pull over his shoul-ders. He had two important appointments. He put the card with the bicycle seller's address in his pocket and bundled the typewriter up in some wrapping paper and a torn tablecloth he never used, and was out of the door before nine o'clock. There was gramophone music coming from Flasch's ground floor apartment. Jazz. Once upon a time that would have got him a visit from the concierge and maybe even the Gestapo, Stave thought to himself. Then two chil-dren began crying simultaneously, the complaint of a couple of lads shut up in their apartment because of the rain and feeling robbed of their normal Saturday run around. The CID man silently wished his neighbour the best of luck, pulled up the collar of his coat and headed off down Ahrensberger Strasse.

He didn't have far to go: across Eichtalpark, the grass as bright a green as an English lawn, the muddy pathways empty save for two young mothers pushing prams covered in rain hoods through the damp morning air. Oskarstrasse on the other side of the park was more like a pathway than a real street, but one that had been missed by the Allies' bombs. On the right side stood tall nineteenth-century buildings with bright plastered exteriors and even brighter window sills, intact roofs and well-tended gardens. He glanced at the now thoroughly soaked piece of cardboard and realised he was to keep to the left-hand side: a row of tiny houses, like dolls' houses glued together. But in a city that had been bombed so heavily even these humble dwellings looked like a bastion of affluence.

The CID man couldn't find any doorbell so he knocked on the door of number 7, hoping he hadn't wasted his time lugging the heavy typewrite out here. He had to wait for a few minutes that felt like an eternity. A man in his dressing gown opened the door, releasing a cloud of stale air made up of cigarette smoke and the reek of day-old beer.

Stave introduced himself and produced his identity papers, restraining himself from producing his police badge. It wasn't a great idea when doing business like this. Not that it was exactly forbidden, but it didn't look good for a CID man.

'Schindler,' the man introduced himself in return. Stave put him at about thirty years old, single and with a tough-looking face. I'm glad I don't have him as a neighbour, he thought.

'This might not be exactly the right time to be doing business,' Schindler said, seemingly oblivious to the fact that his visitor was standing out in the rain while he himself was in the dry doorway.

'Should I come back at another time?'

'No, I mean so soon before they introduce the new money. I hadn't anticipated that when I put the ad up. I'm not all that sure I want to exchange the bike at present. These are uncertain times.'

'Times are getting better,' Stave replied, trying to keep a pleading tone out of his voice. Just don't turn me away, he prayed silently. Be bold, he told himself, pushing his way into the hall without being asked. Before Schindler could say a word, he pulled the tablecloth and wrapping paper off the Olympia.

'Immaculate machine, pre-war quality,' he said.

The man looked at the typewriter and moistened his lips with his tongue. I've got him, the CID man crowed, seeing the greed in the other man's eyes. All of a sudden he was wide awake. Maybe the bike was rubbish? Maybe this was a bad deal.

Schindler hesitated a few minutes as if he was doing calculations in his head. 'Okay,' he mumbled eventually. 'Wait here, I'll fetch the bike from the shed in the garden.' He disappeared into a silent gloomy room at the end of the hall. A few moments later he came back pushing an old, black-lacquered everyday bicycle. The leather saddle was worn, the rubber on the inner-tubed tyres damaged, no hand grips on the steel handlebars, no light, and only a front brake.

'The main thing is, it has all its spokes,' Schindler muttered, not even sounding as if he was convincing himself.

Stave bent down to look at the frame to examine the trademark: a leaping gazelle and beneath it the words: 'No. 10 Heeren Rijwiel.'

'Brought it back from Amsterdam,' Schindler explained. 'I was stationed there. There has to be something to gain from being a grunt. But I have problems with my knee now.'

'I'll take it,' Stave blurted out, before the man could have second thoughts – and before his scruples about taking looted property could kick in.

Just five minutes later Stave felt unimaginably years younger. Even though the rain had soaked through to his shoulders and his thighs, even though every muscle was still aching from his night-time training, even though two links in the bicycle's chain had rusted together, which caused it to catch every time he pedalled, even though the front wheel rim was dented which made the handlebars shudder, and even though he continually feared that one of the tyres would burst, he was in high spirits as he cycled across the cobbles, weaving his way around piles of bricks, bomb craters and blackberry bushes growing out of the broken tarmac on the edge of the streets. Freedom! A minor triumph, a tiny way along the road back to normality. At last he no longer had to concentrate on concealing his limp. Endless routes along which the day before he would have counted his steps out of sheer boredom, giving up only when he got into the hundreds, and now he flew along them. He wobbled to and fro like a five-year-old because it had been so long since he had ridden a bike, but at the same time he felt as elated as a child at long last let out on his own.

The closer he got to the city centre, the busier the streets became. He was taken aback the first time a car passed him, or another cyclist furiously rang his bell at him, though he had no idea why. Pedestrians on either side hurried along aimlessly. Groups on street corners, the men gesticulating. Again and again he heard 'X-day', a new mark. Empty shop windows, displays covered over, nothing on show, no price tickets, not a single pair of shoes, not an electric bulb, not one ball of wool. Empty shelves, as if overnight the city had been completely plundered. It was a good thing the weather was so bad, Stave thought: it made people less keen on wandering the streets.

He would get to the restaurant by the fishing harbour on time, with no need to rush, a completely new feeling. In Altona the roads down to the banks of the Elbe were steep. Stave even took time to get off the bike and push his new acquisition along. It meant there was no risk of him pulling the front brake and flying headfirst over the handlebars.

It was quiet in the fishing harbour at midday. The boats came in late in the evening and sold their catch into the early hours of the morning. Now the last tired workers dressed in rubber aprons were throwing fish heads and guts into the gullies along the stone quays of the Elbe, surrounded by hungry cats.

Stave rode up to the unprepossessing entrance of Sellmers Kellerwirtschaft. It was only then that it occurred to him that he had neither a padlock nor chain to keep his precious new acquisition safe. Not knowing what to do, he just glanced around him, then lifted the bicycle up on to his shoulders and carried it indoors.

When a shocked waiter came up to him, he set the bike down gently, pulled out his ID card and said, 'Police. Where can I put the bike?'

The man was too taken aback to refuse such an absurd demand. 'This way,' he said, showing him into a gloomy hallway next to the kitchen. The chief inspector leant the bike against a wall flecked with damp specks, nodded graciously to the waiter as if he had helped him arrest a murderer and went back into the dining room.

'You're the first man I've known to use the cloakroom for a bicycle rather than a coat,' Anna said by way of greeting.

She was sitting at a small table at the end of the room by a grubby window looking out on to the Elbe. Her slim form was draped in a dress the colour of the river, and her dark hair was held back by an ivory-coloured cloth band, save for the few strands that fell over her forehead, which she played with nonchalantly. Stave had to suppress the urge to carefully brush them back from her face. A light-coloured coat lay over the back of the chair next to her, drops of water falling from the folds to form a little puddle on the floor. He sat down opposite her.

'You're looking good.'

She smiled and his heart skipped a beat. 'Thanks for the invitation. You know this restaurant?'

'I've been here once before. With MacDonald,' he added quickly so she wouldn't think he had brought another woman here.

'What do you recommend?'

'The sole won't kill you.' He waved to a waiter and gave the order. Once again he used the 'forgotten ration card' trick. And why not? After all, he would have given up his new bicycle just to be sitting here with Anna. But at the same time he was anxious about what it was he had to discuss with her.

'How did you come by the bicycle?'

He told her the story, at greater length than necessary – happy to have the opportunity to delay mentioning the topic he would have to broach. Then the fish arrived. Overdone, just like it had been last time, the potatoes mushy, the 'mayonnaise' a whitish yoghurt-like stuff. They talked about the food, but eventually they had nothing but empty plates in front of them. The waiter came over and Stave ordered two cups of ersatz coffee.

'So,' Anna said, looking at him quizzically. 'Just what is it that's on your mind?'

Stave felt she'd seen through him all along. Just don't start stuttering, he told himself. 'I wanted to see you again.'

'That's nice.' She smiled again, and then turned serious. 'I'm not going to claim I can see into the depths of your soul,' she said quietly, 'but we have…' she searched for the right expression, 'a history together. And you don't look exactly like the man who used to be my lover. You look more like when we first got to know one another: a policeman carrying out an interrogation.'

'I was already in love with you back then.'

'But there was something you wanted to find out.'

'All the time I've known you, there was one thing I wanted to find out. Are you free?' Stave blurted out the words, then held his breath, as if he had just thrown a stone and was anxiously watching its trajectory. I can only hope I'm not going to break something, he prayed silently.

Anna looked out of the window. The rain-filled sky was as grey as the river, the downpour so dense that the huge docks of Blohm&Voss on the other side of the Elbe looked like a washed-out watercolour. From somewhere in the distance came the drawn-out sound of a foghorn. Stave noticed the miserable smell of the restaurant: old fish, rancid fat and stale tobacco.

'The problem is,' she said, 'that you're determined to know my history. And I'm determined to forget it.'

Stave found himself thinking of his wife who had been burned to death when their apartment was bombed, while he was elsewhere in the city on duty. Of the nightmares he had had, dominated by fire and heat. Of his son, Karl, who had thrown nothing but curses at him before signing up as a volunteer with the Wehrmacht, which was nearly the death of him. Of the endless time he had spent crawling the station platforms and through the indexes of missing persons in the search for his son. Of the joy and the shock when one day Karl had turned up on his doorstep. Of his helplessness ever since. 'I don't know whether or not you want to tell me your story,' he replied cautiously, 'but I know one thing for sure: no matter how much you want to forget your history, your history won't forget you.'

'I'm married,' she said. Stave tried to read the expression on her face, to see if it was challenging or penitent. Maybe both at once. 'But I assume you already know that. That's your job.'

'Klaus von Gudow,' he muttered. 'A diplomat. I haven't known for long, though. It was a coincidence.'

'And I have this coincidence to thank for this lunch invitation?'

'I have to know it all, now, or else I'm going to go mad,' Stave admitted, realising how anguished his voice seemed. It was good that the restaurant was nearly empty.

Then all of a sudden she leaned across the table and gave him a kiss on the cheek. 'That, if I've understood it correctly, is the nicest compliment any man has ever made me.' Anna fumbled around in her coat pocket, then produced a gold wedding ring and laid it on the table. 'As you can see, my history hasn't forgotten me.' She looked out of the window again. 'I was eighteen years old when I got married. Not even an adult yet. My husband is ten years older. We'd known we'd get married since we were children – and more importantly, as you can perhaps imagine, our families had known it too.'

'But as a mere member of the middle class, I don't need to pay attention to any dynastic inheritance questions when getting married?'

'Don't be sarcastic. Because you didn't have an enormous, ancient family with vast experience in exerting soft pressure on its members, the females in particular.' She sighed. 'I'm afraid I can't even say I was particularly unhappy. My husband was a diplomat. We moved to Berlin. From the eastern provinces to the capital. Things could be worse for a young girl. We lived near Friedrichstrasse. I saw to setting up the apartment. Klaus concentrated on his career.'

'A very brown career.'

Anna gave him a serious, almost angry look. She pulled her arm tight against her breast, that protective gesture he knew so well. 'It may sound absurd today, even pathetic, but I knew nothing about all that. My husband was a diplomat, a trained lawyer. I was proud of him and his title, but I knew nothing about what his work entailed. I just wasn't interested. He went off to the ministry in the morning and came home in the evening, just like all our friends and neighbours.'

Stave, who had never been a member of the NSDAP, and in 1933 had been shoved aside to an unimportant position in the CID, had watched on Kristallnacht as the synagogues burned. Later on he had stood guard over concentration camp inmates who had been sent to do clearance work among the ruins after severe bombing raids. Nor had he been able to prevent his own son enthusiastically signing up in the Hitler Youth. 'There are a lot of people one can accuse of worse,' he muttered.

'In the autumn of 1943 I left Berlin,' Anna continued. 'Klaus insisted. The air raids had become more frequent. He thought I would be safer if he sent me back to the family estates.' She looked at him sadly. 'To escape the American bombers I almost ran into the arms of the Red Army. I only just escaped from the east, but you already know that part of my history.'

'And your husband remained in Berlin?' It occurred to Stave that his own son might have fought alongside Anna's husband.

'To the bitter end. I thought he died in May 1945. At least, that's what a former colleague from the Foreign Office claimed. But to this day Klaus von Gudow is officially "missing in action". No gravestone. Fate unknown.'

'A tragic fate. Or a useful one, if you'd worked in the Jewish department of the Foreign Office and knew the Allies were looking for you and were keeping a spare spot for you on their gallows.'

'Shortly after I arrived in Hamburg I was actually visited by an elderly English officer. Very polite, very tactful. Probably a comrade of your friend MacDonald. At first I thought he was looking for sought-after objects that had survived the war.' She gave a bitter laugh. 'But it was sought-after humans that had survived the war he was interested in. It was only through his questions that I learned what Klaus had been responsible for. I felt...' she searched for the right word, '...dirty. Betrayed. Shamed. I stood there in front of this English officer, as if I was the wife of a thief. Worse than that. The wife of a mass murderer, and ridiculously naïve. To this day I still don't know if the officer in question felt sympathy for me, or despised me for being so clueless. Whatever. He wanted to know where my husband was. I had considered myself a widow, and was surprised by the question. I had nothing to tell him. One way or another he never came back. I reverted to my maiden name and tried to forget the whole story: my husband, his work, our time in Berlin. All of it.'

'But your history didn't forget you.'

Anna nodded, disturbed. 'One day somebody pushed a piece of paper under the door of my apartment – not long after I'd found the place in Röperstrasse. I never discovered who it was. It was a letter from a monastery in Italy. From my husband. He was hiding there, waiting until he got passage on a freighter. To Argentina.'

'How had he got from Berlin under siege to a monastery in Italy?'

'He didn't say in the letter. He referred only to sinister-sounding "helpers" – who would help me too if I wanted, who would smuggle me to Italy. Helpers who had booked passage on board a boat for a woman with papers in another name, with my photograph already on them.'

Stave held his breath. 'Are you going to go?'

She laughed, shaking her head, and almost grabbed him by the hand. 'I got that letter months ago, when I was already in love with another man. Another man whose history then caught up with him, too.'

'A man who had tailed you like a spy and watched as you went into a pawnshop in the colonnades and bought back a wedding ring,' he admitted.

Anna turned the ring lying on the table, carefully, as if it might explode at any time. 'I would never have fled to Argentina with Klaus. Even if I hadn't met you. After everything I've found out about him since, I never want to see him again. Just the thought of him makes me shudder. When I got the letter I was afraid: I had told the British officer I thought Klaus was dead. I had reverted to my maiden name, and that was how everybody in Hamburg knew me. What if Klaus was caught on the ship, or somewhere in Argentina?

What if he had left some traces in Hamburg? Traces that could lead to me?'

Stave closed his eyes. 'What an idiot I am,' he whispered.

Anna shook her head, wondering at herself. 'I would have got rid of the wedding ring long ago. But the inside had his name engraved on it. And mine. And the date of our wedding. What would Lieutenant MacDonald have thought if he had accidentally come across the ring? Or Public Prosecutor Ehrlich? I got my money together and bought back the ring, erasing the traces.'

'Why didn't you just take the letter to the British? Or give it to me?'

'You're a policeman, too. I had fallen in love with you, but I hardly knew you. The more you wanted to know about me, the more under pressure I felt. We'd just become a couple. I was afraid to tell you I was still married. To a sought-after war criminal. You might just have walked out on me. Then your son came back from the prisoner-of-war camp and things between us got even more complicated. Too complicated. I didn't want to have anything more to do with Klaus. I wanted to have nothing more to do with my past. I wanted to live here and now.'

'Very naïve.'

'As naïve as the life I led in Berlin. I wish I knew what to do.'

'I have an idea,' said Stave.

Ten minutes later they were walking along between the sheds. The rain had turned into more of a damp mist, totally surrounding them. The stench of fish oozed from the brick walls of the buildings. Stave led Anna past the last of the sheds to the cobbled quayside. The cobblestones glinted, polished by the soles of thousands of dockers dragging fish from the boats into the warehouses every night. But now there was nobody about.

'May I?' he asked, cautiously reaching out his hand towards her.

She hesitated for a long time, and then let the ring fall on to the open palm of his hand.

Stave closed his hand into a fist – and before he had second thoughts, before he was overtaken by doubt, he relaxed it and hurled the ring away. A golden reflection in the grey waters of the Elbe, then a small circle on a wave, without a sound. Anna took a deep breath. He had half expected she might burst into tears or cling to him for support. But she just stood there, upright and silent.

'Let's go,' she said at last, and Stave was filled with such a sense of relief that it was he who almost needed a supporting hand.

They walked silently along the bank of the Elbe until they came to dingy Röperstrasse. Anna was walking to his right, so Stave was wheeling his bike with his left hand. It was awkward and he was afraid of damaging it in a pothole, but he didn't want anything but thin air between him and the woman by his side. Her basement apartment, her shabby front door. Anna struggled with the rusty lock, then finally unlocked the door.

Suddenly filled with panic at the idea she might just disappear behind it, Stave grabbed her by the hand. 'Will we see one another again?'

Then Anna smiled and kissed him on the cheek. 'Give me a couple of days, just to get used to my new history.'

# An afternoon off

He was only due to meet up with MacDonald to visit Veit Harlan that evening. The chief inspector hung about in Röperstrasse for a long time, long enough for him to notice a curtain twitch in the window of a second floor apartment. Somebody was watching him. He rode off, confused, happy and aimless. Should he go back to CID head-quarters? Wander down the long corridors, sit staring at files with no answers in them? Or just pass the hours sitting in his silent apartment?

Without even noticing, he turned right on to Palmaille, then just a few minutes later – how quickly he could get around now – found himself on the Reeperbahn, grey, dull and abandoned in the rain. North over Heiligengeistfeld, past the imposing flak bunkers, black rather than the usual grey because the damp had saturated the concrete. Through Planten un Blomen park, its muddy path-ways so deeply rutted that his handlebars wobbled from side to side. Dammtor station and beyond: the university.

Stave was looking for an art historian who might be able to tell him something about Toni Weber. He didn't admit to himself that he had an underlying motive for coming here, a hope so fragile that he didn't want to spell it out too clearly for fear it proved illusory.

On the lawn outside the university he had to get off his bike. Two elderly men were driving a pair of oxen pulling a heavy iron plough over the ground. 'Potatoes for the student gentlemen,' one of them called to him, noticing the astonished look on his face. The heavy aroma of freshly turned soil. When had he last breathed in such a rural smell? Once again he began to regret not having bought a lock and chain. He hoisted the frame of the heavy Dutch bicycle on to his shoulders and climbed the first step up towards the main building of the university: a rococo pavilion with light-coloured stone columns against grey fluted concrete which he only noticed on second glance. A building from before the First World War, when concrete was made to look as if it were something much older. The chief inspector, who had never gone to university, felt small and unworthy.

An inscription over the entrance portal declared: 'To research, learning and teaching'. Once upon a time Stave would have considered that pompous, but now, with the oxen and plough below the steps, he found it immensely earnest.

The interior was gloomy and draughty, and smelled of old books and concrete dust. He left the bike in the lodge despite the complaints of the porter. Students pushed past him while he looked around trying to get his bearings: boys and girls in patched cardigans and torn trousers, some of them with briefcases or exercise books, others with schoolbags. A remarkable number of them were missing an arm, a leg or an eye. Their conversation was subdued and serious. There was no laughter. It's a monastery, Stave thought to himself, populated by fanatically earnest monks.

He had to ask around before someone pointed out to him the lecture theatre where Professor Christian Kitt was speaking. 'Trends in the Applied Arts of the Twentieth Century'. The chief inspector crept in. At the lectern was an elderly, haggard man with dark hair, a grey beard and metal-rimmed glasses. In his lectures once upon a time he might have had large-scale reproductions or maybe slides projected on to the wall, but all he was left with nowadays, if he was lucky, were torn art catalogues to hold up. Stave couldn't make out anything of the pictures, which didn't matter as he understood nothing of the professor's lecture. The scholar was using terms he had never heard before. Even after fifteen minutes he hadn't a clue what the lecture was actually about. But the two dozen or so students were eagerly scribbling down notes – many of them on the back of old paper receipts, or on the back of files because they didn't have the money to buy notebooks. The chief inspector wondered if it was a good idea after all to question this professor.

Even so he waited until the end, ignoring the curious glances from the students as they left the lecture theatre, before introducing himself to the professor.

'I'm interested in some information about modern artists and collectors,' he began.

'The police have been interested in modern art ever since 1933,' Kitt replied, not in an unfriendly way, but with a cautiously expectant look on his face. An exile, Stave thought to himself, only come back after 1945.

'What do you know about Toni Weber?'

'I know the name. But that's all.'

'That's all. I thought you were an expert?'

Kitt sighed and gave him the sort of look scholars reserved for complete idiots. The CID man was sorely tempted to arrest him on the spot. 'Have you any idea how much is left of modern art? I mean in the students' heads? Nothing. Worse than that: less than nothing. Totally false ideas, ideas that have been poisoned. What is left for them to refer to? Two thirds of the 60,000 volumes in the university library didn't survive the bombing. The remaining third is no more than what the Nazis left. They were burning books a good ten years before the British and American aircraft. Anyone who wants to study modern art today, let alone carry out research into it, has to start from the beginning. You have to start with the masters: Munch, van Gogh, Klee, Picasso, Matisse, Dix, Kokoschka, I could name dozens. Only when we've managed all of those, which can take decades, can we turn our attention to lesser talents.'

'And Weber is a lesser talent?'

'Every tribe has a lot of Indians but only a few chiefs. There's no point doing research into the Indians if you know nothing about the chiefs.'

Stave thought back to the murals in the black marketeer's house on the Baltic and wondered what Herr Professor Kitt would think of them. 'Is there any way of finding out much about the collectors?' he asked, already with little hope.

'Even less.'

'Dr Alfred Schramm?'

'Ah,' the scholar muttered, licking his lips as if Stave had just mentioned a fine meal. 'A patron. A friend of the Warburg Institute.'

'You know him?'

'Slightly. I was a scientific assistant at the institute when Schramm would call in occasionally. He furthered our work. In non-material ways. And…' Kitt cleared his throat, 'material ways also. At the time I wasn't… established enough, to be noticed by Dr Schramm. And then I was out of Germany for several years.'

'Do you have colleagues who could tell me more about Schramm?'

'Several, but not in Hamburg. The staff of the Warburg Institute, or at least the more competent among them and those who were interested in the same sort of art as Schramm, all went abroad in 1933. Most of them today are teaching in Oxford or somewhere in America. In any case Schramm didn't visit the institute that often and almost never came to the university. He had his people to do that.'

'His people?'

Kitt cleared his throat again. 'Dr Schramm had some of his staff enrol as observers at the Philosophy faculty so they could learn about the history of art and related subjects. They were basically clerks and people like that.' Kitt couldn't manage to conceal his disdain. 'But he trusted them. And he wanted them to advise him in matters of art. Or maybe it was just that he didn't want to be surrounded in his bank with people who could only talk about credit balances but could have an intelligent conversation as well. One way or another there were always one or two gentlemen from the bank here in this lecture theatre where you and I are standing now. Not all the lecturers were pleased about it, but Dr Schramm was a patron so nobody said anything.'

'Did they include Jews?' Stave asked, suddenly thinking of something.

For a long moment the professor looked at him as if he had just mentioned the name of an awkward relative. 'Probably. There were always certain rumours about Dr Schramm's good relations with Jews. And a few of his workers stopped turning up at the university as early as the spring of 1933. That led to certain conclusions, I assume.'

'Names?'

'They were just observers!' Professor Kitt exclaimed, as if that solved everything.

'Thank you,' Stave mumbled, turning towards the door. Could the unknown corpse from the Reimershof, with the Jewish star on his clothing, have been one of Schramm's artistic-leaning staff? Someone who worked at the bank but was also sent by his boss to attend the university? Someone who from 1933 on was employed to watch over banned treasures in the Reimershof? But if so why wouldn't Schramm say anything? Why did he deny everything? As he reached the door he turned and asked: 'Is there a note somewhere of the names of the observers?'

Kitt, who was carefully sorting through his briefcase, looked up in irritation: 'The old student lists were reduced to ashes in one or another bombing raid.'

Stave was walking down the steps outside the main entrance, with his bicycle across his shoulders, when he spotted Karl. He had hoped the occasion might arise. It had been the other reason that brought him to the university rather than just the idea of talking to an art historian. How many students were there here? Four thousand? Five thousand? It hadn't been that unreasonable to hope to spot a familiar face. And as it happened, he had indeed been lucky.

Karl looked at him in surprise. He was wearing a torn, dyed Wehrmacht overcoat to protect both himself and a notebook he was carrying against the rain. Stave gave him a brief rundown on his talk with Professor Kitt. Simultaneously his thoughts were racing. Karl was at the university. He didn't dare ask what subjects he was studying.

'And the bike?' Karl asked. 'Did you pick that up here?'

'It was a good exchange.' Stave told him how he had come by his new possession.

'Excuse me,' his son interrupted him, nodding to his companion. 'May I introduce Manfred Loos, a fellow student.'

Fellow student? Karl had signed on. Stave shook the gaunt young man's hand, though only after he had managed to adeptly transfer one of his crutches from his right hand to his left. Older than Karl, the chief inspector reckoned.

'Manfred is a high-jumper.'

Stave stared at the pair of them, not sure whether they were playing a wicked joke on him. Loos smiled. 'Before the war I was in athletics,' he explained. 'A piece of shrapnel severed part of my lower leg in Russia in 1943. But I've been training and I can get up to 1.77 metres again now.'

'That's just eighteen centimetres below the German record,' Karl added.

Stave realised his son was looking fitter too. His skin had some colour from the sun, his posture was better, his fingers were no longer stained yellow from nicotine. Maybe the two had got to know one another through sport? What did he really know of Karl? Even so he felt strangely light of heart. Even his perpetual fear that his own damaged foot made other people look at him seemed suddenly ridiculous. To jump 1.77 metres, with just one leg. The CID man asked how that was even possible.

He plucked up his courage. 'What are you studying?' It might seem odd to Loos that even Karl's own father didn't know what his son's subject was, but he didn't care.

'History and philosophy,' Karl replied promptly and clearly proud.

Stave realised his son had been waiting for the question. Recognised that he had been right to ask. It was as if he had passed a sort of test, opened a door to his son.

'That's important,' he said respectfully, if only because he couldn't think of anything else to say.

'You can learn stuff from the old days and from thinkers in the past,' Karl said. It was intended to sound casual, but Stave realised he was talking in earnest.

Loos cleared his throat, took his crutches in both hands. 'The lecture starts in five minutes.'

Karl nodded. 'An introduction to Buddhism.'

Stave, still in an upbeat mood, was alarmed. 'A sect?' he asked in shock.

The two kids laughed, but in a friendly way. 'The Burmese monk Bhikkhu U. Thunanda is visiting Hamburg, Father, a great Buddhist from Rangoon. He's on a world tour, to spread his thoughts. He's about to give a lecture about his teaching, the only speech he's going to make in Hamburg. I want to hear it, because I want to be a philosopher, not a Buddhist.' He slapped him on the back encouragingly and bounded up the steps. Loos on his crutches followed him somewhat more slowly.

Stave remained there, staring at the ox plough that in the meantime had divided the lawn into a ploughed field, at the Dammtor station beyond it, at the sky, at the low clouds. He couldn't remember the last time his son had touched him in such a good-natured way.

# An unemployed director

Stave almost felt as if he was on an outing, back before the war. He still had a bit of time so he rode out to Harvesthude, one of the quarters of the city that had been commandeered by the British: it had old nineteenth century houses, well-maintained streets. Calm. If it hadn't been raining, the chief inspector might have been tempted to a racing spurt, but he mistrusted the solitary hard brake on his Gazelle-trademark bike. 'Shitscrapers' they had called brakes like that at school, because the rubber scraped the dirt from the tyres. Unfortunately nor did he trust the profile of the tyre which didn't inspire the chief inspector to take any risks.

The northerly tip of the Alster is shaped like a big 'L': the streets that ran directly along the bank were closed off to all but the British. Stave turned around and the bike took him in just a few minutes back to Esplanade 6: a huge reddish-grey lump of an administrative building amid the smart streets. The seat of the British civilian administration.

The CID man felt a bit shabby and somehow ridiculous as he presented the British sentry on the door with his police ID in the one hand, while the other was gripping the handlebars of an old bicycle. But the young military policeman simply took a note of his name, lifted a heavy black telephone receiver and said a few words of English into it.

A few minutes later MacDonald appeared. 'You're ready to launch a new *Blitzkrieg*,' he exclaimed, when he caught sight of Stave's bike.

The word alone was embarrassing to Stave, especially outside the British administration building. 'Not exactly a bad exchange,' he muttered.

'I can't keep up with that, old boy. We don't have bikes in the army. Maybe I could sit on the basket as we cycle along the Alster? That would give the Nazi film director something to look at. Maybe it would give him an idea for a new film.'

'A comedy, I imagine. I would prefer your Jeep.'

'I thought as much. Do you want to leave the bike here?'

'You're a mind reader.'

MacDonald exchanged a few words with the sentry and the young soldier wheeled the 'Gazelle' into the foyer, touching it the whole time only with his fingertips as if afraid he might catch some infectious disease.

The lieutenant nodded towards a Jeep. 'We could walk, of course, but on the one hand it's raining and on the other, better to make an impression.'

'Provided we don't get a flat tyre.'

MacDonald turned the ignition and they set off at a moderate speed along the street, then turned left along the Alster. The water was grey, tossed with waves and raindrops like an unmade bed sheet.

The lieutenant glanced at his passenger. 'Do you know how I got permission to interview Harlan so quickly from my boss?'

'There are film fans in the British supreme command, maybe?'

'There are government ministers who would like to see this character hang. As far as they are concerned he's worse than many an SS man.'

'So why haven't they just picked him up? Just because his wife is Swedish?'

The young Scotsman sighed. 'There are too many fish swimming in the brown water,' he explained. 'We're only catching the fattest. Or to be more precise, the sharks. The real mass murderers. Those who were at the top of the command tree. We'll leave the rest to you Germans.'

'Thanks a lot,' Stave grumbled. Veit Harlan had been Hitler's favourite movie director: adventure films, epics, big stars, the big wide world. Stave and Margarethe had even gone to see *Münchhausen*. He remembered how she had laughed, and even hours later went back over some of the scenes, on the way home, over supper. Even in bed.

Then there was *Süss the Jew*, in the cinema, long after war had broken out. The sleazy Jew who had financially blackmailed the innocent blonde, raped her, driven her to suicide. Kristina Söderbaum. She had drowned herself so often in all these films that people had sarcastically nicknamed her the 'Reichswaterbaby'. Very pretty, very pure, somewhat naïve. Stave wondered what Harlan must have been thinking when he filmed those scenes: his wife being raped by somebody else. At any rate it was a success. Goebbels put on special screenings for SS men and concentration camp guards, to fuel the hatred of Jews. For a while after it came out Stave's colleagues had talked about *Süss the Jew* over lunch, or a beer in the evening, and all the time with murderous hatred in their eyes. Stave kept quiet. He hadn't seen the film but nor did he dare to argue with any of them.

After 1945 Harlan had obviously ended up in front of the Main Denazification Committee. The experts who worked for it divided thousands of Hamburg citizens into categories: 1. War criminals. 2. Evil doers. 3. Lesser evil doers. 4. Members of the Nazi Party. 5. Innocent. After a few months Harlan was classified in Category 5. A clean bill of the first order.

The chief inspector remembered the protests outside the court, the editorial in *Zeit* newspaper, demonstrations outside cinemas where Harlan and his wife sat among the audience. And now Hamburg Regional Court was pressing another charge against Harlan: 'Crimes against Humanity', based on the argument that *Süss the Jew* had instigated acts of violence. But the result of the case was as yet in doubt.

MacDonald took the curve round the Rondel, a circular pond off the main body of the Alster surrounded by villas and lawns. It was a favourite for lovers who rented out rowing boats to come out here, mostly under the thick-leaved branches of the willows by the banks. Stave's colleagues in the Vice squad used to make jokes about it and would make a point of occasionally patrolling the area. In his young days Stave himself had made a romantic excursion out here with Margarethe, even if he had feared coming across a few gleeful colleagues.

Scheffelstrasse was narrow but smart, with a view out over the Alster: old oak and beech trees with gnarled knots. So abandoned it made the roaring of wind and rain sound unnaturally loud. On the right was a small but elegant villa, two storeys with steep steps but unmissable because of the Swedish flag flapping heavily in the rain. MacDonald cut the engine and Stave inhaled the sweet smell of affluence: damp earth, roses, the almost sweet whiff of the warm water in the Alster. He thought of Karl who at the age of seventeen had been banished to the ice of Vorkuta in Siberia for two years, while men like Harlan didn't even have to leave their villas for a day. He's just a witness in this case, he reminded himself, just a witness.

Outside the heavy wooden door there were piles of letters and parcels with Swedish, British and American stamps. And also some wreaths with black trim.

'It would seem we haven't exactly chosen the best of times to visit,' MacDonald whispered, pressing the bell.

'Maybe it's Harlan who's died,' the CID man replied.

'Would that please you? Or annoy you because you'd have lost your chance to question him?'

'Put it like this, I'd rather be questioning him on his deathbed.'

The young lieutenant was about to reply when the door silently opened and a blonde woman stood in front of them, with sensuous lips, a heavenly nose, bright eyes: Kristin Söderbaum.

Stave had been expecting a housekeeper or a maid, and stood gaping for a moment at the movie star, as if some creature from a fairy tale had just blown into his everyday life. MacDonald got a grip on himself faster and greeted her with a casual touch of his cap, introduced himself and his companion and nodded towards the packages and wreaths next to the door. 'You have mail.'

'Same as every day.' The voice that Stave knew from her films. But somehow even softer. 'I'll clear it up.'

'You've had bad news?'

'No. The letters and parcels have all been sent by friends of my husband. Or sometimes from people who remember my movie roles. The wreaths are from people who'd like to see us dead. I don't know what to do with them. We can't exactly leave them sitting outside the door.' Kristina Söderbaum sighed, glanced back at her two visitors and invited them in. She was looking rather more depressed than she had a few minutes ago.

'We won't stay long,' MacDonald reassured her. Stave gave the lieutenant an inconspicuous nudge. It seemed the young British officer had fallen for the movie star.

'We have a few questions for your husband,' he said carefully.

'I'm certain he'll be able to give you satisfactory answers. We've had a lot of experience answering police questions.'

A brightly lit room, with a table, chairs, pine-framed watercolours hanging on the walls. 'We're just guests here,' Kristina Söderbaum explained. 'The house belongs to Swedish friends. But they're not here most of the time.'

'Life isn't that comfortable these days in Hamburg,' MacDonald said in a friendly tone.

The actress gave him an irritated glance, not certain if he was being sympathetic or sarcastic. 'My husband will be here in a second. He's reading a story to our little one.'

Stave vaguely remembered hearing that Harlan had had a second son. After the war. Life goes on. He felt his anger surging.

A few minutes later the door opened and for the second time that day the chief inspector felt he was standing opposite a living legend. Veit Harlan was nearly fifty years old, chubby, with a bouffant of greying hair, but the goatee beard that had been so well known, and such a subject of jokes in the Nazi days, had been shaved off. His eyes were still clear and attentive behind his dark framed glasses. He was a man who filled every room he entered.

'Are you here about the trial?' It was a voice used to giving orders.

'That's not a matter for CID,' Stave replied.

'I'm glad to hear it.' Harlan flopped on to a chair that creaked slightly under his weight. 'I would like to be able to work again. My wife has a new role.' He nodded towards Kristina Söderbaum.

'I'm playing in an American thriller,' she explained. '*Gaslight*. In the Auslese, a new company. It's refreshing to be doing theatre again.'

'I'm bursting with energy, too,' said Harlan. 'New movies would be good for this country, in this situation. But they won't let me alone.'

'There are a few people who remember some of your earlier films,' the CID man commented.

Harlan waved his right hand as if swatting a fly. 'I was forced, not given a choice. Did you even meet Goebbels, gentlemen? The way he walked on to the set, read through the scripts? Insisted on a cut here and there? And all the time a threat in the background. If you've never experienced that, then…'

'You'll have the chance to explain all that in court.'

'A joint action by Jews, none of whom I've ever seen before. You know not one Jew has ever complained to me in person.'

'There aren't that many left,' MacDonald replied quietly.

The director looked at him for a moment, then nodded and said, 'What is it you want from me?'

Stave pulled the photo of the bronze female head from his overcoat pocket and asked, 'Do you recognise this?'

Harlan glanced at it and smiled. 'Anni Mewes. She was a good actress. Before my time. Silent movies. But her voice was no good for the talkies; she sounded like a scullery maid.'

'That didn't stop her turning up in one of your films – in this form.'

'As a bronze bust? Yes… I recall. I needed props. It was 1938 – modern art. I don't know much about it. I had to have things brought from the propaganda ministry. Goebbels insisted. In person. So I went over and just pointed out a few sculptures: that one, that one, and that one. And then I recognised the likeness of Mewes. I'd seen it before but years earlier. So I took that too and put it on a set where it was clearly visible. A little act of homage to an artiste. Almost a token act of resistance.'

Stave just stared at his hands, and noticed that his fingers were clamped together so tightly his knuckles were glowing white. Try to calm down. 'And then?'

'When?'

'After you'd finished the film. What happened to the artworks then?'

'Back to the warehouse.'

The chief inspector faked a disingenuous expression. 'It's amazing that a director like you who's had to deal with so many things in so many films should remember this prop in particular, when it just sat somewhere in the background for a few scenes.' Harlan hesitated, shot a quick glance at his wife. 'The Mewes bust didn't go back to the warehouse. I remember that. There was someone who wanted to buy it.'

The CID man leaned forward, scarcely daring to breathe: 'Who?'

'I'm afraid I don't remember.'

'I do.' Kristina Söderbaum smiled. 'It was forbidden to mention it back then. But nowadays I think we can speak openly about it. On the last day of shooting a gentleman came to the studio and asked us, very discreetly, about the pieces of art. It was very unusual. I don't know how he knew they were there. He wanted to buy some of them. He had money. But most of them had already been taken away. The bust, however, was needed for the next scene and so it was still there. We offered it to the gentleman and he gave us a good price. Nobody at the propaganda ministry seemed to notice that one less artwork was returned to the warehouse. Goebbels and his people couldn't care less.' She blushed.

'Who was the man who wanted to buy the piece?'

'A Herr Rosenthal. A Jew.' She all but whispered the last word.

'I told you I had nothing to reproach myself about,' Harlan exclaimed, almost with a note of triumph in his voice. 'I recall the story now.'

'Rosenthal? Did he say who he was? A collector? A gallery owner?'

'This was in the thirties,' the director said impatiently. 'Nothing like that was supposed to be possible any more.'

'So what was he?'

'We didn't ask him.'

'You weren't surprised that somebody just turned up and secretly asked to buy some degenerate art from you? A Jew, at that?'

'The final days of filming are always particularly hectic. We had other things on our minds. That very day I had another meeting with the Reichsminister for Propaganda. The thing was an annoyance. I just said, "Good, get on with it, and then get out of here." And that's what he did.'

'Was there a sales contract? A receipt?'

'Where were you in those days? Abroad? Nobody in 1938 was selling banned art to a Jew and asking for a receipt.'

Stave went silent and remembered what Professor Kitt had said: the employees Schramm had sent out to buy things, some of them Jews. Hadn't he even mentioned a Rosenthal? 'Does the name Schramm mean anything to you?'

'Never heard it.' Kristina Söderbaum shook her head too.

He was a neighbour, the chief inspector thought, barely a hundred metres away. Surely they would know him at least in that context. On the other hand Harlan and his wife had only been living by the Alster since the end of the war, and they probably didn't leave the house all that frequently.

'Toni Weber?' he asked.

'Somebody in the movie world? I think I've heard the name. Not that it's exactly unusual, is it?'

Stave ignored Harlan and looked at Kristina Söderbaum: naïve, vulnerable, just like in her movie roles. If I push her too hard, she'll end up in the Alster, he thought to himself. 'Can you tell me any more about this Herr Rosenthal?'

'He was about forty to fifty years old. Thin. Somewhat nervous.' She thought for a moment, then suddenly exclaimed, 'Alliteration! I remember now, when he introduced himself, his first name. He was called Rolf Rosenthal. And he had a limp. He had a club foot, just like Goebbels, although he handled it a bit more elegantly. Not that that matters so much to you, I imagine.' She blushed again.

'Yes it does,' Stave muttered, a wave of gratefulness to Kristina Söderbaum washing over him. 'It's matters a great deal to me.'

'Are you happy now?' MacDonald asked as they climbed back into the Jeep.

'I've solved one problem but given myself others in its place,' Stave replied cautiously.

'Sounds like a typical military manoeuvre.'

The CID man told the lieutenant about Schramm's employees being educated in art history at the university. 'It all fits: I can piece together a story for the bronze bust and the unidentified body. Toni Weber did the sculpture of an actress in the twenties. The Nazis labelled it "degenerate art", and it eventually disappeared into the propaganda ministry warehouse. It emerged again to be a prop for a film directed by Veit Harlan in 1938. Before it could be handed back, Rolf Rosenthal turns up in the studio and buys the piece. It's illegal but lucrative for Harlan. Goebbels had given him a blank chit and he'd made a few hundred, maybe even a few thousand Reichsmarks, cash, tax-free. Who is Rolf Rosenthal? In our interview with Schramm – the banker who paid for art lessons for his staff, including Jews, even after 1933 – he mentioned in passing a Jew called Rosenthal who'd been one of his acolytes. Of course it used to be a common name, but it's still quite a coincidence, don't you think? The body found next to the artworks still bore remnants of a star of Israel, and papers with the forename Rolf, and had a handicapped foot. Given that the Anni Mewes sculpture is in a photo taken in Schramm's villa just a few weeks after the film shoot had ended, there is only one conclusion.'

'Rolf Rosenthal was one of Schramm's agents, who bought banned pieces for him so that Schramm himself – having already had problems with the Gestapo – could remain discreetly in the background,' MacDonald finished off the argument for him.

The CID man gave a tired smile. 'But why would Schramm deny it all? He claims not to recognise the bronze bust. And not a word about the deceased. What he had been doing in 1938 was against the law, but nowadays it would be seen as praiseworthy. Loyalty to a Jewish employee. Saving banned artworks. I don't see why he doesn't admit it. And that's without mentioning that it's a piece of art he probably paid a lot of money for.'

'Schramm doesn't need to worry about money.'

'Do you know a banker who'd voluntarily turn down a single penny? There has to be an important reason behind it – maybe Rolf Rosenthal didn't die in a bombing raid. There's that strange injury to his skull, as if he had been hit from above. Scratch marks in unusual places on the soles of his shoes. It's all a puzzle to me.'

'But you look rather pleased with yourself.'

'Things have been worse,' the chief inspector admitted.

A little later Stave was cycling around the Gorch-Fock Wall and the bomb craters on the Esplanade. It was only a few hundred metres but his trousers were sticking to his legs and water was running down into his shoes. You're going to have to get yourself something for protection against the rain, and he wondered what he could barter on the exchange market for a waterproof cape. Or whether there would even be an exchange market any more after X-day. A truck passed him by, an asthmatic pre-war model, hardly going any faster than he was. Blue clouds were pumping out of the exhaust and hanging over the street like a thick fog in the rain-sodden air. It stank of oil and petrol. He was on Karl-Muck-Platz – he could keep straight on and ride into the CID headquarters foyer. He would enjoy the looks from his colleagues. But he turned right towards the public prosecutor's office.

'I believe you're visiting celebrities these days,' Ehrlich said when he saw him. His eyes behind the thick lenses of his glasses twinkled mischievously, but Stave noticed that they were red in the corners from exhaustion.

'Think of it as an archaeological expedition to the ruins of a former UFA star.'

'Did you dig up any treasure?'

'I identified a club-footed mummy.' The chief inspector told him about the interview and the conclusions he had drawn from it.

'What a pity you no longer work for Homicide,' Ehrlich commented. 'However, we have another meeting coming up. Probably in July. The court will summon you as a witness.'

'The ship's mate from the *Tirpitz*, the one who shot me,' Stave mumbled.

'Who also has the fate of his own family on his conscience. We have his confession. But you know how things are: we will still need to hear all the main evidence. And some of it might be a bit awkward for CID.'

Stave closed his eyes. 'The beating he was given. I heard about that. I saw nothing, I had other things on my mind at the time.' He gave a gentle tap on his chest.

'The defence may call Herr Dönnecke into the witness stand.'

'He won't do his client any good. The mate is for the chop anyhow.'

'Sometimes the right ones get what they deserve.'

Stave ought to be going but somehow he couldn't bring himself to get up from the uncomfortable chair. Nor did Ehrlich look as if he had anything better to do.

'Are you also in charge of the investigation into Harlan?' the CID man asked.

'For inciting racial hatred? No, one of my colleagues is doing that. He'll do it well but I still feel sorry for him.'

'Because he has no chance of success?'

'That's the way it looks. Nasty films aren't a crime in themselves; at least not so far. And in any case Harlan claims he was under pressure from Goebbels.'

'All the old Nazis say that.'

'And they nearly all get away with it. Anyone who didn't actually have a finger on the trigger or the gas tap, in other words anyone who doesn't directly have blood on their hands, doesn't need to worry too much. Everyone had a pre-1945 superior who gave him this or that order which he was obliged to follow.' The public prosecutor took a sip of tea. 'So far more than 300,000 citizens of Hamburg have appeared before the tribunal – and nearly all of them have been given a "Persil paper". And in the event that somebody really doesn't get cleared there's always another way around: a coincidental car accident, for example.'

Stave nodded. Karl Kaufmann, the former Gauleiter and effective ruler of Hamburg during the 'brown years', was injured in a quite spectacular car accident, which was sufficient to halt his trial. And then there was the former mayor Krogmann, whom he had seen recently in a restaurant. The former Gestapo agent Greiner, who walked around freely. And Anna's husband, the diplomat in the Jewish bureau, hiding in his monastery on his way to a new life in South America.

'Not all the Nazis got off so lightly,' Stave replied cautiously. 'Anyone who worked in a government ministry is investigated.'

'In the foreign ministry, perhaps?' Ehrlich asked, with a thin smile on his lips. 'I knew you'd sooner or later pick up that trail.'

'Klaus von Gudow.'

'A man from the past.'

'How long have you known?'

'After I got to know Frau von Veckinhausen, and was impressed by her knowledge of the art world, I made a few enquiries about her.'

'Discreetly?'

'Very discreetly, via English friends. No Germans.'

'Does Anna know about your inquiries?'

'No.'

'Are you looking for her husband?'

'Yes.'

'Are you using Anna as bait?'

'Yes, but the prey isn't biting.'

Stave stared at Ehrlich. 'Your employment of Anna to track down your missing pieces of art was just cover, then?'

The public prosecutor shook his head energetically. 'Let's call it collateral. She had some success.' He nodded towards the sketch on the wall. 'Frau von Veckinhausen came up with a couple of pieces.'

'But in reality, the reason you employed her was so you could keep an eye on her.'

'In case her husband made contact? Yes.'

The CID man thought of the wedding ring from the jeweller's shop and wondered if the man opposite him knew about it.

'Klaus von Gudow is somewhere in Italy,' Ehrlich went on. 'Still. Have you ever heard of the "ratlines"? Escape routes via Austria to Italy? Set up by old Nazi Party comrades and some priests who're open-minded on the issue. There are a few bishops who see the murder of six million Jews not so much as sin but the justified vengeance of God.'

'Anna has nothing more to do with her husband.'

'Unfortunately that's the conclusion I've also come to myself: no trips, no secret meetings. She's severed all links between herself and her husband. A new start in life. A new lover.' He watched Stave carefully with those tired eyes behind thick spectacle lenses.

'So, what happens now?' Stave asked, scarcely daring to breathe.

'I have turned the search for Klaus von Gudow over to the chief public prosecutor's office in Frankfurt-on-Main, the American Zone. Given that I assume the gentleman in question has no intention of remaining in Italy, but will pursue his travel arrangements to South America, I expect their colleagues will be better equipped to cooperate with the authorities out there. They may still catch him before he disappears to Argentina or Paraguay.'

'Argentina. Does Anna know about all this?'

'Not a word.'

Stave closed his eyes. He felt as if a rucksack full of boulders had been lifted from his shoulders.

'Good luck,' Ehrlich mumbled, getting to his feet. 'I mean, with Frau von Veckinhausen.'

'I'll try not to make a mess of things,' he replied, shaking the prosecutor's hand.

Stave decided not to go back to headquarters: there would be nobody there, certainly not in Department S. Tomorrow was X-day. The chief inspector asked himself if tomorrow suddenly everything would be different.

He pushed the pedals down against the damp northerly wind. When he got to Ahrensburger Strasse 93, he lifted the bike on to his shoulders. Flasch, who was looking out on to the pavement from his ground floor apartment, appeared surprised, then made a gesture that might have signified amazement or sympathy. Stave nodded back to him and pushed open the heavy entrance door to the block. What did it matter. If he hoped to use the bike again tomorrow, then for better or worse he had to lug it up to his apartment; the door to his storage area in the cellar was made of little more than a few planks nailed together.

He was out of breath by the time he reached the landing outside his apartment. His left ankle hurt, and his shoulders ached from the steel bars of the bike frame sliding with every step he took. His chest wound throbbed. He was fumbling with his right hand in his trouser pocket for the key when all of a sudden the door opened.

Karl.

'You look like you need wringing out!' his son exclaimed.

'It's only rain,' Stave muttered, not wanting to admit to his son just how exhausted he was. He set the bike down and wheeled it into the hallway. 'I'll get changed quickly. You're staying a bit?' He hardly dared ask the question.

'Let's see. Have you got anything in the larder? I bartered for some lettuce and carrots up at the allotment, and the first sour cherries.'

'I've got potatoes, bread and lard and ersatz coffee,' came a shout from the bathroom.

'Do you think we'll get a bit more to eat any day soon?' Karl asked half an hour later as they sat at the kitchen table with two seductively steaming plates.

'Things can only get better.'

'I heard that after the bombing raids. And when I was fighting with my comrades on the streets of Berlin. And in the POW camp in Vorkuta. "Things can only get better." It was never true. Things just got worse and worse.'

Stave didn't want to depress his son. He's just twenty years old, he thought. And if he can't be optimistic, who can? 'The new money will be worth something,' he replied, trying to sound more confident than he really felt.

Karl gave a brief laugh and shook his head. 'The famous X-day. What if nothing happens at all?'

'It's not just something the British are doing. It's the Americans too. And they're the real bosses. If they organise something, it happens.'

'They certainly organised the bombing raids well.'

'And the CARE packets. Without those a few more people would have starved to death.'

His son shook his head again pensively: 'I wish I could believe in a better future,' he muttered. 'Do you?'

Stave wanted to say yes, but he also wanted to be honest. 'I hope the future will be better,' he replied cautiously. 'I'm working on it. That things will be better, I mean. What else is there to do?'

'Leap out of the window.'

'If that was really what you thought, that there was no hope left, then you wouldn't have survived two years in Vorkuta.'

Karl looked at him in surprise, then smiled appreciatively and clicked his fingers: 'You've got me into a corner there. There's something true in that.'

'And you're a student now,' his father let slip, proudly.

'Of ancient history. Somebody needs to get to the bottom of this mess. I mean, right to the bottom.'

'Two thousand years back?'

He shrugged his shoulders. 'There has to be an origin to it all. Maybe it was the Romans who conquered Europe? Or Christianity? One way or another, the Nazis weren't the first to have the idea of taking over the whole continent. Nor were they the first to want to kill every Jew they got their hands on. That goes way back too.'

'What's the point of looking for reasons in the distant past?'

'To make sure the same thing doesn't happen again.'

Stave leaned back, genuinely surprised. He had never looked at things like that. History was always about something that happened yesterday, never about tomorrow. He hoped it was optimism in Karl's case.

'In fact it was primarily because of that that I invited myself to supper. You have a radio.' He glanced down at an old watch on his wrist. Where had he got that from, his father wondered. Probably in exchange for tobacco.

'The mayor is about to make a speech. I was thinking it might be interesting.'

Stave stood up and turned the old radio on. He hoped his electricity ration for the month would be enough to hear the speech to the end. To make sure, he turned off the light, which had his one remaining working bulb. The soft yellow glow of the radio valves flooded the room, the sound crackling and hissing as they warmed up. And then a voice. NWDR, North West German Radio.

They listened to Mayor Max Brauer's voice, cautiously optimistic. 'The German people will remain poor for years yet and unable to afford any particular luxury. But there is no shame in poverty, and we above all do not need to be afraid of it as long as all decent German men and women are paid honest money for their work, money with which they can buy things, and still save some, which is what we all will have to do.'

'He certainly has a different way of speaking compared to Adolf,' Karl said when the broadcast ended.

'Honest money doesn't sound bad.'

'But he also said we would remain poor for years.'

'At least he wasn't telling lies.'

Karl looked out of the window, streaming with rain. Darkness falling on Ahrensburger Strasse. 'What would you buy first? After X-day, I mean. If the "honest money" isn't just a load of nonsense. What would you buy with your next paycheque?'

Stave thought long and hard. 'A pair of shoes,' he answered finally. 'Decent men's shoes. Leather, comfortable, with good soles. Shoes you can walk around town in, without looking like a tramp. What about you?'

'Books. American books, English books, French books. Maybe even Soviet books. I feel as if it wasn't just two years I spent in that camp, but my whole life.'

Let's hope the new money is a success, Stave prayed silently. Something has to work in this country sooner or later. Shoes. Books. Not a bad start for a new era.

Karl rubbed his eyes. 'I'm tired,' he said. 'Can I spend the night here? Is the little room still free?'

'Who else is it for?' Stave replied, scarcely able to believe his own happiness.

# Deutschmark

*Sunday, 20 June 1948*

Stave woke up at 4 a.m. exactly, as always without an alarm clock. If he decided the night before to get up at a specific time the next morning, he woke up at precisely that time, as if he had an internal clock. He crept into the kitchen so as not to wake Karl. X-day. Grey light, rain, far too cold for the beginning of summer. He cut the mouldy pieces off the grey bread and threw them into the bin. He cut one third of the rest and completed his breakfast by washing it down with tap water. It would take too long to heat up the old iron stove. Maybe he could get an ersatz coffee somewhere later.

The chief inspector carried his bicycle down the semi-dark stairwell. The only glimmer of light came through the gap under Flasch's door. The CID man wondered in passing how his neighbour was going to get to the Landeszentralbank.

As he rode down empty Ahrensburger Strasse it occurred to him that the whole city seemed to be holding its breath, before bursting into... Into what? An adventure? A whole new era? Or a huge disappointment?

He arrived at the square in front of the city hall just before 5.30 and leaned his bike against a patrol car. There were a few uniformed police in place outside the bank, and English military police patrolling the doors. Trucks with their engines running stood alongside the building, an armed guard next to every driver.

'It all kicks off today,' Constable Ruge called out.

'Back to your place,' an overtired senior shouted at him testily. Ruge made a face but did what he was told.

Stave joined a group of detectives standing around Cuddel Breuer.

'Okay, boys,' their boss announced, 'this has to go smoothly. In that building there are 600 million marks, 600 million Deutschmarks, worth so many Reichsmarks you couldn't write it on a single sheet of paper. Our colleagues in uniform and the British soldiers are about to share them out between the 1,300 distribution centres throughout the city. It is our job to make sure they all get there safely. After that you can have the rest of the day off. You can go to your own allocated distribution centres and get your own ration of the new money. And tomorrow we'll all be rich.'

The first truck rolled up outside the door. There were no more wooden boxes, Stave noticed. They had transferred the banknotes into sealed bags. It took only a few moments to fill it. Then the next arrived. And the next. There were no passers-by on the windy Rathausplatz, no suspicious movements to be seen on the side streets. No noise, save for the raindrops falling on the brim of his hat. The chief inspector spotted Flasch among the officials whose job it was to run alongside the bags of money, holding umbrellas over them so that they wouldn't get wet in the few metres from the doorway to the truck. At one point Flasch recognised his neighbour and touched his cap to him. Stave returned the gesture.

After the last truck had trundled away down Alter Wall, a few post office cars came past, also laden with bags of money. Then buses. Sooner or later the vaults have to be empty, Stave reckoned. It had to have been about 6.30 a.m. before the last vehicle left the Landeszentralbank.

'Back to mummy, everybody,' Cuddel Breuer called out. 'Our work here is over. Time to change money.'

Whereas most of his colleagues hurried off, Stave walked over to the bank building, showed his ID to the British military policeman on the door and was allowed in. Once inside, he stopped the first bank employee he met and pulled out the five- and ten-pfennig notes from his coat pocket. 'Is this the new currency?' he asked the confused man.

'Where did you get those from?' the official stuttered. 'You're not supposed to be able to exchange for them yet.'

Two minutes later the chief inspector was back outside. He watched a small group of uniformed police who were still guarding the building. They had pulled their caps down as far as possible over their foreheads, in the vain hope it would give them better protection from the rain. Ruge was among them. Stave went up to him and whispered so that nobody but his colleague would hear: 'Might you be interested in a little expedition this afternoon?'

'In my free time?'

'Yes. And in plain clothes.'

'I'm on. What's it about?'

'We'll meet at 4 p.m. On Goldbekplatz.' The chief inspector touched his index finger to the rim of his hat in farewell and strolled off.

'Are we going to solve the case?' the young constable called after him hopefully.

'You can bet a new Deutschmark on it,' Stave replied.

The chief inspector rode back home and put his bike away. The apartment was empty. Karl was a grown-up, no need to worry, he told himself. He hurried off to the neighbourhood ration store to get the new money.

There was a long queue on the pavement, at least 300 metres. Figures under soaking wet capes, umbrellas. Blue plumes of cigarette smoke in the cool air. The smell of old shoes and unwashed bodies. Everywhere people were whispering; it was like a buzz of electricity filling the air. The tension was somewhere between that in a movie premiere and a dentist's waiting room. The CID man could only make out a few whispered words: 'Deutschmark'; 'new pots and pans'; 'nothing will come of it'; 'no good for the little man'; 'Yankee paper'; 'new times'; 'nylon stockings'.

The crowd crawled slowly along. How many years of my life have I wasted standing in queues? Would it ever end? He looked around. The way policemen did. Then he relaxed a little. It didn't seem likely that there would be unrest. Nobody was talking loudly, nobody pushing. Men and women were standing patiently in the rain, resigned to their fate. He could have done with a hot ersatz coffee.

After a good hour or so, he reached the entrance. There was a poster on the wall: 'Information about the change in currency.' Nobody read more than the first two lines. Onwards! It was as if everybody was afraid that the door would be slammed in their face and they wouldn't get the new money.

He showed a tired-looking steward his bluish British Zone identity card and then his current ration card, to prove his identity.

'Move along,' the man said, waving forward the next in line. Anyone who couldn't show their papers was refused the new currency. On this one day alone we'll catch more illegal dealers as in even the biggest black market raids, Stave reckoned.

There was a lot of pushing and shoving inside, the air was musty, voices muffled. A row of tables spread across the room, like a barrier. At each one sat four city civil servants, and against the wall behind them British and German police. Boards hung above the tables designated the customer alphabetically.

The CID man stood in the 'S-Z' queue. He glanced over the headscarf of the woman in front of him at the table: rubber stamps, a large black telephone, bundles of old Reichsmark notes, scrappy and tattered. They looked like paper rags next to the piles of green, blue and brown notes that seemed as if they had been ironed. All of a sudden his heart began to beat faster. He looked at the clock.

'Your identity card.' A sweating bald official was looking at him through watery eyes. Stave pulled out his papers again, as excited as a schoolboy about to take an exam. The bald man examined his documents, the man next to him noting something down in a list, then looked through his files to find the reference to Stave's name.

'Head of the family?'

Stave stared at the official blankly, sighing deeply. 'The head of the family is entitled to exchange money for all other family members. What is the situation in your case?'

He thought of Karl who was registered under his own address and was hopefully waiting at another distribution centre. 'No,' Stave answered. 'I'm exchanging only on my own behalf.' It sounded somehow like the acknowledgement of a divorce.

'Then you get the pro capita sum of 40 Deutschmarks.' The official's voice was a dull drone, a sentence he had said hundreds of times over the past few hours. Stave could hardly make him out. 'You give us 40 Reichsmarks in exchange. In two months' time you can exchange another 20 Reichsmarks. Coins and notes worth less than one Reichsmark are not exchangeable. They remain valid, but at just one tenth of their former value. Do you understand?'

The chief inspector nodded, as if in a dream, and handed over his bundle of notes. They were the best-preserved Reichsmarks he had found in his briefcase. The third official behind the table counted them out quickly, then added them to the pile of old notes. The fourth man handed him a neat pile of new notes.

'Please sign the receipt. Next.'

Stave moved aside, leaned with his hip against the table and looked in amazement at the notes in his hand. A blue note with a design that resembled an oak leaf: 'One half Deutschmark – 1948 issue.' A turquoise note, yellow and brown, a heroic man thinking, paper in his right hand, a globe in front of him, a ship behind him. 'Five Deutschmark.' Majestic blue and red, a representation of Justice, with scales and shield: 'Ten Deutschmark.'

He stroked the solid virgin paper with his fingertip, inhaling the aroma: worth, reliability. But it's just paper, a voice inside him said. Yet somehow it felt quite different to the old Reichsmarks. And in that single second, on the fringe of the scramble in the distribution centre, he realised that never again would he have to pay for something with cigarettes or butter. This is a revolution I'm holding in my hands, he thought, and nothing in Germany is ever going to be the same again.

He quickly flicked through the rest of the notes. Right at the bottom were the five- and ten-pfennig notes. I've seen you before, he whispered contentedly, and walked out into the open air.

Karl was waiting for him back at the apartment. He had spread out his own DM notes on the table as if they were a deck of cards. 'It's going to take a while to get used to them,' he said quietly.

Stave wasn't sure whether he heard hope or fear for the future in the sentence. 'In six months' time we won't even remember what the old Reichsmarks looked like,' he said.

'You really think the Yankee money will be a success?'

'It's our money now, Karl. It's the Deutschmark, not the Allies' mark. It's a new beginning.'

'Sounds as if you're proud of this money?'

Stave looked at his son in surprise. 'You're right. There's no logical reason behind it, but yes, I am proud.'

'Who would have thought that you would let yourself be distracted from logic,' Karl replied genially. Then he looked back down at the notes. 'A lot of books there,' he muttered, looking at the table as if the works themselves were already lying on it.

'You can pick up the latest weekly subscription novels for a few pfennigs each. With that amount of money,' Stave nodded to the notes lying on the table, 'you could buy a whole library.'

'But you won't fill your shoe cupboard that quickly.'

'How do you mean?'

'Are you going into town later?'

'Yes. To Goldbekplatz. On business.'

'Take a detour via Mönckebergstrasse. Take a look at the shops.'

'It's Sunday. There are no shops open.'

'That doesn't mean that the grocers are sitting on their backsides. Go and take a look.'

'Are you coming with me?'

'I need to get back to my allotment. We'll see one another in the next day or so for sure.'

A tiny black flower of disappointment fell on Stave's heart but he refused to let it depress him. 'See you in the next day or so,' he replied and forced a smile.

'Maybe I'll find a kiosk that's open on a Sunday. See if they have these weekly subscription novels.' He shuffled the banknotes back together and waved the bundle of notes. 'Heil Deutschmark!' he exclaimed. But he didn't sound bitter. He was laughing. Karl, laughing. Laughing like a young man, jovially, ironically, carefree. When was the last time I heard him like this, Stave asked himself. And then he joined in laughing, so hard that his chest wound hurt, but even that he treasured.

The chief inspector set out earlier than he actually needed to as he decided to take Karl's advice. Even before he reached Mönckebergstrasse he realised what his son had been reckoning on: the shops were full. 'New currency – new prices!' stood on two huge posters above the display at a women's clothing shop. Everywhere men and women were standing like curious children with their noses squashed against the shop windows. Stave got off his bike and pushed it. Despite the bad weather there were people everywhere. Eventually he stopped and stared down Mönckebergstrasse.

'I simply don't believe it,' he muttered. Then he realised he had been talking to himself out loud. Don't let yourself be bowled over, he told himself, but nonetheless he had the impression that the ground had been taken out from under his feet.

There were cigars in the shop window, bottles of Rhine wine, smoked sausages piled in artistic bundles on porcelain plates. A car dealer had even a shiny black Opel Olympia in his showroom, with '6,785 DM' on a cardboard placard behind the windscreen. The CID man took a moment to realise what the two letters stood for.

And shoes, shoes, shoes. Men's leather shoes. Brightly coloured women's shoes with heels. Children's shoes. Working boots.

'Where has it all come from?' whispered an elderly lady, standing next to Stave at a shop window.

A young girl pointed to a sign in the corner of the window display: 'Not hoarded stock,' it said. 'All lies,' she hissed.

Stave turned towards her, too astonished to be angry. The humiliating feeling of having been betrayed. The realisation that during years when one had to creep out on to the windy black market squares like an embarrassed john visiting a prostitute, to offer the family jewels to grinning young crooks when all the time these scarcities, these treasures, these essentials actually existed: hidden away invisible, hoarded in warehouses, cellars, back rooms. Hoarded by merchants you gave your ration cards to, people you had known for years, neighbours even. People who had hidden away what they had despite the misery, all in waiting for today: X-day. New money.

The shops, however, were still closed. Stave looked around. Would the disappointed citizenry smash the windows and storm the shops? It doesn't look like it, he thought. Everyone seemed somehow intimidated by the riches glittering before their eyes, separated by just a pane of glass.

That's the end of the black market for sure, the CID man realised. I need to hurry up.

He arrived punctually at the street adjoining Goldbekplatz. Ruge was already waiting for him. The chief inspector only recognised him when he nearly bumped into him. Out of uniform he looked like a schoolboy.

'Obviously I'm not carrying a weapon,' Ruge whispered.

'I only asked you to come so you could look after my bicycle when I pounce,' Stave hissed back. Ruge's face fell. The CID man clapped him on the shoulder. 'I was only joking,' he assured him. 'You needn't worry about this old "Gazelle", and we won't need a weapon either.' For a moment he remembered his own gunshot wound, but quickly dismissed any fear. Don't make yourself go crazy.

Stave had brought a rusty padlock and some thick cable from his cellar and used it to chain his bike to a lamppost.

'Even my granny could break that,' Ruge said.

'Well let's hope your granny isn't on her way here to do some black market business. I'll buy a new lock tomorrow.'

'Or a new bicycle.'

'One way or another, I don't need anything from there,' the chief inspector said, nodding towards Goldbekplatz.

'The black marketeers are running around as if a hand grenade has just gone off,' the young policeman joked.

Stave wondered for a moment if Ruge had also been a soldier at the front, but said nothing. 'Have you been here long?'

'About a quarter of an hour. Same as ever actually, black marketeers, a few little squirts, men with briefcases, lookout boys, mothers with shopping bags. Cigarettes, coffee, a bit of butter. The shops are still closed. But you can feel how nervous everybody is. Tomorrow the shops will open and all this will collapse, everybody knows that. The black marketeers are trying for one last big deal but nobody really knows whether it's better to hold on to the last few things they have or on the other hand to buy up whatever is still available.'

Stave and Ruge strolled casually out on to the square. Prices were being whispered, jackets rapidly opened and closed. But canny glances this way and that, fingers being rubbed together, laughs that were that bit too loud. Tomorrow you're all finished, the CID man thought. I wonder what job you'll switch to the day after. I bet you'll still be CID customers.

'Who are we looking for?' Ruge asked impatiently.

'An acquaintance of mine,' Stave replied. 'Be patient, the man is harmless. In fact I feel sorry for him.'

Suddenly he nudged the young policeman in the ribs and nodded straight ahead: 'There's our man.'

'He certainly does look harmless,' Ruge replied, clearly disappointed.

Kurt Flasch. Small, thin, half blind because of the raindrops running down his soldered-together nickel-framed glasses, zigzagging across the square. Distracted, jittery, an unhappy expression on his face.

'Are you sure he's the forger?' hissed Ruge.

'He's never forged a note in his life,' the chief inspector replied and walked up to his neighbour from behind. 'Herr Flasch, you're under arrest,' he said softly. 'If you don't do anything silly I'll save you the embarrassment of being handcuffed here in the square.'

Flasch turned around in shock, stared at Stave, shot a glance at Ruge, then turned back to the CID man. His pale skin turned ever so slightly paler. 'I've broken no laws,' he stammered.

'The Allies would see that differently,' the chief inspector replied, laying his right hand on Flasch's shoulder. He could feel the man's collarbone through his thin raincoat. When he worked in Homicide he had never felt sorry for the people he arrested. After all, they had taken another human being's life. Now he was thinking of Flasch's overweight wife, his rowdy children, and felt what he was doing was almost shabby. 'Maybe you'll get away with a fine,' he said, only half believing it.

'What are you accusing me of anyway?' But the eyes behind the glasses made it quite clear to the chief inspector that Flasch already knew.

'You sold some of the new pfennig notes on Goldbekplatz,' the CID man replied. He had by now led the man over to the wall of the abandoned chemical factory and pushed him into the broken-open doorway of the building. They could have been taken for three men doing a run-of-the-mill black market deal.

'Herr Ruge is going to search you. It won't take long and nobody will pay any attention,' Stave reassured him.

Ruge set to and hand-searched the arrested man. His hands were deft. This is no longer the kid I met last year, wet-behind-the-ears with just eight weeks' training. He may well join CID soon. Ruge produced a wallet, a few cigarettes and a load of Reichsmarks – along with a dozen of the new five-pfennig notes, held together with a paperclip.

'You were sitting right at the source,' Stave growled, looking at the notes.

'I got my pro capita allowance this morning, just like everybody else,' Flasch said defensively.

'Everyone was given four five-pfennig notes, not twelve.'

'I've already bought something and got change,' Flasch said in his own defence.

The chief inspector held one of the notes up to the light. Yellowish-green colour. The pattern just slightly to one side. He opened his briefcase and took out a five-pfennig note. The same colour, but the design wasn't to one side. Flasch slumped his shoulders and stared down at the dirty ground. 'You owe me an explanation,' the chief inspector said.

'How did you find out?'

'It wasn't difficult. A few questions and pretty soon I was sure these weren't forgeries, but real banknotes. The new currency. Who could get their hands on these notes before the day they were to be issued? One of the Allies. But why would one of them be down selling them off on the black market? What would anybody paid in British pounds have to gain? So it had to be a German. That meant somebody from the Landeszentralbank. The notes first turned up on Goldbekplatz. You're a regular at Goldbekplatz. It was absurdly simple.'

'It was pure chance I was there that day.'

'You were the one who warned me about the dealers who sold poisonous torpedo oil as cooking oil. That was something only someone who traded here regularly would know.'

'Just shows that no good comes from doing good,' Flasch muttered resignedly.

Stave shook his head. 'Even if you'd said nothing, you still wouldn't have got away with it.'

'In that case why didn't you arrest me sooner?'

'Because there were two things I didn't understand and I thought I'd better clear them up before pouncing. But now that the new currency is out I have to arrest you, but I still don't understand everything. Why did you sell these notes before X-day? If you had waited until today, nobody would have been able to accuse you of anything. And why take such a risk for pfennig notes rather than mark notes?'

Flasch made an anguished face. 'I wanted to wait for the right moment,' he admitted. 'When they brought the new currency into the bank in wooden boxes, we sorted them into bundles. We very soon noticed that there were some five- and ten-pfennig notes where – you saw yourself – the colours and patterns aren't quite in perfect alignment. That always happens. It was the same with the old Reichsmark, but it happens in particular with new issues, until they've got the printing blocks sorted out. The "misprints" end up in the drum.'

'The drum?'

'A sort of waste bin. The misprints are shredded down to the size of grain. Two employees deal with the drum, throwing bundles of notes in and watch over the whole process until there's nothing but the tiniest of shreds remaining. The drum looks a bit like a washing machine, one that only opens at the top. You can look down and watch the notes being shredded.'

'Not just "look" down, but reach down too,' said Stave, beginning to understand.

'That's why there's always two of us. One to watch the other. But my colleague had a cold. He was coughing and blowing his nose noisily, and he turned away when he did so. Only a second or two. But I took the chance to stick a hand into the drum and pull out as many as I could.'

'How many notes?'

'Eight ten-pfennig notes, about twenty fives.'

The chief inspector closed his eyes and tried not to laugh. All this fuss for a few pathetic pfennig notes!

'I shoved the notes into the belt of my trousers,' the bank employee went on, 'and waited until the end of the work day. Then I went to Goldbekplatz, where I'd done a bit of business before. Honest business.'

'Nothing on the black market is legal,' Ruge commented.

Stave preferred to say nothing, just looked at the arrested man. 'But you of all people knew that the new currency was about to be released. Why not wait a few days more? Why get rid of the notes straight away?'

'I have a wife and children,' Flasch whined. 'If I'd waited until today then I'd only have been a few pfennigs richer. That's a joke. Not worth the risk. I told myself, sell the notes first and you'll get a better price. Maybe a pair of children's shoes. Or even,' he blushed, 'ladies' stockings.'

Flasch dropped his head and stared at the ground.

'Oh, it doesn't matter,' the chief inspector muttered consolingly. 'In any case the British got hold of the notes soon enough and made a huge fuss about it.'

'I never thought of that. I never thought they would become widespread. Just a few pfennigs. Now nobody would pay any attention.'

'Now is too late.'

'Let me go, please. It was just a few pfennigs,' Flasch begged.

Stave hesitated ever so slightly. Remand in custody. Trial. An English judge would pass sentence. A year in jail? In any case he would lose his job at the bank. No job and a family at home. All of that for just a few pfennigs? Then he glanced at Ruge, who had witnessed the arrest. 'I can't let you off the hook,' he said apologetically, wondering whether or not to handcuff Flasch after all. Not because he thought he would try to escape, but because he might throw himself underneath a car or a tram. In the end he decided against.

'Let's take a walk down to CID headquarters,' he said.

'A pleasure I'll try to avoid in future,' Flasch replied and trotted obediently alongside the two policemen.

Later Stave sat alone in his office; Flasch was already in custody and Ruge had gone home. He reached for the telephone receiver. MacDonald would be pleased, he thought. As it was a Sunday he called the lieutenant's private number. 'Hallo?' A female voice. For a moment Stave was so taken aback that he couldn't get a word out. Then he recognised the voice.

'Frau Berg!' he exclaimed. 'I mean, Frau MacDonald,' he hastily corrected himself.

'Too late, Herr Oberinspektor, I recognised your voice. Still in the office, as ever?' Her light-heartedness. Suddenly Stave felt his heart ache with nostalgia. Nostalgia for the good old days, Homicide, Erna's irrepressible optimism. Sentimentalism. You're getting soft, he told himself. But there remained a twinge of longing. A nostalgia for a Sunday afternoon at home with a woman laughing down the telephone.

'How's Iris?'

'She's sucking me dry, cries all night, gives off more wind than a company of soldiers with dysentery. Everything as it should be.'

Stave would have liked to ask about her son, about their plans. What they would do after their imminent move. Whether or not she knew yet where they were going? But it felt indiscreet. 'Is Lieutenant MacDonald at home?' he asked instead.

'You're not going to drag James away from me on a Sunday, are you?' He could hear an inkling of concern in her voice.

'Quite the opposite: I'm going to make his weekend better.'

'In that case the answer is yes, James is at home.'

'Old boy, not at church?'

Stave was confused for a few minutes. 'I'm going later. To stuff a few notes into the collection box,' he answered at last.

'Five- and ten-pfennig notes? You've got our man?'

'The King of England and the President of the United States can sleep quietly at night again. The saboteur of the new currency is safely behind lock and bars.' Stave told him how the case had unfolded.

'Eight ten-pfennig notes and twenty fives,' MacDonald summed up, bursting into laughter. 'A total of 1.8 Deutschmarks and the British Empire quakes in its boots! Obviously you're not surprised. I'm just pleased there aren't any much larger holes in the system. Imagine if it had been one of the Allies. Or the bogeyman: Uncle Joe Stalin, who is very "not amused" that the Deutschmark has been introduced in the western zones and might have sent some NKVD saboteur to dig into our skin like a tick. What would we have done if Stalin had really been behind it? Been marching to Siberia? Good God, I'm relieved it's such a pathetic individual.'

'Pathetic is right,' Stave mumbled.

'You know him?'

'He's a neighbour. A poor devil.' He told him part of the background.

'Come on, out with it,' the lieutenant demanded when he had finished.

'Out with what?'

'Old boy, I know you as well as your bathroom mirror. You can't pull the wool over my eyes. You want me to intervene on behalf of this Flasch.'

'You do have certain connections.'

'But you've already arrested him and put the thing in the hands of the prosecutor.'

'I had no choice. I wasn't on my own.'

'I see.' There was a long silence on the end of the line. 'You know what? The case will end up before a British summary court. I can see to that. As a standard black market offence. Your files doubt-less leave no loopholes, but happily they are written in German. I will translate it into an English case for prosecution. Something like "Apprehended during a raid in possession of an unusual amount of cash, but no rationed goods." A ten-minute case. Sentence: two weeks in jail. Next, please! Not exactly pleasant but routine. It's almost the truth. Flasch will suffer some disciplinary measure at the hands of the Landeszentralbank. But they won't fire him.'

'If I hadn't promised Erna otherwise, I'd get on my bike and ride over, grab you by the arm, drag you into the nearest pub and have the pair of us drink our fill.'

'I have to say I wonder why our two countries ever fought one another. Problems can be so easily solved. I'll remind you of that offer another time.'

Stave was sitting at his desk putting his files in order. It was quiet in the giant building save for the fine hissing sound of the rain on the windows. He pushed pieces of paper here and there, but it was no good. He was bursting with energy. Maybe he should just jump on his bike and cycle around Hamburg for the sake of it. Pointless. Just go home? But there was nobody waiting for him. Eventually he realised that there was only one thing for him to do. Just don't make a mess of it this time, he told himself.

Seconds later he was cycling down Holstenwall towards the Elbe. Past the Bismarck monument, high as a tower and dark with rain, right into Hafenstrasse, then Palmaille. There was hardly a car on the street, the pavements were empty, except for in front of the shop windows, where there were still crowds of people, knots of umbrellas, overcoats, rain capes. As he cycled past, the chief inspector saw only the rear of people's heads; everyone was staring at the displays, their amazement almost like a strange smell over the tarmac.

The further he went, the heavier he trod on the pedals. Past the large shared family house on the left. Its central entrance, which looked like a gate into a courtyard, actually led into a small cul-de-sac: Röperstrasse. Stave was hurtling along and grabbed the brake so sharply outside house number 6 that the wheel nearly grated the rubber off the brake block. So what, he thought, I can buy a new brake block. Hastily he fumbled with his own home-made lock until he had fastened up the Gazelle. He took a deep breath to stop his heart hammering in his chest, before knocking on the shabby door to the basement apartment. Please be in, he prayed. He could hear steps behind the door, the scratching sound of a bolt being pulled back. Anna.

'You,' she said simply. She opened the door wide.

Stave didn't know how to reply. She had her hair tied back in a loose bundle, but strands fell over her face. She was wearing a light-coloured dress he hadn't seen before. He should have brought flowers, or something. He walked in, feeling rather embarrassed. He inhaled her perfume as he walked past into the hallway, while she carefully closed the door behind him. The flat consisted of the one basement room plus an old laundry room. The brick walls were painted chalky white and pictures Anna had salvaged from the rubble were hanging on nails that had been hammered into the grouting. A table, two chairs, a little living room cupboard, without doors, below the high basement window. On the shelf on the wall a few old books lying flat and a couple of tatty weekly subscription novels. Another table with an oil painting on it, the frame loose and the canvas torn. More booty from some ruin, a piece in the process of being restored, and the big square basin from the laundry room. The walls were wet with damp. It felt like paradise to Stave.

'I surprised myself,' he admitted. And then he did what he should have done months ago. He took one step towards her, took her in his arms and kissed her.

# The final clue

*Monday, 21 June 1948*

In the grey light of dawn Stave slid out of the narrow bed without waking Anna. He got dressed, took a key from his lover's purse and carefully closed the door of the apartment behind him. He didn't want the neighbours to hear. It was foggy but there were people on the street. More than he had expected so early in the morning. He pulled the collar of his coat up high and walked the few paces to the bakery he knew from previous visits was nearby.

He stopped dead a few paces before it; there was a smell of fresh bread. Real bread, made from real flour. He felt faint. The bakery was packed, excited voices filling the small space. He thought he was dreaming. On the glass counters lay loaf after loaf of white bread, rolls piled up in baskets, biscuits even. When had he last seen so much? Eight years ago.

He was so mesmerised that he nearly didn't notice he was at the front of the queue. 'What can I get you?' the young, dark-haired baker girl asked. Friendly, but impatient. Just like back in peacetime.

'Two round rolls,' he said, realising his voice was a croak. 'No, make that four,' he added quickly. Why save money? On the wall behind the baker hung a handwritten sign declaring, 'No points required! No rationed goods!'

Stave pushed a few of the new pfennig notes over the counter. He inhaled the smell of the bread, felt the firm, pale golden crust. Still warm. Somebody pushed him out of the way.

When he got back to the apartment at 6 Röperstrasse, Anna had already made ersatz coffee. That will go soon, too, he thought. 'Look what I've brought us!' he exclaimed, holding up the paper bag with the rolls. 'My finest gift for the bride.'

'Your second finest gift for the bride,' she said seriously, kissing him and pulling his coat from his shoulders.

Later the pair of them sat at the wobbly table; Stave no longer noticed the shabby walls, the cracked cups. He was chewing thoughtfully at his roll, savouring every bite, delaying as long as possible before swallowing.

'It's unbelievable,' Anna muttered, 'that all of a sudden everything is there again. One day we're starving, the next everything is the way it used to be in the good old days.'

'They must have had all this, the flour for the bread, the stockings and pans in the shop windows. Just nobody bought them. But now we have the new money and big business is all the go.'

They chatted about what they wanted to buy. About how much he would get in his pay packet now every month, and whether there would be enough money to go round if everybody bought all the things they had been without for so long. There won't be enough to last years. But what did that matter. They said not a word about the past, his or hers. But when they had polished off the last crumb, Anna looked at him over the rim of the cup, still steaming from the ersatz coffee. 'Where do we go from here?'

'Marry me!' Stave burst out, almost shocked by his own outburst.

She went pale, then a blush came over her cheeks. 'You know that's not possible,' she whispered. 'I'm not divorced. And if I do get divorced, people will ask questions, want to see paperwork, do background checks. The whole story will come back to haunt me.'

He got to his feet and took her in his arms. 'Nobody is going to do background checks,' he whispered, and then a moment later shook his head, realising what he had said. 'That is the strangest thing a chief inspector should say,' he explained. 'There is no Anna von Gudow. The papers with that name were burned in Berlin. Either that or they're mouldering in some local archive in a village that today is either in Poland or the Soviet Union, harder to reach than the moon. You are Anna von Veckinhausen. You're free.'

'What about you? Are you free?'

He told her about Karl. About him being a student. About their dinner together and their complex conversations. 'His childhood is gone forever. Irreplaceable. Destroyed. But his youthful years are not. He has rediscovered himself. He's starting over again.' Stave kissed Anna. 'I think we've all earned the right to start over again.'

She smiled in a way she had never smiled at him before, pushed the strands of hair back from her face and said, 'You're going to be ever so late at the office today.'

It had been years since Stave had felt so light-hearted. He felt free and full of energy cycling along Palmaille late morning. This time I'm going to hold on to Anna, he told himself. And Karl, too. I'm going to come through once again. He would even ask to take a holiday. For the first time since 1941. If it weren't for the loose ends in this case: the death of Rolf Rosenthal, the works of art found in the Reimershof, the banker who denied everything. Like a sharp stone stuck in an otherwise comfortable shoe.

He was overtaken by a black car, which for some reason or another struck him as strange. It was only a few seconds later that he realised why. It was a taxi. When had he last seen a motorised taxi? Before the war? In the early years of the war? Certainly not since 1945 with the initial ban on driving for Germans, followed by the need to fill out log books and the petrol rationing.

A number 31 tram came rattling towards him, barely half full. That was also something new. Up until yesterday the few trams that were running were jam-packed, with workers and office employees, black marketeers, housewives with children, people going out to find food in the country, all squashed together until the doors would hardly close. Now the black marketeers and those going to search for food had disappeared. Stave found himself wondering if Bahr at Department S would find him another case. And if he did what might it be?

The CID headquarters was buzzing like a disturbed beehive. Bahr rubbed his hands when Stave walked into the fifth-floor corridor.

'Where have you been, then?' his boss asked him.

'I've been working on the investigation.' Amazing how easy the lie tripped off his lips.

'I understand. I was down at the Hansaplatz myself this morning. I wanted to see our clients sweat. All the fuss of the currency reform has been worth it just to see the sullen faces of the black marketeers.'

'They can pack their bags.'

'That's exactly what they're doing. Literally. They're flogging off whatever they've got left and packing up the stuff nobody wants. Take Lucky Strike cigarettes. They'd be lucky to get 25 new pfennigs for what was seven Reichmarks a few days ago. And the price is dropping. Cigarettes remain cheaper on the black market than in the tobacco shops, but only because the fences are emptying their warehouses. You can get a pound of butter now for five Deutschmarks.' Bahr laughed as triumphantly as a general who'd just won a war.

'So what happens to Department S?' the chief inspector asked.

'You can go over to Vice if you want. There are more than enough "swallows on the wing". The ladies of the night used to pay for their rooms with cigarettes, but now they're not worth anything any more, they've been thrown out and are walking the kerbs in broad daylight. With the introduction of the new mark ordinary German men are as viable a customer as Allied soldiers and black marketeers. Vice won't be short of work.'

'That's not exactly my thing.'

'Well then, that leaves the two of us. There will still be economic crimes. I'm going down to patrol the station. A few wise guys spent the last few days buying railway tickets with the old Reichsmarks and are now standing by the tracks selling them on at exaggerated prices in DM. Whispering to passers-by just like on the good old black market. People always think of something. Want to come along?'

'I've still got one case to file away.'

'The art stuff down at the Reimershof? What is there left to do?'

'Give me a couple more days,' Stave replied and closed his office door behind him.

The CID man worked his telephone until he got Kienle on the end of the line. 'Can you look in?' he asked the photographer.

'A work thing?'

'Sort of.'

'Sounds like it might not be totally legal. I'll be there.'

Just a few minutes later the slim, red-haired man was standing in front of the chief inspector, the leather bag with his Leica slung over his shoulder.

'Can you also take pictures of small objects,' Stave asked him. 'About as big as your hand. Indoors. Without a flash.'

Kienle laughed. 'When I was working for Signal on the frontline, none of the squaddies would have been very happy if I was following them around with a flash.' He glanced into his bag and pulled out a thin lens. A 1.5 Summarit. A five-centimetre lens with wide aperture. I can take photos under the bed sheets with this.'

'I'm not working for Vice yet,' Stave mumbled. 'With that lens you can put the Leica in your jacket pocket. Nobody would notice.' He fumbled around in his desk until he found a wooden ruler. 'You'll need to hide this on you, too.'

'I'm supposed to be incognito?'

'Leave the rest of your equipment here. You'll come with me and I'll introduce you as working for CID. It's not exactly a lie.'

'Where am I supposed to take these secret photos? And what's the ruler for?'

'I'll explain to you on the way. We'll take a car.'

'You're too late there. Now that you can get fuel at every petrol station colleagues like Bernd Rosen have been racing around the streets. Any excuse is good enough to put your foot down.'

'In that case we'll go on foot. It's not that far.'

'A black market in the neighbourhood?'

'That's not what we do any more, Kienle. Germany's on the way up. We're going to see a banker.'

As they left the head office a massive figure confronted them near the bronze elephant at the doorway. 'Are you joining the foot patrols now, Stave?'

Dönnecke. Right at that moment there was nobody Stave wanted less to meet. His deep-set dark eyes flicked between Stave and Kienle. Stave could actually smell the suspicion emanating from his colleague. He's nervous, wondering what I'm doing with the photographer, he thought. Let him wonder.

'There's still work to do,' he replied loudly, trying to push his way past Dönnecke.

But two heavy paws landed on his shoulders. 'You deal with the black market,' the older policeman growled. 'The black market no longer exists, since we've got the Allied money. So why do you need our snapper?'

'A confidential investigation.'

'You're not going down to the Reimershof? I don't like it when people stick their noses into things that don't concern them.'

'Neither do I,' Stave replied and wrenched his shoulder free from Dönnecke's grip.

'Our colleague Herr Dönnecke in top form,' Kienle muttered when they had gone a few paces. 'The success of the mark has given him bulging veins. He would have preferred to see half Hamburg starve to death. Then the other half would be calling for a new Führer.'

'Do you want Dönnecke as an enemy?' Stave asked.

'No way,' the photographer answered in horror.

'Then maybe you'd better not come with me,' the chief inspector said with a sardonic smile. 'Because you're going to be sticking your lovely Leica lens into our esteemed colleague's case.'

They walked through Valentinskamp and the Gänsemarkt as Stave explained to Kienle what it was he had to do. He was speaking in a quiet voice but he need hardly have bothered. The pavements were heaving with people and nobody was paying the slightest attention to them. Everyone's eyes were trained on the shop windows. Awed amazement, indignant snorts at some of the prices. Men coming out of shop doors with triumphant expressions and wrapped parcels. Pipes in a tobacco shop. The chief inspector wouldn't have believed they were still being made in Germany. Now there they were, lying on shelves everywhere as if the years between 1939 and 1948 had never happened. A clothes shop: poplin shirts from 8 DM. A bright red silk dress. Anna would look wonderful in that, Stave thought. Two hundred marks.

'Not for your salary,' Kienle remarked, following Stave's gaze. 'But that'll soon level out.'

'Level out?'

The photographer nodded towards the window of an electric shop. 'Electric iron, 17.50 DM,' he read aloud. 'I came by yesterday as they were just putting out the first price notices next to the goods. I've been looking for an iron for years. Yesterday it was 27.50 DM. The good people who came by this morning have got a shock. The wholesalers have been hoarding this stuff for weeks, goods they either bought in Reichsmarks or got in barter exchange. They're pricing it all randomly, but it'll all level out. Before long a dress won't cost a month's pay.' The he added, curiously, 'I didn't know you were married.'

'I'm not,' replied Stave. 'Yet.'

On the Jungfernstieg by the Alster there was a market. Traders had put tables together and set out their wares. All perfectly legal. Hundred of people were pushing their way between them. It seemed as if Hamburg hadn't bothered to turn up for work. The embarrassed whispers and milling around associated with the black market was no more. Housewives and office workers were picking things up in their hands, looking at them and discussing the quality and price – still uncertainly, as if with a lack of self-confidence they were testing out skills long forgotten.

Stave and Kienle walked through rows of vegetable stands, behind which somebody was offering an electric kettle for DM 27.50 and a matt-yellow porcelain dinner service for DM 2.60. A typewriter for 300 marks. The man who swapped his old bicycle for my Olympia could do a good deal now, the chief inspector thought. He didn't care.

They pushed their way through the crowds until they reached the quiet streets on the east bank of the Alster. Once there, they could walk more quickly.

'You've understood everything?' Stave asked, just to be sure, before they entered the driveway to Schramm's villa.

'I know what I have to do,' Kienle replied, tapping his coat pocket where the Leica was concealed.

'You don't give up, do you? Heydrich would have been proud of you,' said Schramm when they were sitting face to face a few moments later.

'Heydrich isn't my boss,' the chief inspector answered. Don't let him provoke you. 'Does the name Rolf Rosenthal mean anything to you?' He held his breath.

Dönnecke had let the case go to pot. He had never even interviewed the banker, so Schramm probably knew none of the details about the corpse found in the ruins, Stave hoped. 'We came across a piece of paper in the ruins of the Reimershof,' he said, praying the man wouldn't realise it was a lie, 'and made out that name on it.'

Schramm stared at him, his right eye half closed, the left eye wide open behind an old-fashioned monocle. 'As I told you, I used the place to store things I didn't want in the bank,' he eventually replied. 'For example personnel files of Jewish employees. Herr Rosenthal joined the firm as a fourteen-year-old apprentice in 1917. Even back in the Kaiser's day a Jew with a crippled foot found it hard to find a job. But I spotted his abilities immediately: he was a natural with numbers. Discreet. Ambitious. Not a gossip. By 1930 he had almost become my right-hand man.'

'And three years later?'

'What do you think? That I got rid of him. I kept him in my employ. But his personnel files disappeared into the Reimershof.'

'Did Herr Rosenthal continue to work there?'

'From time to time, but occasionally he also had to work in the head office.'

'Was he also advising you on art matters?'

Schramm glanced out of the window. 'Herr Rosenthal was one of my buyers. Why are you asking such curious questions?'

'What happened to Herr Rosenthal?' Stave asked.

'Herr Rosenthal had a large family. His parents were still alive, and he had brothers and sisters. Nearly all of them stayed in Europe, too long. Only a niece emigrated, in 1939, to New York. In the summer of 1940 after France had been conquered, Herr Rosenthal told me that he and his family wanted to make their way via Paris to Marseille, and from there find a way to Portugal or North Africa. They had everything prepared. That was the last time I saw him. I assume he was arrested on the way.'

'Do you mind if I wash my hands?' Kienle interrupted. 'It's this damp weather...' He smiled apologetically.

'Of course, go ahead. The first door on the left in the hallway,' Schramm replied, mildly irritated, then stared again absent-mindedly out of the window. 'It's remarkable how few traces we leave behind in this world,' the old banker commented. 'A piece of paper in a pile of rubble. That's all that remains.'

Not altogether, Stave was thinking.

A few minutes later Kienle came back into the room and gave the CID man an inconspicuous nod.

'We're about to close the file on this mysterious case,' the chief inspector said, getting to his feet. 'Many thanks for your full and frank answers.' He tried to keep any sarcasm out of his voice.

'You must be very busy at the moment,' Kienle said. 'As a banker. With all this new money.'

Schramm stared at him through his monocle as a botanist might regard a misshapen plant. 'The new currency has made many of my customers paupers overnight. Yesterday they might have had a thousand Reichsmarks in their account. Today it's just 65 Deutschmarks. Many of them are about to find out that they don't have enough money for all the nice new things they'd like to buy.'

When they were a few metres along Fährtstrasse, the chief inspector asked Kienle, 'Did you get the photos?'

'You'll have them in your hands within the hour.'

'You don't need to whisper.'

'That guy frightens me.'

'Schramm survived twelve years under the Nazis, despite the fact that the Gestapo made regular house visits. He's a hard old dog. And a liar.'

'What banker could afford to tell the truth all the time?'

'Not every banker has the corpse of one of his art buyers in the ruins of his office. Rosenthal didn't try to escape via France in 1940. He remained in Hamburg until 1943. It was his body you photographed in the ruins of the Reimershof. Ruins that were created by the bombing raids of 1943.'

'I thought as much. I didn't come across anything like a piece of paper with a name on it during the crime scene investigation. What now?'

'You know yourself what was left of the body. There weren't many clues, but there were two: the soles of the shoes, first of all. Dr Czrisini pointed out the scratches on the leather soles to me. A sign that in his death throes the man had been moving. Which from my point of view suggests he wasn't killed by collapsing rubble or the shock wave from an explosion. That would have been too quick. And then there's the wound to his head.'

Kienle whistled through his teeth appreciatively. 'I'm beginning to see where you're coming from.'

The photographer kept his word and within an hour delivered half a dozen still-damp prints. 'I've used my last sheets of photo paper on these,' he said, 'and worked to expose the finest detail in the darkroom.'

'This ought to do,' Stave muttered. Schramm's walking stick. Kienle's task had been to photograph the banker's walking stick in the wicker basket in the hallway – in particular its heavy silver handle. L-shaped. Now he held in his hands black-and-white pictures of the handle from every angle, and the ruler next to it. The photos were a bit grainy and the relief on the silver ever so slightly blurred.

'I had neither a flash nor a tripod,' the photographer said apologetically.

'You can make out the shape well enough. And with the ruler next to it you can work out the size to the nearest millimetre. That will do.'

'Do you want to smuggle the photos into Dönnecke's files?' Kienle asked. 'Or do you plan to go straight to the public prosecutor?'

The chief inspector rubbed his temples. 'These aren't evidence. They're just drawing plans, for an artist.'

He shook the photographer's hand in farewell. 'Don't say a word to anybody, least of all Dönnecke,' he stressed. Then he sat down by the telephone and called MacDonald.

'Want to come with me to the most derelict hovel in Hamburg?'

'As draughty as a castle in the Scottish Highlands? I wouldn't have thought that was possible.'

'I need you to pay for something for me.'

'Already blown all your new money? You wouldn't be the first from what I hear.'

'I don't need you to pay with Deutschmarks or English pounds. I need you to use your good connections.'

'Who do you want to annoy now?'

'If it works: a respectable fellow citizen. If it doesn't work, then it'll be me. And one way or the other a few American officials.'

'We're going to annoy Americans? I'll pick you up in ten minutes.'

The Jeep bounced in and out of potholes as they headed for St Pauli. Stave told the lieutenant where they were heading and what they would do when they got there. Then he looked to one side: there were still crowds of people staring into shop window displays. A motorcycle and sidecar with a dozen shiny polished pots in it. Two men pushing a bicycle with a rolled-up carpet fixed to the frame.

'It certainly looks as if the currency reform is working,' MacDonald said with a smile.

'The hangover is yet to hit,' said Stave, 'at the latest when the next pay packet comes in.'

'People get hangovers when they drink too much whiskey. But that doesn't stop them drinking.'

'I need to find a new job. Department S has become redundant.'

'Just like cavalry. But the cavalry officers found new jobs. What will you do?'

'I shall have to go and see Cuddel Breuer first of all: see what he wants to do with me. It may also depend on how I do with this case. It's likely to be the last for Department S.'

'You'll go down in the annals of crime history.'

He turned into Lerchenstrasse. 'Are you sure someone won't steal my Jeep here?' the lieutenant asked, looking distrustfully at the ruined, dilapidated houses and the gutted cavity of the Schiller Theatre.

'I would be fairly certain someone would make off with it after dark. But not now. Too many witnesses.' Stave nodded at a few refugee women who were using the interval between rain showers to hang piles of washing on lines outside the theatre.

'Let's get a move on then.'

'There's more than one reason to get a move on. Don't breathe deeply when you go through this door.'

Paul Michel opened the door when they knocked, wiping green paint from his hands with a dirty rag. 'You again,' he said resignedly. 'You promised never to bother me again.' Then he glanced nervously at the lieutenant. 'And now you've enlisted help from the Allies. I can't escape you.'

'I've got a job for you,' Stave replied, pushing the door open again. A stench of faeces and decay wafted over them. 'It's particularly bad today,' said Michel, apologetically.

'It smells a bit like the school kitchen when I was young,' Mac-Donald said nonchalantly, and walked into the dismal apartment as if he were at home.

'I'm not a grass,' Michel muttered as he hunkered down at the kitchen table with them. 'I'm not up for that.' He rapped his prosthetic leg.

'I want to hire you as an artist.'

'And the Führer used to paint postcards for you. Don't give me fairy tales.' Stave laid out on the table the photos Kienle had taken little more than an hour earlier. 'I want you to make me as close a copy as you can of this walking stick handle,' he explained, watching the artist closely. 'Last time I was here you said you could do something like that.'

Michel examined the photos. 'Is it silver? I don't have any silver,' he answered cautiously.

'The material doesn't matter. It's only the shape that matters. I want a copy that's exactly the same shape and size. As far as I'm concerned you can carve it out of wood. Can you do that?'

'Clay would be better. Easier to shape. But I need to get hold of some. And then I'll need to fire it in a friend's oven.'

'Can you have it done by the end of the week?'

Michel took the photos in his hands, which were shaking slightly. Hopefully from excitement, Stave thought to himself. The one-legged man studied the photos carefully, then shrugged. 'I did very different things at the UFA studios, and I'm a bit out of practice. But it should work.' He licked his lips. 'Depending on whether the pay is good enough.'

At that MacDonald gave him a beaming smile.

'I'll get you and your family an American visa,' he said.

When they were back out in the open air, the lieutenant stroked the wet bonnet of the Jeep. 'Glad it's still here. God, it must have been like that in there during the last war. When there was a gas attack in the trenches. My legs are shaking. I wouldn't have been able to make it back on foot.'

'I did warn you,' Stave growled.

'Why did you have to be so generous? The man was so poor he'd have done it for a couple of pounds. Or a few Deutschmarks. Why a visa for America?'

'Because he'll be a lot happier in Hollywood than here.'

'Are you intending to send every police grass to Douglas Fairbanks?'

'That handle is an important piece of evidence in a murder case.'

'I see. You no longer work there but you still want to meddle in a colleague's business.'

'Which is something I'd rather remained in the dark. If Paul Michel is in Hollywood then he won't bump into that colleague and say anything he shouldn't.'

'When I'm transferred you'll have one less friend in Hamburg,' MacDonald said, looking seriously worried.

Stave gave him a thankful smile. 'This case is important,' he explained. 'I'll be more cautious in future, I promise.'

'You sound like a man with a mission.'

'I was there when a murder victim was found. I have an idea who the murderer is. Nobody else seems interested, except for Public Prosecutor Ehrlich. Shouldn't I at least try to get the perpetrator convicted? Present the public prosecutor with evidence to charge him?'

'With a copy of a walking stick handle?'

'With a copy of a walking stick handle, a bit of luck and one or two semi-official investigations.'

'I had imagined German policemen differently.'

'I hope I'm not letting you down.'

'On the contrary, old boy!' MacDonald laughed and turned the key in the ignition. 'I'll drop you off at headquarters. Then I have an appointment with an American liaison officer.'

A little later Stave was sitting opposite the public prosecutor in his uncomfortable visitor's seat. Ehrlich was staring at him through spectacles as thick as magnifying glasses. 'It's not enough,' he said unhappily.

The chief inspector sighed. He had just told him that he had traced one of the art works in the Reimershof more or less definitively back to Schramm.

'It's not a crime,' the prosecutor continued. 'Schramm denies having owned the bronze bust. Maybe because he acquired it from the film studio – or should we say the propaganda ministry – under dubious circumstances, and he finds it embarrassing. But even if you can link it to him, so what…? The banker rescued a work of art that would otherwise have been melted down by Goebbels' henchmen. No judge is going to pass sentence on him for that. File the case away. The objects found in the Reimershof will become public property and given to a gallery. Not the worst thing that can happen to an artist's work.'

'It is the worst thing that can happen to a policeman's. Rolf Rosenthal's body was also found among the same ruins. An art buyer. A Jew.'

'Most Jews are dead these days.'

'And most of their murderers are still at large. But Rosenthal wasn't burned to ashes in a camp. We have his body. We have clues and we have a suspect.'

'You have a suspect, Stave, but you're the only one in CID who does. And you're not officially working on this case. We just have our own little private agreement. And the prosecutor's office has nothing that would justify pressing charges. Where is the evidence? Your colleague has none, and nor do you.'

'Dönnecke doesn't want to produce any evidence because he doesn't want the case to come to court. Because if a dead employee of Dr Schramm becomes the object of a trial, then Schramm himself will become a centre of attention. And if Schramm becomes the subject of an investigation then things could become difficult for Dönnecke too.'

Ehrlich pulled out a large handkerchief and began exhaustively polishing his glasses. 'And what about you? Do you have any evidence?'

'Sort of. Or I will have in a few days.'

'Sort of? I'd make a laughing stock of myself if I based charges on "sort of" evidence.'

'I can't dismiss that possibility.'

'You've told me better stories in the past. I'll take a look at your supposed evidence and make up my mind then.'

Ehrlich accompanied him to the office door. 'By the way how's Frau von Veckinhausen,' he asked.

'She's very well,' Stave answered swiftly, and hoped the blood wasn't rushing into his face.

'Have you seen her in recent days?'

'Frau von Veckinhausen and I are very close.'

'I understand.' Ehrlich reached out a hand. 'Give her my best wishes.'

He left the office early as he had nothing much to do but wait until Michel had finished his work. He took a detour on his way to Berne via the allotment gardens, just to see if Karl might be there. Stave was lucky – his son opened the door to him and invited him into his shed. There were shelves on each wall. Books.

'Have your spent all your money already?' he found himself saying. Karl laughed. 'Now you sound like a real father should. I handed over a few new mark notes to a bookseller. But most of them I got in exchange for a few cartons of allotment gold.'

'A good deal. The shops are full of tobacco and cigarettes again. Before long your leaves won't be worth the effort.'

'I've got other work. The university is keeping me busy.'

Stave took down a book with a dark cover: Ronald Syme's *The Roman Revolution*. He leafed through the first few pages: Oxford, 1939.

Karl smiled. 'Caesar and Augustus. The standard text on the end of the republic and the rise of a dictatorship in ancient Rome. Unavailable in Germany for years.'

'Books by English authors weren't exactly in tune with the Zeitgeist.'

'Least of all ones that came out a week after the war began.'

'Is your English good enough to read it?'

'I'm learning. It's one of the advantages of living in the British occupation zone.'

Stave put the book back on the shelf. In doing so he noticed between the books a couple of yellowing sheets of paper, with writing in pencil. And in handwriting he recognised; his own. It was the letter that he had written to Karl the previous year, in the midst of a complicated murder case: about the 'brown years' and Karl's membership of the Hitler Youth. About his own job in the police. About Stave's hopes that things would at long last get better. His son had never mentioned the letter.

'I always meant to reply to you,' Karl said, embarrassed, and took the letter from him. 'It's not easy to put it all down on paper.'

'If we can talk to one another, then we don't need to write,' Stave replied. All of a sudden he was overwhelmed by a feeling of total relaxation, the sort of relaxation you only felt when you've finally completed something really important

That evening he chained up his bicycle in front of the theatre. He had imagined himself feeling out of place with his old bike among women in evening dress and men in black tie, Mercedes and Opel limousines. But in fact he was almost alone.

Stave stared around in amazement, then spotted Anna. He hurried over and kissed her. She was wearing a dress the colour of Bordeaux wine with a light bright-coloured summer raincoat. Her hair, loose, her scent.

'You look magnificent,' he whispered.

'We'll attract attention in the theatre,' she replied, smiling.

'Has the play been cancelled?' *The Devil's General* by Carl

Zuckmayer. Ever since its German premiere in November 1947, it had been booked out. Stave had been pleased to get any tickets at all, even those costing three Deutschmarks, a small fortune.

'It's the new money,' Anna said. 'Nobody wants to spend a mark on art – not that it's worth something once again. Frying pans are more important, shoes, coffee.'

Indeed there were barely two dozen people in the sumptuous auditorium. Stave glanced around in embarrassment. He found it somehow wrong that actors had to take the stage in front of such a tiny audience. 'If people won't spend a Deutschmark on the theatre, then they won't pay even a pfennig for antiques,' he conjectured during the interval.

'Are you worried my business won't make any money now? There's always a market for antiques. They're more durable than acting. But I'll have to change my trade, even so.'

'In what way?'

'Wait and see,' she replied and kissed him.

Later he took her home, sitting side saddle on the old bike's luggage rack, her hair fluttering in the wind, her arms around his hips. An open-top British Jeep overtook them and the two soldiers wolf-whistled and shouted something merrily at them. Stave felt as if he were eighteen again and in love for the first time.

As he braked into Röperstrasse she jumped nimbly off the bike. 'You're staying,' she exclaimed. A statement, not a question.

The only light was that from the old wooden-cased radio that Anna turned on. The 'barcarolle' from the *Tales of Hoffmann* opera. They undressed, whispering to one another as Offenbach's bright and cheerful music wafted through the room, the soft yellow light falling on their bodies.

'What if the neighbours hear us?' Stave said.

Anna just smiled at him tenderly and turned up the radio.

Later the two lay together on the narrow bed, naked and happily exhausted. Stave no longer feared falling asleep by her side and being woken by nightmares. It hadn't happened the night before, maybe it would never happen again. And if memories did come back to taint his dreams, he would explain to his beloved. He felt himself sliding into the soft twilight of half-sleep when the operatic melodies that had soothed them for more than two hours were interrupted by the sharp voice of a man announcing important news. Just like the old days.

Turn the box off, said Anna, her eyes already closed. Stave had just reached the radio when his fogged brain realised what was being announced. The Soviets had blockaded Berlin, closed all the roads, railway lines and canals: there was no gas, electricity or coal reaching the western part of the city, the American, British and French occupation zones.

'What was it they were saying?' Anna mumbled when he lay down next to her again.

'Nothing important,' he whispered reassuringly and put his arms around her.

# Murder weapon

*Thursday, 24 June 1948*

Stave would never have believed the Department S floor could have been quieter than it had been over the past two weeks. But now it really was as dead as could be, until Paul Michel walked down the corridor leading towards his office. Stave had been waiting impatiently for this moment for the last 72 hours, looking at the clock again and again, feeling like a caged animal. At last. The one-legged artist sat down, staring around him in amazement but saying nothing. He was carrying an old cardboard box in a string shopping bag slung around his neck. The knuckles on his hands gripping his crutch had gone white.

'Relax,' the chief inspector said, opening the door of his office for him. 'You're here to do me a favour, not to be interrogated.'

'That's not what it feels like.'

'Show me your work.'

His guest sat down on a chair and set the box carefully on the desk. 'Even though the clay has been formed it's still fragile,' he explained, taking out the bundle of old newspaper inside. 'I don't want it to break now.' He wrapped the newspaper and eventually produced a brown object as large as a hand.

'Perfect,' Stave mumbled in amazement, taking up the object carefully in his right hand: a copy of the silver handle of Schramm's walking stick. He laid Kienle's photos on the desk next to it: the same shape, the same pattern as on the handle, reworked in the finest relief.

'It was actually a real pleasure,' Michel admitted, blushing. 'At last I could work in my own profession again, and legally.'

Stave was thinking of Chief Inspector Dönnecke and that on no account should he see this. 'You've well earned your American visa,' he said.

'That isn't a joke, then?' Michel said, incredulously.

The CID man wrote down MacDonald's name and room number in the offices of the British civilian administration and handed them over. 'Introduce yourself to the lieutenant and he'll send you and your family on a long journey.'

'I'm on my way!' the artist exclaimed.

'Not quite so hasty,' Stave got to his feet. 'I'll take you downstairs,' he said, not wanting Michel to bump into any of his colleagues on the way and start talking.

Immediately after, Stave got on his bike, the pottery copy of the walking stick handle hidden in his coat pocket. He rode along the Alster. The elegant district seemed deserted – nobody collecting the cigarette butts of English soldiers, no one-legged men poking around in their bins. Things were on the way up, people no longer felt humiliated. In Neue Rabenstrasse he came across a group of medical students, young people with pale faces coming out of the pathology building.

'I have an experiment involving one of your corpses,' Stave said to Dr Czrisini when he found him.

'If you want my job, you can have it,' the pathologist said, coughing. 'Which corpse would you like?'

'The one from the Reimershof.'

'Still tiptoeing through the minefield, are you? Come into the cold store. I've dealt with the students and most of my colleagues are on their lunch break. We'll be on our own. I imagine you don't want witnesses.'

'I'm grateful to you.'

'You'd better be quick, though,' Czrisini muttered.

The CID man wondered what that last cryptic comment meant as he followed the doctor down the steps to the cellar.

Czrisini pulled open the drawer with the mortal remains of Rolf Rosenthal in it, and Stave produced the pottery copy from his coat pocket.

The pathologist gave a wry smile. 'I understand now. I won't ask where you got that or to whom it belongs.' He took the pottery model carefully and laid it against the skull of the dead man. 'It fits,' he said in a satisfied voice. 'This handle fits perfectly into the hole in the skull: same size, same L-shape.'

'Imagine a walking stick with a heavy silver handle: could it have caused the fatal blow?'

'Use the subjunctive. It's hardly proof. Not even with a clay model of such a potentially deadly handle.'

'But a clue.'

'Straight out of the book. It might even be enough to push Chief Inspector Dönnecke into relaunching his investigations.'

'I wasn't so much thinking of my colleague as the public prosecutor,' Stave explained.

'I don't think it's enough. An L-shaped wound to the head and an L-shaped walking stick handle aren't enough to press charges. And no pathologist would swear in court that a head wound and a walking stick are the same as a lock and a key. If that was the case every lame man in the city could be charged with the Reimershof murder.'

On the way back up from the cellar the pathologist fell into a serious coughing fit. Czrisini bent double, his thin hands grasping the banister like a drowning man holding on to a piece of driftwood. He held his handkerchief tight against his mouth. When he stood up again, there were beads of sweat on his forehead. The handkerchief was blood-red.

'You really need to get that cured,' Stave said, shocked.

'The cure for lung cancer hasn't been invented yet,' Czrisini coughed, forcing his blue lips into a grimace that the chief inspector thought didn't so much resemble a smile as the expression on the face of the dead man he had just seen in the morgue.

'I'm sorry to hear that,' he stammered. He felt as if he were in some absurd dream. It seemed somehow undignified to hear a man he was as close to as a good friend casually pronounce his own death sentence in a dirty, badly lit stairwell.

'That's how much English cigarettes cost,' the pathologist blurted out as he forced himself up the remaining steps.

'Maybe there are new treatments, in America or England?' The CID man tried to encourage him. He was thinking of MacDonald. 'Maybe I…'

'I'm afraid there's nothing you can do for me,' Czrisini interrupted him. 'The Americans haven't yet found a way to explode atomic bombs to destroy tumours in the lungs. Thanks all the same for the offer.'

Stave followed him silently until they reached the pathologist's office. Once upon a time it was piled high with files, reports and specimens. Now it was ghostly empty. 'How much time do you have left?' Stave asked falteringly.

'It's a miracle I'm still alive!' Czrisini replied, lighting up a Woodbine. 'Normally a cancer like this kills its victim within six months. I'm well overdue. No idea why I've been given so much time. It'll be the last post-mortem I'll be present at.'

'Should I take you home?' Even while he was saying the words, it occurred to the CID man that he didn't even know where Czrisini lived.

'I spend as little time as possible in the house,' the pathologist replied. 'That increases the probability that I will drop dead at my workplace, as befits a man in my position. Also it means my colleagues won't have to bring the body so far.' He laughed, before falling into another coughing fit.

Stave didn't know where to look, what to do with his hands. He wanted to say something to Czrisini to give him hope. At the same time he was eager to leave, leave the smoky office and the scent of death, which he felt he was inhaling with every breath. 'I'll drop by again soon,' he said, knowing himself how false it sounded.

'*Auf Wiedersehen,*' the pathologist said indifferently. 'Either here or somewhere else.'

Stave took his hand and held it longer than normal. He knew it would be the last time.

He had agreed to meet MacDonald for lunch in Sellmers Keller-wirtschaft. 'This is the last time I'm inviting you,' the young lieutenant said jovially. 'Since you've had the Deutschmark, I've felt like a visiting poor relative with my British pounds. I have to ask myself who actually won the war.'

Stave studied the menu. There was no longer a waiter wanting a 'deposit' for 'forgotten' marks. The prices on the menu were the ones that actually had to be paid: a cup of real coffee for DM 1.30, a three-course meal for DM 3.50.

'The victors won't live cheaper,' the CID man muttered. He wouldn't be able to afford the restaurant much longer.

'The lunch menu is still the same old burned sole,' the Briton warned him.

'No wonder the room is half empty. I'll have one anyway. Otherwise the sole will have died in vain.'

'That's the right attitude. So let's be sure two fish didn't die in vain.' MacDonald waved the waiter over. Then he pulled out a large envelope from a briefcase next to his feet.

'It's Erna,' the chief inspector exclaimed in surprise. A portrait of MacDonald's wife – head and shoulders, intense eyes, hair like blond flames, her cheery round face outlined in bold black brush marks.

'Very modern,' Stave said carefully.

'As if it came straight from the Weimar Republic. You can tell Toni Weber hadn't been able to do any expressionist work for a long time. He really put his foot down.'

'Has Erna seen it?'

'Do you think she'd give me a thick ear for it? I'll wait for the right circumstances to present this little darling to my little darling.'

'If you want my advice, I'd wait until you've been posted to Calcutta and left Erna behind in Europe.'

'Smart idea,' the lieutenant said, putting the painting back into the envelope. 'There's only one little thing wrong with it: I'm not going to Calcutta, I'm going to Berlin.'

'I thought as much,' the chief inspector replied, a feeling of despondency running through him. 'When?'

'Tomorrow. We're setting off from the Landungsbrücken.'

'From the Landungsbrücken? The quayside? You're going to Berlin on a boat? But the reds have closed off the city.'

'You'd be surprised. We're going to tweak Ivan's nose.'

'You said "we". Are Erna and your daughter going too?'

'Erna's never been to Berlin.'

'You're having a laugh. A million Red Army troops have cut the city off. Nobody says it but everybody knows what they've done there since 1945. And you're asking your wife and daughter to go there with you?'

MacDonald sighed and gave a tired smile. 'I would prefer to persuade Erna at gunpoint to remain in London. But she wasn't exactly…' he paused, searching for the right expression, 'about to compromise,' he said at last, and shrugged his shoulders. 'She said she'd already let one husband go off to war. And we know that story didn't end well. She wasn't about to let it happen again. She'll come with me, but live in the British barracks: a privilege granted officers' wives.'

'We'll come down to the quayside tomorrow to wave goodbye.'

'You said "we".'

'Anna and I.'

A broad smile appeared on MacDonald's face. 'That'll be a greater honour than having a bagpiper come to see me off.' He nodded towards the waiter. 'Here come our soles. Let's hope for the best and be prepared for the worst. And while we hack our fish to pieces, you can tell me about your case. I'm going to miss the CID investigations here when I get to Berlin.'

I may be missing the CID investigations, too, thought Stave to himself, as he walked down the Department S corridor a little later. He might not have much more time to deal with what could be his last case in this department: he had an appointment with the public prosecutor. Once in his office, he collected up all the documents about the body and the artworks found in the Reimershof. He hesitated for a moment, then included the grey index card given to him by the former Gestapo man, Philip Greiner. The card with a précis on it of the old Gestapo investigation into Schramm. The card that included the note 'Cäsar Dönnecke, *K.z.b.V*', the 'Special Purpose Detachment'. Stave had added to the file a note of Greiner's statements about Dönnecke's investigations carried out in February 1945, which ended in two executions. It was from memory, but it was better than nothing. And also Dönnecke's involvement in the murder of children from the concentration camp. Stave glanced up at the ceiling. The Homicide department was on the floor above. You'll regret the day you started running a dossier on me, he thought to himself.

A quarter of an hour later, Ehrlich was sitting listening to the chief inspector's report. 'You and I have a confidential agreement which goes against a dozen regulations. Under dubious, not to say illegal, circumstances, you had a copy of a walking stick handle made,' the prosecutor summed up. 'Made by a man who has already been involved in making illegal copies. It just happens that by chance this copy fits the hole left by an injury to a skull, which for the past eight years has been lying in a bombed-out building. You don't seriously think I can press charges on that basis? Against a respectable citizen, an opponent of the Nazis and protector of Jews? You can't even prove that the dead body is that of Rolf Rosenthal. According to what Dr Schramm has said, it can't be. Apart from all of that, can you even prove that at the time in question, 1943, Schramm used that walking stick? It would be embarrassing to say the least if he could prove in court that he only bought it in 1947.'

'A silver handle? Nobody's been able to buy anything like that since 1939.'

The public prosecutor raised his hands to prevent argument. 'The silver handle isn't even the problem – your whole story's the problem. If you really want to know the truth: you haven't remotely convinced me.'

'It all fits perfectly.'

'Just like the silver handle and the skull injury. Indeed, it could have come from a Sherlock Holmes story. But let me play the dim Dr Watson here and ask you: why would Schramm have killed one of his employees? What's the motive? During the Nazis' time the banker protected Jews; he didn't go around bashing their heads in.'

'It has to have something to do with the artworks, seeing how Schramm so vehemently denies ever having owned them.'

'And that's all you'll be able to say when the judge summons you to the witness stand? "Something to do with artworks"? At that point, at the very latest, the case will be an unconditional dismissal and your career will be ruined.'

'It's already ruined.'

'You can always fall further than you think.'

'So you're not going to raise any charges?'

'I don't want to go down with you. Are you really surprised?'

'No.' Stave admitted, taking a deep breath. 'If I were still working in Homicide, I'd keep digging.'

'Even then I wouldn't bet a single Deutschmark on your chances of success.'

'I have one more thing for you, by the way,' the CID man said with a thin smile. 'Let's just say it's a postcard from a colleague.' He laid on the desk in front of Ehrlich the Gestapo man's index card, and his own notes, and told him everything he knew about Dönnecke's past during the Nazi era. 'This Greiner, the Gestapo man,' he said in conclusion, 'is one of the men you're investigating. I suspect he'd testify against Dönnecke if you spoke nicely to him.'

'You mean if I let him off the hook?'

'Greiner might be a bastard, but Dönnecke's a sadist and a murderer.'

'Killers like him very rarely get caught; they leave too few traces.'

'This is one.'

Ehrlich picked up the old filing card. 'Are there any more of these?'

'As far as I understood from Greiner, yes.'

The prosecutor took off his spectacles and began polishing the lenses. 'That would be enough to press charges against Dönnecke.' His tone of voice was businesslike, but behind it Stave could hear a determined decisiveness. His heart beat a little faster: they might send Dönnecke to the scaffold!

'You have to promise me something,' said Ehrlich, pointing the frame of his glasses towards him: 'You will appear in court. As a witness for the prosecution.'

'It'll be a pleasure,' Stave promised him.

Stave went silent for a long time, contemplating the trial to come. Dönnecke would be the worst murderer he had ever got convicted, and that when he was no longer working for Homicide.

Eventually his glance fell on a copy of *Zeit*, the latest issue, lying on a side table. 'The newspapers are full of stories about Israel,' he said. 'This new state in Palestine. Utopia. A safe harbour for Jews.' And to Ehrlich, 'Why are you doing all this here? In Hamburg you were humiliated, sacked. Your wife was driven to death here. Your children have been at boarding schools in England for ages. Yet you hear stories here about some guy who hung unconscious children in a cellar and decide to press charges that could keep you fighting in court for months if not years. Why don't you just leave and let all the culprits come back to this heap of rubble?'

'Look at me,' Ehrlich proclaimed with an expression on his face that projected sadness and pride at the same moment. 'Do I look like some Zionist with a spade in one hand and a gun in the other who wants to go set up a kibbutz in the desert? My place is here in Hamburg, precisely because it was here I was so humiliated. Precisely because children were murdered in cellars here, and a crippled art buyer killed in an office building.'

Stave smiled. 'I'm glad to hear not everyone's leaving. I'll talk to

Greiner again and put together some more facts on Dönnecke. If I ever turn in a watertight case, this'll be it.'

'What about your other investigations?'

'I'll keep looking for clues on Rolf Rosenthal, clues that at some stage might point the finger at a certain Hamburg banker. The artworks can go to a museum and the files into a cabinet.'

'You can't win them all.'

That evening he held Anna in his arms. She was spending the night with him. They hadn't even tried to conceal the fact. The neighbours were going to have to get used to it. Gusts of wind blew the rain against the windowpanes, as if someone was flicking a wet handkerchief against the glass. A motorbike spluttered down Ahrensburger Strasse, its misfires ringing out like gunshots.

NWDR Radio was broadcasting a play about pigs that egged on the animals on a farm to stage a revolution against their masters, but in the end they themselves became dictators. 'Just like animals,' the announcer called it.

Stave caught himself as he was about to contradict him with 'just like people'. Don't start talking back to the radio, he warned himself. Anna had fallen asleep much earlier, but he sat there listening to the talking pigs, and thought about war and revolution.

His thoughts drifted to MacDonald who was taking his wife and child to a besieged city. A new war? Berlin had to be a paradise for spies – a city where you only had to cross the road to be in another sector. A city where the ghosts of murder and rape hovered amid the ruins. Where men had still been making propaganda films in an inferno until one of them lost a leg to a grenade. Where a diplomat called Klaus von Gudow had last been seen alive. A city that just a few days ago you could reach in two hours on the train, but was now as sealed off from the world as Moscow.

Might Karl be dragged into a war again? Could he once again find himself wandering through the ruins of bombed houses looking for bodies? The wearier he became the more his thoughts wandered. Dr

Czrisini who was coughing himself to death and didn't trust himself to go home to his empty house, who was maybe even this minute breathing his last. Chief Inspector Dönnecke who might even be listening to the same radio play. Would that make him too uncomfortable? Or did someone like him sleep easily, always convinced of being on the right side? Kurt Flasch from the Landeszentralbank, downstairs in the basement. Was he able to sleep? Or after two days in jail for black market offences, would he forever fear that his breach of the regulations at work would one day come to light and ruin him? If a few misprinted pfennig notes could yet signal his doom?

Who still cared about a few damaged works of art found in a bombed building? Who cared about a corpse with a curious wound to the head? What did any of that matter to the way the world turned? You can't win them all, the public prosecutor had said. And Ehrlich should know.

The play ended about midnight. Without hope. The battle between rebellion and suppression was eternal. Nothing good lasted; it all fell to pieces. Stave got to his feet cautiously and tiptoed over to the radio. He was about to turn it off when he looked around: Anna sleeping in the yellow light given off by the radio tubes. The sight made him deliriously happy; he wanted to dash to the window, throw it wide open and proclaim his revelation to the empty street. Instead he crept back into bed, put his arms once again around his lover and whispered into her hair what he had not dared to shout aloud: 'Our lives are not in vain. We will not lose. Not this time.'

# St Nicholas's tower

*Friday, 25 June 1948*

The wooden boards of the Landungsbrücken glistened in the rain. Waves danced on the Elbe, tossed by hundred of barges, tugboats and freighters. An American 'Liberty' freighter was heading downstream towards the North Sea, the black plume of smoke from its funnel hanging in the damp air like a dirty sheet forgotten on the washing line. Anna had taken Stave's left arm. She had turned the collar of her coat up against the gusting wind and hidden her black hair under a headscarf. Stave was holding a bouquet of flowers in his right hand, trying at the same time to protect it with his torso against the rain.

'Haven't you got a Union Jack to wave us off with?' MacDonald was hurrying with long steps down the gangplank that connected the Landungsbrücken to the Elbe embankment by Baumwall. He was wearing his dark dress uniform, the insignia shining, his shoes immaculately polished, all despite the rain. Erna was by his side in a white coat, pushing Iris in a pram, a little bundle also in white, like a tiny Egyptian mummy. Stave's former secretary was even rounder than he remembered though her cheeks were pale. Maybe she's already pregnant again, the chief inspector wondered. Or maybe it's just excitement.

The women embraced as if they'd known one another forever, while Stave and MacDonald stood by awkwardly.

'It's been a pleasure working with you,' the chief inspector said, realising it hardly sounded impressive.

The young Scotsman laughed, clapped him on the back and shook his hand. 'These months in Hamburg have been the best I've spent in the army,' he exclaimed. 'I've just a few more years to serve, then I'm free. Maybe I should apply to Scotland Yard?'

'I'll write you a reference,' Stave promised, smiling, although he felt dismayed to be losing his friend.

Gradually more and more British officers turned up in dress uniform – but without companions. Stave wondered where Erna's son might be, and whether she'd ever see him again. And wondered if she was thinking exactly the same thing.

A long blast on the ship's horn and suddenly there was a flurry of excitement. Suitcases, kit bags hauled on board, hasty words, handshakes, embarrassed waves. If Anna hadn't nudged him in the ribs, Stave would have forgotten to hand over his bouquet. He coughed and awkwardly gave it to Erna.

'Sometimes I miss the office,' she said, blushing slightly.

'Without you, Hamburg CID will never solve another case,' Stave replied.

'What are you going to do now that you've left Homicide and Department S is being disbanded?'

Stave shrugged his shoulders: 'I don't know yet.'

'Promise me you won't move to Vice.'

Stave laughed and nodded. 'I can do without the hookers and their pimps.'

'Don't be cross with me,' Erna said to Anna, winking at her, before standing on her tiptoes and kissing Stave on the cheek.

'It's a good job we're not both on duty,' he mumbled.

'Excuse me for butting in,' MacDonald said. 'But I'm British and we find sentimentality awkward. Time to get on board.'

'You still haven't told me how you're going to get from the Elbe to Berlin.'

'We're going to fly, old boy. Uncle Joe in Moscow has a thing or two to learn if he thinks he can keep out a lieutenant of His Majesty.'

MacDonald pointed downstream. By the other bank of the Elbe, hardly recognisable through the rain, two grey shadows swam on the waves. Stave, who hadn't paid attention until now, had just assumed they were freighters. Only now did he realise they were huge four-engined flying boats. On the sides of their nearly 25-metre fuselages were red, white and blue British roundels.

'The Elbe-Havel Express,' the lieutenant explained. 'Our American friends are flying food, coal and medicines, everything the Russians have blockaded, into the city on board DC-3s. We're using a couple of Short Sunderlands. They were used to hunt U-boats during the war. Now they're flying tinned foodstuffs back and forth. You can make a career of that too. And between the sacks of salt and tins of corned beef, they've found a place for me and my good ladies.'

Stave recalled the fleets of bombers flying through Hamburg's sky, the exploding flak shells in the beams of the floodlights, the burning planes and the tumbling silhouettes of pilots on parachutes falling into the darkness. 'It won't be a holiday excursion,' he said.

'Don't worry, old boy. The Russians won't shoot at us. Not yet at least. We'll be flying over the Brandenburg Gate within the hour.'

'The weather isn't good.'

'We're British. We only worry when the sun comes out.'

'You have an answer to everything.'

'As a good policeman should have. I really should consider going over to Scotland Yard.'

'It has the advantage of working in London rather than Berlin.'

Two German sailors and the British soldiers carefully carried the pram on to the barge. Erna climbed on board with Iris in her arms. MacDonald shook his hand again. 'We'll be in touch.' It was a statement, not a question.

Stave smiled and tried to touch his hat with his right hand in a military salute. Then the engine roared and the barge pushed off into the waves on a course for the other side of the river near Finken-werder. The people on board were crouched down against the rain and spray coming over the side of the boat. Only one stood upright by the stern waving.

'He's a lucky dog,' Stave whispered, taking Anna's arm. 'There won't be another James MacDonald.' He sounded as if he wanted to persuade himself of something he didn't quite believe.

Anna had linked arms with him as they climbed up the knoll on the summit of which stood St Michael's church. Stave began to walk more quickly as they passed the ruins where he had been shot a few months earlier. Anna knew nothing about that, even if she had seen the scar on his chest long ago. She was waiting for him to tell her about it, he knew. And he would.

'Karl's coming round this evening,' he began, cautiously.

'Dinner for three?' A jovial expression. But he could feel the tension in her words.

'We have a lot to talk about. His future. He's a student now. Did you know that? And our future. We're getting married, did you know that?'

Then she kissed him and laughed. 'I'd already almost forgotten.'

Behind the church they turned towards the Alster. Stave looked at a truck that roared past them, loaded with sand and beams. 'You won't always be able to hunt down treasures in the ruins,' he said. 'There are going to be builders everywhere soon. At some stage somebody is going to find you out.'

'I know. In any case I think it might be more fitting for the future bride of a chief inspector to find a legal trade.'

'That sounds as if you're a street walker. It's not quite that bad.'

'I'm going to open a shop,' Anna announced. 'An antiques shop. I'll trade under my maiden name, if you don't object. Old aristocracy, tasteful objects, the two go together – and my East Prussian past ought to be good for something. I'm just looking for premises. Something near the Alster would be perfect. You get the right sort of customers strolling along the Jungfernstieg.'

He gave her a sceptical look. 'Are you sure there are enough people who might wander into your shop?'

'There's enough money about. It's just been hidden away. Now, with the new currency, it's creeping out again and looking to be spent.'

'But on old things? New, new, new – that's what I hear from everybody. New shoes, new coats, even new cars. That doesn't leave a lot to be spent on expensive antiques.'

She gave him another smile. 'You'd be surprised to see just how much money there is to be spent in Hamburg already.'

'I ought to get up to date,' he answered embarrassedly. 'I need to find a new job.'

'You're not going back to Homicide?' Anna's voice had risen a touch – as if she had difficulty suppressing a cry of joy.

'Fraud is going to be the crime of the future. Can't be bad to get in there at the beginning.'

'Frank Stave, have I ever told you I love you?'

'I don't mind if you say it again.'

They didn't part until they reached the Jungfernstieg, where Anna wanted to see what shop premises there were for rent.

'Don't forget we have a date for dinner,' Stave reminded her.

'What do you plan to do with the afternoon? Are you going back to headquarters?'

'I will later. But first I want to visit a crime scene.'

'A new case?'

'Quite the opposite: the old business about the bronze bust. For better or worse I need to put the file to bed. But I just want to revisit the place where it was found. Take a final look.'

'Will it take long?'

'It's only a few hundred metres from here on foot. An old ruined office building nobody cares about any more, except for a chief inspector who wants to take another look around, even though there's nothing more to be found. I'll be back in headquarters in an hour at most.'

The Reimershof. Stave had passed the city hall and walked through the ruined nave of St Nicholas. From the bridge leading across to the Reimershof he took a good look at the remains of the office building: eight rows of empty windows, no glass, not even the wooden frames. No roof, no ceilings. Just drizzle, soaked into the fire-scarred outer walls. The muddy water of the Nicholas fleet lapped against filthy wooden support piles by the bank. Early afternoon in midsummer but it had hardly even got properly light yet. Nobody about. Even the *Trümmerfrauen* weren't to be seen – they must either have salvaged everything of use from the Reimershof or it was too dangerous for them to go into the unsecured ruins after the endless days of rain.

The chief inspector walked through the arched walls where the main entrance would have been. Piles of rubble, broken bricks. No chimney pipes any more, no heaps of tangled cables, no undamaged stone. There was a chattering, chirping sound coming from somewhere: a nest of rats, the CID man guessed. He walked into the ruins. Half of the interior lay in the inky shadow of the walls: the collapsed cellar in which the damaged works of art had been found, the same place where the corpse of Rolf Rosenthal had lain. Stave wondered what secret might yet lie beneath that rubble. Suddenly he heard a noise. Stave lifted up his head, held his breath. Footsteps.

The chief inspector glanced around quickly. A thick clump of blackberry bushes growing out of the rubble near the external wall opposite the entrance. He dashed over, squeezed between the wall and the thorns and ducked down, blood oozing from a scratch on his right hand, damp coming through his light summer trousers at the knees. He fumbled hectically in his coat pocket for his FN22. In vain; his pistol holster was still hanging on a hook in the cloakroom of his apartment.

Schramm. It was the old banker standing in the burned-out entrance, staring suspiciously into the interior. A dark coat, a dark hat on his huge skull. The walking stick with its silver handle. Stave hardly dared breathe, bent further down to get his hands on a lump of brick. Better than nothing.

Tentatively, the banker ventured into the ruins. He clambered with some difficulty over the first pile of rubble, struggling at the same time to put his monocle into his left eye. The shattered ceiling of the vault where the artworks had been, Stave realised, that's where he was heading. He was looking for something.

Taking careful steps Schramm climbed down into the crater, poking with his walking stick into the brick dust and charcoal remnants of woodwork. Flakes of lime plaster dirtied his dark coat, but he paid them no attention. Schramm bent down, studying the rubble with the eye behind the monocle. He pushed a dinner plate-sized concrete block to one side, brushed away mortar dust and pulled up a beech sapling, complete with roots.

Stave's knees ached and he was shivering in the cold, because by now both his trousers and the shoulders of his overcoat were soaked through. He was holding the half brick so tightly that the scratch on the back of his hand began bleeding again.

Suddenly, the banker too fell to his knees, dropped his walking stick and began foraging with both hands in the rubble. He picked up something that looked like a damaged key, its edges serrated, covered in dust but part of it glistening black. Schramm lifted up his discovery and used his stick to support his massive frame as he clambered out of the ditch and staggered to the external wall, where more light was coming through what had been a window. It was a ceramic skull, Stave realised. Schramm had found the other half of the broken male head, the lower half of which he himself had discovered along with the bronze bust and concrete sculpture. The banker looked long and hard at the fragment, the expression on his face as inscrutable as that of the piece of sculpture he was holding. For a moment it made the chief inspector think of Hamlet holding up the skull of Yorick. These are all his things, Stave thought. He's the only one who knows what else lies buried under all this rubble.

The banker was holding his discovery in his right hand, leaning on his walking stick with his left, limping towards the doorway. Stave waited until he had disappeared behind the external wall before jumping to his feet and hurrying after him. As he came out of the ruin he glanced around and saw Schramm on the bridge – his big dark shape above the opaque water.

The CID man was thinking feverishly. There was no cover. Where would Schramm head? If he ran after him he would be noticed as soon as he reached the bridge, if not before. He suppressed a curse and waited. By now Schramm had reached the other side of the bridge and was stumbling through yet more rubble to the ruins of St Nicholas's, his shadow visible through the remains of a window, between remnants of walls and stumps of blown-up pillars. And then he vanished.

Stave sprinted as fast as his left ankle would allow: the bridge, the rubble on the other side. The church nave. Nothing. He looked around in confusion. On his right, the remains of the choir, walls towering ten metres high, coming together like the prow of a ship, between them nothing but rubble. A Gothic portal leading nowhere. In front of him was a bombed side wall and beyond it the disembowelled remains of other office buildings. A movement to his left. Not next to him. Above him.

The ripped open, fire-scarred tower of the St Nicholas church. Two of its walls were gone, but the floors were still there, with damaged walls and a half-intact stone staircase reaching into the grey air like the bare skeleton of some enormous backbone. Ever since 1943 it had been banned for anyone to venture into the towering, dangerously unstable ruin.

Schramm's figure appeared on the crooked staircase, hurrying upward, seemingly untroubled by the abyss beneath his feet.

Stave rushed towards the bombed tower ruin looking for the entrance to the staircase.

# The sky above Hamburg

The stones at the base of the tower were red from old fires. On the steps was a slimy black layer of dirt. Pigeon feathers. The stench of cement and excrement. Stave sprinted up the stairs two at a time. The first landing. He lurched backwards. Air. A gust of wind pulling at his coat. He didn't dare look down. No walls, no banisters. Pull yourself together. That's barely ten metres. Keep going.

He took the steps more slowly now, watching his feet constantly. Schramm couldn't get away from him. What was the guy intending to do up there? Rainwater on his shoulders. At one point Stave stopped. Next to him was the shell of a blown-out window, filigree arches and rosettes. If I fall against that, it will all give way and carry me hurtling to earth, the CID man told himself. He thought he could hear the banker panting for breath somewhere above him. But it might have been his imagination. The wind was whistling in the walls, the gusts getting stronger. How high was the tower? Twenty metres? Thirty? Keep on.

Dented bells hanging in a wooden frame. The verdigris-covered bronze housing shook in the wind. A beam creaked. His ankle ached with every step. His right hand hurt because he was still carrying the lump of brick. His chest wound hurt as if somebody was perforating his lungs with a needle. He shivered, his body wet with rain and sweat. At least fifty metres up. He wondered where the banker got the strength to charge up the tower at such speed. Onwards.

The last landing. Seventy-six metres up. Don't look down. It felt as if the church tower was swaying. It's just an illusion, he told himself; it has to be an illusion. Yet he could feel the stairs trembling even through the soles of his shoes. The wind was howling around him like an organ pipe.

Carefully, Stave climbed on to a half-destroyed floor beneath the pointed spire of the church tower. A Gothic demon figure, burned black, perched at the top of the wall, grimacing down at the city: the houses blown apart, the stumps of walls, the empty windows, the black traces of fire. Grey sky, low black clouds, streaming rain. The sinister figure stared ironically down at the apocalyptic landscape as if its curse was responsible for the destruction. The evil eye, Stave reflected. Then suddenly he stopped. Schramm was standing at the opposite side of the devastated platform with his back to him. From where he stood the tower fell away to a view of the bridge and the Reimershof, looking from this height like a collapsed doll's house. The banker was staring down, his shoes almost touching the edge of the crumbling stonework, beyond them – nothingness.

The chief inspector didn't know what to do. He forced himself to take long, slow breaths as he watched the other man. Schramm stood there on the edge, almost totally immobile for ages. Eventually he lifted up his right hand and dropped the upper half of the black head into the abyss. For a second, two seconds maybe, the fragment of the artwork fell downwards. A dark speck in the sky. Then it exploded on a narrow strip of land between the church and another ruin. Just like a bomb, Stave thought, except that he was too high above it to hear a sound.

And then he finally realised what had driven Schramm up here.

The chief inspector took a step forward. 'Don't do it!' he called out.

Schramm spun around, so shocked that in the action of turning he almost tumbled into the abyss. The walking stick in his left hand was trembling. Stave dropped the brick in his hand. 'Don't do it,' he repeated, more gently this time. He took a step forward.

'Stay right where you are. I've had enough of you and your likes.'

'This is not an interrogation,' the CID man went on. 'Nothing's going to happen to you. Let's go back down the stairs, and then we can talk. If you want to.'

Schramm gave a bitter laugh. 'You want to get me to talk? You already know my story. Otherwise you wouldn't be here.'

'It's a coincidence,' the chief inspector told him. 'I just want to close the case. All done and dusted. Honest. I just came to take a last look at the scene. And then you turned up.'

'I thought I'd seen a movement somewhere before I went into the Reimershof.'

'Why were you there?'

Schramm nodded towards the ground. 'I wanted to see if I could find any more pieces of art.'

'There were all yours. Your collection.'

'Collection?' Schramm gave another bitter laugh. 'More like a refuge, set up by an idiot. From 1933 onwards I bought up all the pieces those barbarians had stolen, all the ones I could. There were few enough, and I didn't get anything spectacular most of the time. The Nazi gentlemen sold those abroad. But I could get my hands on some of the lesser-known pieces. Like that male head. I hid them away. Hoping for better times to come.'

'In your villa.'

'How do you know that?'

'The family photo on the wall was a giveaway.'

The banker looked at him, confused, then nodded in resignation. 'You always make some mistakes. It's a good job you weren't Gestapo. Your colleagues' visits forced me to hide my works of art elsewhere. In the Reimershof.' He shook his head. 'What an idiot. Not one slate on the roof of my house was even scratched throughout all those years. And take a look at the office building.' He nodded downwards again, wobbling a bit once more. It occurred to Stave that the man had to be exhausted.

'It was clear to me from the start that the link between the works of art and myself would come out before too long,' Schramm continued.

'I could never have proved it though. Just as there are other crimes I can never prove.' The chief inspector nodded towards the walking stick in the hand of the man facing him. In the meantime he had taken another step forward. 'You used that to kill Rolf Rosenthal. In the summer of 1943. Your employee. Your right-hand man. A Jew you had protected for years at great danger to yourself. I've been asking myself, why you did it.'

'I ask myself the same question, and have done ever since.' The banker rubbed his eyes with his right hand. But he had forgotten about his monocle. All of a sudden the little round piece of glass flew away from his face, a flicker of light in the air, and then it was gone. Stave used the distraction to take another step forward.

'It had never occurred to me that in a moment of panic you can wipe out a life. Or even two.' Schramm's face was grey now, the voice used to giving orders suddenly sounded tired. 'I didn't lie to you. I had rented the rooms in the Reimershof a lot earlier, in order to carry out certain discreet bits of business. Bits of business that wouldn't have pleased our local Gauleiters and certainly not the gentlemen in Berlin. From the middle of 1939 onwards, I also began hiding my art objects there.'

'Including the bronze of Anni Mewes.'

'The finest piece in my whole refuge. I had actually seen Mewes on stage once, when she was still young.' He laughed wistfully. 'I kept the artworks on a shelf, hidden behind files. Only the Mewes was kept in view in front of them. I just couldn't bear to let this young woman's face be consigned to darkness. Sentimental.' The banker fell silent for a while. Stave prayed the wind fluttering the man's dark and now dirty overcoat out over the abyss behind him would die down. 'Then from September 1941 I let Herr Rosenthal hide in the offices.'

'In September 1941?'

Schramm stared at him, his eyes flashing with rage. 'Where were you when the Jews still living in the Reich had to wear a yellow star?'

Stave said nothing.

'From that time on, many Jews were carted off to concentration camps,' the banker said in an expressionless voice. 'It was an autumn night in 1941 when Herr Rosenthal came hammering on my door. He had fled his apartment and was in a panic. So was I, as you can imagine. I didn't dare let him stay in my house. What if the Gestapo had discovered him there? Just before dawn we went from my villa to the Reimershof. And that's where Herr Rosenthal…' he searched for the right phrase, 'made himself at home.'

'He went into hiding?'

'You could put it like that. I brought him food, clothes, newspapers. Not that he enjoyed reading the headlines.'

'Who knew about this?'

'Nobody. Herr Rosenthal's relatives had no idea, because I never dared get in touch with his family. I was afraid of the Gestapo. I'm sure you can understand that. None of my co-workers had a clue – you could never be sure there wasn't an informer among them. The cleaning lady glanced in the rooms once a week, but she always came at the same time, and Herr Rosenthal hid in the heating cellar each time. I would look into the Reimershof from time to time. Nobody paid attention because I'd had an office there for ages.'

'So why did Rosenthal have to die?'

Schramm closed his eyes a moment. Too short a time for Stave to intervene. 'Because I lost my head. On the first night raid in June 1943, incendiary bombs fell on the Reimershof. The attic caught fire and it spread to the upper storeys. The building was damaged but nothing like as badly as it looks today. I rushed there the following morning. One of my two office rooms was gone, and the artworks with it. Buried somewhere under tonnes of rubble. The other room was half destroyed, ripped open like a cardboard box. Herr Rosenthal was in there, cowering, half crazy with fear, having had to spend the night in the building effectively powerless. There was no shelter. Imagine it: all alone in a huge building, bombs falling, fires breaking out all over the place. His nerves were shot.'

'Did he attack you?'

'Not with his fists.' Schramm closed his eyes at the memory. He was swaying. Stave dared come a few centimetres closer to him. 'He jumped at me the minute he saw me. "You've got to get me out of here, Herr Director," he was screaming. Really loud, like he always did. I became frightened. What if someone heard us? And in any case

I had nowhere to hide Rosenthal. I didn't even know how I could get him out of the Reimershof without being seen. In the wake of the attacks the city was full of police, firemen, air raid wardens, homeless. I couldn't have just walked out with a Jew.'

Stave remembered the chaos after the bombing raids. The fires, the survivors wandering through smoking ruins as if drugged, the unexploded bombs, the looters, the vile stench of burned flesh and sewers blown open.

'I tried to calm him down. But it was as if he just wasn't listening to me. And then, all of a sudden, it was as if he had suddenly become somebody different. That frightened me a lot more. Rosenthal, who had normally always been quite restrained, suddenly dashed across the devastated office, despite his club foot, and pulled a packet of headed paper out of a desk drawer. The paper was singed but the letterhead was still clearly legible: my name, my address. Rosenthal was screaming: "I'll report you. I'll write to the Gestapo and tell them you're hoarding degenerate art unless you find me a hiding place somewhere, right now!" He'd gone crazy with fear. Blind, effectively. Sadly I didn't keep a cool head. All of a sudden I was in as big a panic as he was. If he really did report me, the Gestapo would break my bones, I thought. I wanted to make Rosenthal see reason, wanted him at the very least to stop running around screaming in the ruins, with all those people out on the street, just a few metres away. And I lifted my walking stick and hit him. Just once. I really just wanted to shut him up. Wanted to bring him to his senses. Like giving a slap in the face to a hysterical person, you know what I mean.'

'But it wasn't just a slap in the face.'

'I heard the bone break,' Schramm admitted. 'The minute I hit him I regretted it. Rosenthal rolled his eyes and fell over backwards, as if he'd been struck by lightning. All of a sudden there was blood everywhere. His legs began shaking uncontrollably, his shoes kicking over the heavy old office chair. And then his feet were suddenly still, terribly still. I ran out, horrified at what I had done.'

'Did you come back?' Stave was so close now that he could have reached out and grabbed him. But he didn't dare raise his arm. What if Schramm jumped the minute he grabbed him and pulled him over with him? He had nothing to hold on to.

'The following night there was yet another bombing raid. When I ventured down to the Reimershof again, the whole interior was destroyed. There wasn't a trace of my office, of my artworks – or of Rosenthal. Everything had been buried under the rubble. I went back home and tried to forget the whole business. By and by, it came to seem as if it had all been a nightmare, unreal. It couldn't have been me who had done it. It simply hadn't happened. It's amazing what a human being can suppress if he just works hard enough and long enough at it.'

'But then I appear at your house and show you a photo with the bronze bust.'

'That's when it all came back. The memory. And the fear of being found out. Then you started rummaging around in that old business. When you left I only had to make a couple of calls to find out Rosenthal's body had also been found in the Reimershof. And that of all people, it was Dönnecke who was investigating the case.'

'But he never came to see you. In fact he didn't investigate the case at all. He was every bit as scared of you as you were of him.'

'But you weren't scared of me at all. Gradually I came to understand that nobody in Homicide was interested in the corpse; not one of them even came to interview me. But by then it was too late. All the memories had come back. As did the shame over what I had done.'

'I was on your tail. But I could never have proved anything against you.'

'And you still can't. This is hardly an interrogation. You have no proof of any of what I've just told you.'

Stave thought feverishly for a few seconds, wondered if he should try to bluff, but in the end decided to tell the truth. 'That's true,' he admitted. 'I have not a shred of evidence against you.'

Schramm smiled a smile of weak triumph. 'Even the Gestapo boys never managed to pin me down,' he whispered. 'But you can't fool your own conscience. In the end you never escape your memories. Ever since your visit I've thought of Rosenthal again and again. In my dreams I still hear his pleas from back then in the ruin. I have him on my conscience, and I can't persuade myself otherwise. So I have to face the consequences.'

The chief inspector looked desperately around for something to hold on to. Nothing. 'I admit that if you jump I won't be able to arrest you,' he said. He wanted to sound beseeching but his words sounded hollow. Then he reached out with his right hand and grabbed Schramm's coat. 'If you jump now, you'll pull me over with you.'

The banker gave him an angry look. 'Don't be ridiculous. Let go of me. Whether I jump now or end up hanging from the gallows is all the same to you. You've solved your case. And I will have my peace at last.'

Stave's thoughts raced. Dönnecke. The Gestapo agent in the café. The Nazi mayor sitting at the restaurant table. Not one of them had ever had a bad dream. So many dead. So few punished. 'You're one of the good ones,' he blurted out. 'You turned the Gestapo away. You protected Jews. You saved works of art. The Nazis couldn't hurt you. Do you really want to let them win?'

Schramm gave him a tired look, and said, 'I really couldn't care less.'

And Stave let go of him.

The chief inspector took two steps backwards. Sweat was running down his brow. His heart was pounding like that of a boxer after a fight. 'I'm going back down,' he said, his voice no more than a croak. 'And the minute I'm back down there, I shall forget every word I heard up here. The Reimershof. The bronze bust. Rolf Rosenthal. None of them exist any more as far as I'm concerned.'

Then banker looked incredulously at him. 'You really are trying every trick in the book,' he whispered.

Stave shook his head. 'I'm being serious. That was no murder back there among the bombs that night in 1943; it was just a second of frightened madness. A tragic mistake. Nobody can do anything about it now. And you've already been punished enough without having a judge pass sentence on you.' He moved backwards to the first step on the staircase, then turned one last time and said: 'And in any case, I don't work for Homicide any more.'

With that Stave began walking down. Step by step. Fearing that at any second he would hear a shrill scream followed by a terrible dull thud. Another step. And another. He was shivering with damp, cold, vertigo. One more step.

When he had gone down two floors the chief inspector heard a noise. He stopped, held his breath, listened. The scraping sound of a walking stick on stone. The grating of brick dust underfoot. Heavy steps on the staircase, somewhere above him.

Then Stave hurried down the ruined tower. All of a sudden he was no longer afraid of the chasm beneath him

# Afterword

No single event from the prehistory of the Federal Republic has become such a powerful myth as the issue of the new currency. Even so, that rainy day in the early summer of the year 1948, on which all West Germans were allowed to collect their 40DM pro capita money, was also a day of loss and disappointment – and crime. The five- and ten-pfennig misprints which attracted the attention of MacDonald and Stave, did actually exist. Several days before the twentieth of June they were discovered being sold by employees of Hamburg's Landeszentralbank who had grabbed them out of the shredding drum supposed to destroy them. (The sale of toxic torpedo oil as cooking oil also took place.) For dramatic reasons I moved the place where they were sold to the black market which operated on Goldbekplatz. In reality they were sold on the *Kiez*, officially known as the Reeperbahn, in the St Pauli district. Kurt Flasch, the bank employee and Stave's neighbour, is a wholly fictional character.

On the other hand the speech given by Mayor Max Brauer is 100 per cent authentic, as are the conditions referred to for the exchange of Reichsmarks into Deutschmarks.

The massive building of the Landeszentralbank is still there today next to the city hall, and gets a lot of visitors, mostly from patrons of the arts, as it is today the Bucerius Art Forum. And if you stand on the square outside the city hall and look up you will still see on the building's gable five massive stone figures, a crest and the word 'Reichsbank'.

The history of those works of art created under the Weimar Republic, then condemned by the National Socialists as 'degenerate' but kept as props for movies, has been adapted for this crime thriller.

At least fifteen expressionist objects from the twenties have indeed been discovered in building works, covered in earth, damaged or battered. The discovery was not, however, made in Hamburg but in Berlin, and then not until 2010.

The Hamburg Museum für Kunst und Gewerbe displayed these works in 2012, with a nod to one local element. The bronze bust of the actress Anni Mewes was not created by my fictional artist Toni Weber (whose name – if not his biography – I borrowed from an amateur painter represented along with others at a 1947 exhibition in the C&A department store), but between 1917 and 1921 by Edwin Scharff, an artist who would spend the last ten years of his life working in Hamburg,

The propaganda film in which many of these items confiscated by the NS propaganda ministry and then 'loaned out' as props was entitled *Venus in Court*. The director Veit Harlan turned out many influential films for the NS regime, but not this one. It was actually Hans H. Zerlett who was responsible for the script and direction. Harlan, however, did indeed live in the circumstances described on the banks of the Alster along with his Swedish wife Kristina Söderbaum, and defended himself as described here, both in court and in public, against accusations he was a propagandist for National Socialism.

The story of the art collector-banker Dr Schramm and the tragic events he was involved in during the bombings of 1943, however, has no historical basis.

Unfortunately, there is a historical basis for the mild punishments or even lack of punishment dished out to leading National Socialist activists, even in the immediate post-war years: Hamburg's Gauleiter Karl Kaufmann, who was politically and in other ways responsible for the Neugamme concentration camp, spent some time in various internment and detention centres up until the beginning of the 1950s, but never for very long. From the mid-fifties onwards he lived as a respected citizen and partner in both an insurance company and chemical factory in Hamburg. The Nazi mayor Carl Vincent

Krogmann escaped with not more than a brief spell of internment, and later worked without problem in trade and industry. The case against Captain Rudolf Petersen, who had sailors shot even after the unconditional surrender of the Nazi regime, brought in this novel by Public Prosecutor Ehrlich, genuinely did take place: he was acquitted.

Anyone who takes enough effort to do their research will find a few examples of artistic licence. For example, the water pump outside the city hall, which Chief Inspector Stave leaned against, was not erected until 1950. The sell-off of silver and jewellery by auctioneer Herbert Nattenheimer in the Winterhude Fährhaus restaurant actually took place in October 1947, rather than the spring of 1948. George Orwell's *Animal Farm* was broadcast by NWDR as the radio play *Just like Animals* in July rather than June of 1948. The anonymous accusation Stave read in Department S is genuine in both content and grammar. The accused transit operator, however, is an invention. The casino in Travemünde only got its licence back in 1949.

Several venues mentioned, unsurprisingly, have vanished without trace. Nothing remains of the Ley huts on Langenhorner Chaussee. The house at 23 Lerchenstrasse with its miserable little apartment no longer exists, although the Schiller theatre opposite remains a derelict monument. The Ohlendorff villa with its park is still there in Volksdorf. (It really was a British officers' club and yes, on more than one occasion a gentleman did ride through it on horseback.) The Jewish cemetery in Jenfeld remains as a little-noticed witness to a culture all but extinguished.

The Reimershof has been rebuilt after the serious wartime damage. You can still get a good view of the office building from the bomb-scarred tower of St Nicholas church – except that today you can get to the top in an elevator, at no risk to life or limb.